Praise for Stuart Kaminsky and his Inspector Rostnikov mysteries

"Kaminsky has staked a claim to a piece of the Russian turf. . . . His stories are laced with fascinating tidbits of Russian history. . . . He captures the Russian scene and character in rich detail."

—*The Washington Post Book World*

"Rostnikov is quite simply the best cop to come out of the Soviet Union since Martin Cruz Smith's Arkady Renko."

—*San Francisco Examiner*

"As always, Kaminsky provides a colorful, tightly written mystery (he doesn't waste a word) filled with twists, counter twists, and a surprise ending that is plausible and clever."

—*Chicago Tribune*

"Stuart Kaminsky has created a sympathetic and engaging hero who solves mysteries in spite of the peculiar handicaps imposed by the police bureaucracy and exacerbated by KGB interference."

—*The Cincinnati Post*

"Kaminsky's Moscow is as convincing as it is compelling. . . . His people throb with life."

—*The Philadelphia Inquirer*

Also by Stuart M. Kaminsky:

Inspector Porfiry Rostnikov Mysteries
DEATH OF A DISSIDENT*
BLACK KNIGHT IN RED SQUARE*
RED CHAMELEON*
A FINE RED RAIN*
A COLD RED SUNRISE*
THE MAN WHO WALKED LIKE A BEAR*
ROSTNIKOV'S VACATION*

Other Mysteries
DOWN FOR THE COUNT
EXERCISE IN TERROR
THE FALA FACTOR
HE DONE HER WRONG
HIGH MIDNIGHT
THE HOWARD HUGHES AFFAIR
THE MAN WHO SHOT LEWIS VANCE
MURDER ON THE YELLOW BRICK ROAD
NEVER CROSS A VAMPIRE
POOR BUTTERFLY
THINK FAST, MR. PETERS
BURIED CAESARS
BULLET FOR A STAR
LIEBERMAN'S FOLLY*

**Published by Ivy Books*

DEATH OF A RUSSIAN PRIEST

An Inspector Porfiry Rostnikov Novel

Stuart M. Kaminsky

IVY BOOKS • NEW YORK

Ivy Books
Published by Ballantine Books
 Published in the United States by Ballantine Books, a division of Random House, Inc., New York, and simultaneously in Canada by Random House of Canada Limited, Toronto.

Library of Congress Catalog Card Number: 91-58638

ISBN 0-8041-0836-6

Printed in Canada

First Hardcover Edition: August 1992
First Mass Market Edition: September 1993

To Evan Hunter
for his support and inspiration

With special thanks to the two Moscow police officers who showed me a night side of Moscow of which few are aware, and to the Moscow Branch of the International Association of Crime Writers for their generous hospitality.

. . . in his period of piety, fasting, visiting monks, and going to church, when he was seeking help in religion to curb his passionate nature, Nikolai had not only failed to find anyone to encourage him, but everyone . . . had laughed at him. They teased him, called him Noah, a monk; and then, when he returned, no one came to his aid. Instead, everyone turned away from him in horror and disgust.

—Leo Tolstoy, *Anna Karenina*

ONE

AN HOUR AFTER DAWN ON A CHILL DECEMBER MORNING, the assassin stood before the white wooden church in the village of Arkush.

He was careful not to touch any of the gathering faithful who entered prepared to cross themselves, stand, bend, pray, and sing during the three-hour ceremony that would be conducted by the priest who would one day be a saint.

The assassin looked up at the domes of the church, four bulbous shapes meant to represent colorful flames reaching up toward heaven, but looking to child and nonbeliever only like pastel onions. The assassin, filled with disgust, hid behind a suffocating mask of piety. He entered the church and found a place to stand where the priest could be clearly seen.

The church was filled with men and women of all ages, families with children, not just old babushkas. They had come to hear the holy man who evoked the spirit of St. Basil and St. Philip. They had come to pass their candles forward and then be blessed by him.

Through the moving, talking congregation the assassin could see the iconostasis, the wall of holy paintings that, according to dogma, served as the door to the Lord, the Holy Mother, or the depicted saint. The assassin paid little attention to the crowd, the icons, the lighted candles. He watched the actual door in the iconostasis through which the priest would soon be coming.

In the sanctuary beyond that door, Father Vasili Merhum held out his arms in homage to the Savior so that his grandson Aleksandr could help him put on his vestments for the Eucharist. As the ecclesiastical robes slipped over his arms the priest's heart beat madly in anticipation of what he planned to do this very afternoon.

Into his mind there came a vivid picture of a low wooden building in Moscow, the Department of External Affairs of the Russian Orthodox Church.

In a conference room in the building, where Father Merhum planned to go that afternoon, was a large painting. It was Father Merhum's favorite painting. In the painting a large angry man in golden robes partially covered by a dark monk's cloak looks down at a bishop, the object of his scorn. The bishop, in full white vestments, appears quite calm as he looks up at the irate giant.

The golden giant in the painting is Ivan the Terrible. The bishop is Metropolitan Philip of Moscow. Legend has it that Ivan entered the church in disguise to demand that Philip cease speaking out against the policies of the czar. The bishop refused. Ivan had him arrested and strangled in prison and Philip became a saint of the church.

Father Merhum was a large man, over six feet tall and shaped like a brown bear. He was sixty-six years old and his beard was curled and gray. His unflinching gray eyes announced that he was a priest who fully believed he had the ear of Jesus. With faith in his mission Father Merhum had stood up to commissars, the leaders of his own church, the KGB, and state leaders from Stalin to Gorbachev. And now, days after the end of the seventy-year-old failure of Soviet socialism, he stood ready to take up the demands for reform with Yeltsin himself.

Father Merhum had no illusions. He did not believe the

new *Sodruzhestvo Nezavisimykh Gosudarstv*, the Commonwealth of Independent States, would suddenly bring freedom. He did not believe that the men against whom he had fought for more than half a century would suddenly become tolerant because they wore new hats and waved a flag of red, white, and blue instead of a red flag with a hammer and sickle. Yeltsin had come to power without a party behind him. He and the leaders of the other new nations had no choice but to rely on the old bureaucrats. The people would continue to suffer, with starvation, with the gradual realization that different is not always better, and ultimately, with attacks on their faith.

Vasili lifted his robe and held up a leg so his grandson could help him put on the *stitcharion*, the long, smooth undergarment. "My soul rejoices in the Lord," the priest said softly. "He has dressed me in the garment of salvation and put upon me the vestment of joy. Like a bridegroom, He has placed the miter upon me, and like a bride, He has surrounded me with adornment."

Across the shoulders of the priest his grandson, who stood a full half foot shorter than the old man, placed the *epitrachelion*, the stole. Its dangling ends, sewn together over the chest, signified the burst of joy of the Holy Spirit.

As he donned the stole the priest said, "Praise be to God who has poured out His grace upon His priests like precious ointment upon the head; it flows down upon the beard of Aaron; it flows down upon the hem of his garment."

Then, as the girdle was placed about his ample waist and belly, Father Merhum recited, "He has girded me with strength and made my way irreproachable."

Then the *epimakinia*, the cuffs, reaching from wrist to elbow.

"Thy right arm," he said, "was glorified in strength, O Lord; Thy right arm, O Lord, shattered the enemy."

And then for the left arm. "Thy hands have created me

and formed me; teach me, that I may know Thy commandments."

Then he put on the chasuble, the "house," seamless like the tunic of Jesus.

As Father Merhum said his prayer the assassin stood off to the side of the railed platform from which the priest would soon address his flock. An ancient nun, covered in black from head to foot and wearing a beehive-shaped head covering, stood head bent, praying the rosary. The assassin watched her gnarled hands that cradled a rosary of silver and green beads.

At her side a small choir of six men and women sang softly, almost to themselves. Nun and choir went silent as the ornate gold-painted door opened and Father Merhum, a giant in full vestments, stepped forth and bellowed, "Forgive me my children."

"*Spasi gospodi.* God save you. God will forgive," echoed all but one voice in the church.

The service lasted more than three hours. Then it was time for the sermon. There was a great silence as Father Merhum turned his back to the congregation to look at the icons and gather strength from them. His broad shoulders sagged and then rose with determination.

A small child cried out for something to drink. Angry voices whispered to quiet the little boy, but the priest, who had now turned to face those before him, held up a hand and smiled.

"It is right that that thirsty child should ask for water," he said. "The Lord did not make children with the power to dissemble. Children are taught pretense. We live in a world of pretense taught to us not only by those who once told us to worship the false God of Lenin, but by all those who would reject the true God and our Lord Jesus Christ. Give the child water."

The ancient nun in the corner rose and the crowd parted.

She moved to the child who had asked for drink and took his hand.

"Your soul," the priest continued as the nun led the little boy to the church door, "may wear its earthly masks. Women may paint their faces." His words echoed from the ancient stone walls. "Men may perfect their masks. But the true God can see the soul and hear its cry for water, food, meaning."

The assassin was certain that the burning eyes of the priest met his at that moment. He forced himself to keep from blinking and turning away.

"The struggle is not over, though the statues are down and the empire is dying. We speak openly, but those with clubs and guns, the murderers of the soul, wait in the shadows. New freedom is not only for the just but for the unjust also. Those who stole your bread will be replaced by others who will steal your bread and your water. The struggle is not over.

"Look you," he bellowed, stepping forward. "New false gods already dwell behind the golden doors of Moscow, Tiblisi, Kiev. Deny them. There is no new kingdom and there was no old kingdom. It was always the kingdom of our Lord Jesus Christ. This very day I will go to Moscow. This very day I will be expected to join in the rejoicing of those who claim a new kingdom called Democracy. This day even those in vestments in our own church will smile and give thanks and be mesmerized by hope. It is not hard for an evil king to clothe the seduced in the vestments of priests, but God, not the kings of the earth, determines the holy. In the name of our Lord I will not be mesmerized by a crucifix of gold while someone reaches into my chest to take my soul, our soul, and claim the kingdom of the Lord."

At the end Father Merhum blessed the worshipers and patted the heads of those who came forward to kiss the hem of his vestments.

Assassin and priest's eyes met again for an instant. Had the cleansing weapon not been hidden outside, he would have climbed over the backs of the fools, the stupid animals who knelt in front of this preening pot of filth. The pot had to be broken. *Krov*, thought the assassin, blood. He imagined the broken priest split in two, a putrid foul gas escaping from his body.

The priest was gone. Through the golden door.

The assassin pushed through the crowd. The priest would change quickly. Feigning humility, he would walk through the woods to the train station, where he would travel to Moscow to do battle with the state in the name of God and the people. But he would do other things in Moscow of which he told no one.

Hypocrisy, he thought, willing himself to move at the pace of those who stepped out into the cold daylight, dazzled, still in a religious swoon, a state of stupid ecstasy. They moved slowly and so did he.

Father Merhum, with the help of his grandson, removed his vestments carefully, with reverence. He was aware of his hands, his thighs, the rippling gray hair between his legs as he slipped off each vestment and handed it to Aleksandr.

"I have a question for you," said the priest, and the boy's legs trembled as he placed a cloak neatly on a wooden hanger. Aleksandr was sure that his grandfather had discovered his secret.

"You ate this morning?" Father Merhum asked, pulling his head through the top of his black cloak and smoothing his unruly hair and beard.

"Yes, Father," said Aleksandr. He placed the sleeves gently in the wooden box on the table.

"You ate all your bread?" asked Father Merhum playfully.

"All of it," said Aleksandr.

"Good," said his grandfather. "Are you still going to be a priest?"

As he had said dozens of times before, the twelve-year-old answered, "As my grandfather and his father before him."

They said nothing of Aleksandr's father, Peotor, who had forsaken his tradition for the life of a shopkeeper. Peotor claimed to be an atheist. In the four years during which Father Merhum had been imprisoned for his articles, for his attacks on the puppet priests who had been appointed by the government as metropolitans and bishops, not once had Peotor written to him.

"Your father has lost his soul," said Father Merhum, adjusting the heavy cross on his chest. "He inherited the weakness of his mother, whom our Lord has taken to his breast."

The small, thin boy, who most resembled his sad and pretty Georgian mother, nodded his head. When his grandfather talked of his father, Aleksandr imagined not the sullen man at home but one of the sinners in the icon of the Lord and the gates of hell that hung in his grandfather's house. The sinner in the icon was a thin, pale creature in rags, his right arm trying to cover his face from the wrath of the Lord.

"It is not that Peotor honestly turned from God," said Father Merhum, "but that he believed in the Lord yet turned his back upon him and the Holy Mother for a few extra bottles of wine and a shank of meat on earth. I respect an honest atheist, even an honest Communist, but I despise the coward who thinks only of preserving what sheathes his body and fills his belly, the coward who abandons God and his soul."

Aleksandr nodded dutifully.

"You understand?" asked Father Merhum. "Speak."

"I understand," said the boy.

"My words are hard, but it is better to face reality than to waste time constructing lies and excuses. We are what we must be, but the Lord gives us the opportunity to choose. Your father has chosen. You must choose. Today. Tomorrow."

Aleksandr nodded.

"Do you understand even half of what I say to you?"

"I think so."

"Good," said Father Merhum. "Go."

And the boy turned, grabbed his coat, and ran out the door.

With his grandson gone, Vasili Merhum surveyed himself in the tall mirror and contemplated the approaching struggle. He would fight for political and religious freedom in this new Russia. He would demand that those who tortured and murdered under the old regime, even if they be officials in the new commonwealth, be brought to justice. He would supply the names. He would read them in Red Square atop the empty tomb that had held the profane icon of Lenin, which the foolish had stood in line to worship. And if he were martyred, then so be it.

He would name the ones who had changed their masks, from the highest generals to the party members and even the pathetic mayor of Arkush. And to that list he would add two bishops. It would begin with a public meeting in snow before St. Basil's this very day. The foreign press had been invited. Yeltsin himself had been invited but would certainly not come. Even Gorbachev had been invited, though it no longer mattered if he came or not. Father Merhum expected only the people and the television cameras. He would speak in Russian, English, French. He anticipated the day not far in the future when he would be offered a position in the Russian government. He pictured himself righteously refusing the offer.

After he put on his coat, Father Merhum checked the floorboard under the leg of the table, found the hidden space below it and its contents as he had left them. Then he rose and stepped out the door onto the stone path behind the church. He crossed the small concrete churchyard, went across the brick-lined street, and entered the woods.

As he walked, watching his cold breath cloud before him,

the priest allowed himself a brief thought of the appointment he had made for that evening in the square building just across from the church where Pushkin had been married. The appointment and what it would lead to would be both the earthly reward and punishment for the explosive speech he would make that day. Father Merhum's challenge to Yeltsin, his demand for immediate punishment for those who now hid behind the shadowed pillars of the Kremlin would be on the lips of every Christian and non-Christian in Russia and beyond. He planned to demand the immediate resignation of many of those in the new Commonwealth governments. He expected no such thing to happen, but the demand would signal that a respected member of the Church had joined in the call to overthrow not only the old reactionaries but the new bigots and self-seekers.

Father Merhum was soon no more than fifty yards from his house. He would not turn toward the house but would continue straight on to the station. Walking on the narrow path of stones, he was aware of the scuffling of animals in the snow-covered grass and the rustling of wings of the gray-black crows in the trees above.

He paused at the birch tree where at the age of sixteen he had cut a cross to impress the young large-breasted daughter of the then mayor of Arkush. There was no longer a trace of that cross. He stopped now because something was in his shoe, a pebble perhaps. As he paused, reached down, and removed the shoe, Father Merhum was aware of a rustling in the leaves behind him, a rustling that suggested something larger than a ferret or rat. With his right shoe in one hand and balancing himself against the familiar birch with the other, he turned his head and saw not a person but an upraised ax.

There was no time to think, pray, or respond. The priest fell backward as the blow came and his shoe sailed into the woods. He tried to turn his back, but he had no time. The next blow brought no great pain, just a sudden throbbing as he rolled onto his back and looked up.

"You," he said. "You."

The assassin was going to strike again, but he stopped in midblow. The priest had fallen backward, eyes opening and closing in confusion as his mouth let out a deep breath and a cloud of steam. The assassin stared at the bearded, wide-eyed dog who looked up at him, blood and something yellow coming out of the back of his head, staining the leaves on the ground dark. Instead of striking again, the assassin turned his back and walked into the woods, ax at his side.

Father Vasili Merhum, not yet dead, rolled over onto his knees, touched the back of his head, and felt the soft cushion of his own brain flecked with sharp edges of bone. He began to crawl, trailing his bloody handprints in the snow and along the stone path. Were he to live, it would truly be a miracle.

Through the clearing he could see his small house. The heavy cross on the chain around his neck scraped against the stone path as he crawled forward, slowly losing sensation in his shoeless foot and his right arm. He could imagine his cross sending up sparks.

At the low wooden gate to his house he saw his father, who had been dead for more than forty years. His father flew toward him, his vestments prepared for Easter. The old man's cross bounced on his chest. His beard, long, gold gray, and silken, trailed behind as he approached his son.

And then, as his father knelt at his side, Father Merhum could see that it was not his father but a woman from his childhood, Yelena Yozhgov, and suddenly it was not she but Sister Nina, her rosary of silver around her neck. She sat, put his head in her lap, and wailed, a wail that was pain and justification to the dying priest. He would be a martyr. He could simply be quiet now and die a martyr, but he could not keep his mouth from moving.

"Sister, Oleg must forgive me," he said, and she leaned forward to hear what he would say next, but there were no more words and the priest was dead.

TWO

IT WAS NOT AT ALL CLEAR TO GALINA PANISHKOYA HOW she came to be sitting in the back room of the former State Store 31 with a gun in her hand pressed hard against the neck of a young woman in a faded and not very clean white smock.

Galina was a sixty-three-year-old grandmother, a babushka, in a cloth coat. She had two arthritic knees and she had two granddaughters to take care of. If there was one place she should not be, it was here.

She shifted on the rickety wooden stool in an attempt to get a bit more comfortable. The movement made the gun in her hand shift, and the young woman in white sitting in front of her gasped as the barrel tapped bone just above her ear.

"I'm sorry," said Galina.

The young woman, whose name was Ludmilla, sobbed, and tried not to look at the body of Herman Koruk, her boss, who sat on the floor, his legs spread, eyes wide open in surprise. There was a spot in his neck just below his chin where Galina had shot him. There was very little blood.

"Please let me go," said Ludmilla.

"Shhh," said Galina, looking at the partly open door to the shop.

She was trying to hear what the policemen were saying, but they were too far away. The first policeman through the door had been a young man. Most policemen seemed to be young. For that matter, most people seemed to be young. She had already sat the shopgirl on the floor in front of her when the young policeman had entered.

"Stop," she had told him, and though he was young, he was not stupid.

He stopped and moved his hand away from his holster.

"Don't hurt her," he had said.

"Go away," Galina had said.

"I . . ."

"Away," Galina repeated, and he had gone away.

Ludmilla, who was twenty-five years old and just a bit on the scrawny side, wanted to do two contradictory things at the same time: become invisible, and plead with the madwoman with the gun to let her go. She started to turn her head slightly to address the woman and felt, even smelled, the steel of the gun barrel against her ear. She decided invisibility would be the better choice.

When the call went out on the police band that someone had been shot and a hostage taken at former State Store 31, Porfiry Petrovich Rostnikov had been seated next to the driver of a new Mercedes police car speeding to the morning meeting of the Special Affairs Department. The car happened to be passing the massive gray block of the Lenin Library, which meant that State Store 31 was five minutes away.

"Go," said Rostnikov.

When they arrived in front of the store at the entrance to Arbat Street, two uniformed policemen were trying to keep a crowd from pressing up to the store window and possibly getting their frozen noses shot off by the madwoman inside.

Rostnikov stepped out of the Mercedes and closed the door.

The cold began immediately to work its way up Rostnikov's left leg. The leg, a tyrant in the tradition of the Czars, was quick to complain of changes in weather or requests for activity. The leg, rather badly served by a German tank during the Great War, placed full blame on Porfiry Petrovich's youthful patriotism. In the forty-six years that had passed since the event Rostnikov had learned to endure the accusations of his leg.

He addressed the appendage—internally, of course—and made deals with it. Give me only minimal discomfort today, he would bargain, and I will prop you up tonight with a pillow and not move for three hours.

Porfiry Petrovich Rostnikov, wearing an imitation leather jacket over his still-serviceable black suit, moved slowly through the crowd that parted resentfully.

"Go home, all of you," shouted the young policeman who had seen Galina in the back room of State Store 31.

"Why?" asked a gravelly voice that could have belonged to a man or a woman. "There's nothing to eat at home."

"We've got a free country now," came another voice, a younger male voice. "We can't be ordered home by the police anymore."

"Yes," shouted several people as Rostnikov broke through to the front of the crowd.

A snaggle-toothed little man wearing an orange wool hat pulled over his ears and an oversized coat pushed his face toward Porfiry Petrovich and squealed, "No more pushing around."

Rostnikov could smell alcohol on the man's breath.

"The police will always push," came the gravelly voice from the rear. "No matter what color they wear."

Two more uniformed police had arrived and were helping push the crowd back. The young policeman spotted Rostnikov and broke away from the man with whom he was arguing. Rostnikov, hands plunged into his pockets, was looking at the bare windows and the partly open door of State Store 31.

"Inspector Rostnikov," the young man said, assuming a position something like attention.

Some people in the crowd laughed at the young policeman. He tried to ignore them. He had joined the police when he came back from Afghanistan, thinking he could make a living and command some respect. He was wrong on both counts.

"What is your name?" asked Rostnikov.

"Misha Tiomkin."

Misha Tiomkin's nose was red. His fur uniform hat was pulled down over his ears and he looked like a boy dressed up like a soldier.

"It is an old woman," said Tiomkin.

"Go in and shoot her, why don't you?" said the drunken little man with bad teeth. "Solve all your problems that way. People get hungry, shoot them. Bullets are cheaper than food."

Rostnikov and Officer Tiomkin moved away from the crowd, closer to the store's open door.

"It's not clear what happened," said Tiomkin. "People were pushing and shoving, complaining that there was so little in the store, that it was too expensive, ten times more than last week, even bread is—"

Tiomkin stopped himself.

"The situation got tense," he continued. "Someone broke a glass case, took some cheese. Others started grabbing. The manager had a gun. He fired in the air. People were screaming. And then someone took the gun from the manager and . . . I don't know. She's in there with a clerk, a young girl."

"Tell me, Misha Tiomkin," Rostnikov said, looking up at the gray sky and then at the angry crowd, "is it your impression that winters are getting milder in Moscow?"

Tiomkin pondered the question. "I don't know."

"I think they are," said Rostnikov. "Mild winters are like full moons. People grow mad. The blood is affected like the tides, perhaps."

"Perhaps," agreed Tiomkin.

Rostnikov patted the young policeman on the shoulder, motioned for him to move back to control the crowd, and moved to the door of State Store 31.

"He's going to shoot her, look," called a woman.

"Who?"

"The one in the fake leather jacket, the one there by the door. Use your eyes, the one that looks like a barrel."

Rostnikov stepped into the shop, closed the door behind him, and looked around. Broken glass and the beads of the store's broken abacus lay before him on the floor.

There was nothing that resembled food in the store except a spongy splat of white on the floor. The splat, which may have recently been cheese, bore the footprint of a large shoe.

Rostnikov moved around the splat, behind the counter, and up to the door behind which someone was sobbing.

He knocked twice.

"Who?" came a woman's voice.

The voice sounded dreamy, as if the woman had just awakened from a deep dream.

"My name is Porfiry Petrovich," he said. "I would like to talk to you."

"Are you a policeman?"

"Would anyone but a policeman want to come in and talk to a woman with a gun?"

"Do you have a gun?" she asked.

"No," he said. "I'm not fond of guns."

"Me neither," said the woman. "Why do you want to come in?"

"Perhaps I might be able to help."

"You are alone? There is no one out there with you?"

"No one."

"Come in and close the door behind you. I want to see your hands."

Rostnikov pushed the door open.

The room held a small metal table, some empty shelves against the walls, several chairs, and a stool on which the older woman sat. The walls were gray white. The room was not large, but he was at least ten feet from the two women.

"What is wrong with your leg?" asked Galina as Rostnikov came forward slowly.

"Old injury, the war, Nazi tank," he said. "May I sit?"

Galina shrugged. "I don't own the store. Sit if you want to sit."

Rostnikov moved carefully to the nearest chair on his right, almost a dozen feet from the two women. He sat awkwardly, his left leg extended, his right bent. The young woman on the floor looked at him with moist frightened eyes.

"You were telling the truth," said Galina.

"The truth?"

"Your leg," she said, pointing at his leg with the pistol in her hand. "I thought you might be pretending so you could jump at me when I didn't expcct it. But . . . you are too young to—"

"I was not yet fifteen when this happened," he said.

Galina nodded knowingly.

"Your name is . . . ?" asked Rostnikov.

"Galina Panishkoya," said the woman.

"And you are . . . ?" he asked, looking at the frightened girl on the floor.

"Ludmilla, Ludmilla . . . I can't remember my last name," she said between tears.

"That's not possible," said Galina.

"It happens to some people when they are very frightened," said Rostnikov. "It happened to me once."

"To forget your own name," said Galina, shaking her head.

"Perhaps if Ludmilla got up and went outside, she would be less frightened," Rostnikov suggested.

"But then," Galina said, raising the barrel of the pistol to the girl's head, "your police would come in here and shoot me."

"No. You would still have me," he said.

"You? What would I do with you?"

"Talk," he said.

"Talk, there is nothing to talk about," said Galina. "This stool is too low. When I was a girl in Georgia, I milked goats on a stool like this. Sat for hours. Now, backaches."

"You remember a—"

A loud noise rose from beyond the door, on the street, laughter or anger—it was hard to tell which. Ludmilla looked at the dead man near the door and began to shake.

"You remember a great deal about when you were a child?" Rostnikov asked.

"One forgets the details," said Galina. "Where was the chair? The bed? What color were the walls? These are important things. If we cannot remember our lives, what do we have?"

Rostnikov nodded. "Ludmilla is growing more frightened," he said.

Galina looked down at the young woman in front of her as if for the first time. "I have two granddaughters," she said. "Little. Eleven and seven. My daughter is dead. Her husband left them with me. He"—she nodded toward the sprawled dead man—"looked like him."

"Is that why you shot him?"

"I don't know if I shot him," she said, looking directly at him. "But . . ."

"I believe you," he said, and he did believe her.

"My savings are gone. My job, I used to work at the Panyushkin dress factory, gone. My legs, gone. And my memory is going. I can't even remember if I shot a man a few hours ago."

Rostnikov did not correct her. The manager of State Store

31 had been shot no more than ten minutes ago. "I suggest you put the gun down and I take you and Ludmilla out."

"No," Galina said, looking toward the door. "I'll go to jail. I'm too old. I'm a good Christian. I'll die knowing my girls are starving. It's better I die here."

Rostnikov could now barely hear her over the sobs of the girl on the floor. He put a finger to his lips to quiet her and she made an effort, which resulted in more subdued sobs.

"He came out," Galina said, trying to remember what had taken place less than an hour earlier. "He shouted. He had a gun. He had no compassion. This one . . ." She touched the top of Ludmilla's head with the barrel of the gun, and the girl closed her eyes. "She had no compassion. Now she cries, but we cried, my babies cry with hunger."

"It's my work," Ludmilla said, addressing the policeman. "I feel, but—"

"Go," said Galina, standing. "Go."

Ludmilla looked up at her and then at Rostnikov. "You'll shoot me."

"Go," Galina repeated, and Rostnikov nodded his head yes.

Ludmilla stood, knees week, sagging arms and shoulders shaking. "You won't shoot me?" she said, looking down at the corpse near the door.

"No."

The girl took two steps to the door and stopped. "I can't walk."

"Ludmilla," Rostnikov said gently. "It is time to go."

"I've made in my pants. There are people out there. Customers. They'll see me. Laugh at me . . ."

"Go," Galina said gently. "Now."

Ludmilla sighed deeply, brushed back her short hair, and ran out the door, slamming it behind her. They could hear the sound of her feet running on broken glass, a door opening, and then the mixed cheers and boos of the crowd.

"I don't even know what kind of gun this is," Galina said, sitting back on the stool.

"May I?" asked Rostnikov, putting his right hand up to his jacket.

Galina nodded.

Porfiry Petrovich reached into the inner pocket of his jacket and extracted a pair of glasses, which he placed on his nose. He looked at Galina and the weapon in her hand. "A Femaru, Hungarian pistol," he said. "Probably a 7.65mm Hege. Possibly a Walam model. Look at the handle."

She loosed her grip slightly and looked down.

"A Pegasus in a circle?" he asked.

"Pega . . . ?"

"Flying horse."

She nodded.

"The Hege," he said, putting the glasses away carefully.

"I thought you didn't like guns," she said, lifting her arm to aim the weapon at him.

"It is, in my work, a good idea to know weapons. One is not required to like what one may be required to know."

"I think," she said, "it would be best if I shot myself." She raised the weapon and pointed it to her head.

"I have a son," Rostnikov said. "His name is Iosef."

"I had a daughter," said Galina. "We were told not to have more than one child. We all listened except the Ubekistanis. Arabs. They were right. We were wrong."

"Your granddaughters," he said.

"I am not young and this gun is heavy."

"It makes an unpleasant hole," he said, shifting his weight slightly. "A painful hole. I think you might not be in jail long, if at all, Galina Panishkoya. Have you ever committed a crime?"

"I was born. I had a daughter. I'm sorry, I can hold this gun no—"

"You shall see your grandchildren," he said. "You shall talk to them, prepare them. Where are they now?"

"Home, waiting for me, hungry," she said.

Rostnikov said nothing. He imagined two frightened little girls waiting all day. He looked into the deep brown eyes of the woman across the room and knew she was thinking the same or something very like it.

The gun came down slowly.

"You promise?" she asked.

"I promise," he said.

"All I wanted was a small bread," Galina said, taking a step toward the policeman and holding out the weapon to him. "I had the money to pay for it."

Rostnikov took the gun, placed it in his pocket, and moved to the woman's side to take her arm and keep her from collapsing.

The central police headquarters known simply as Petrovka stands at 38 Petrovka Street. It is, to those who see it for the first time, a surprisingly pleasant pair of white L-shaped buildings. Behind the black-and-white iron gates of Petrovka is a garden. In the spring the red flowers that bloom there recall the summer palaces of the long-extinct nobility and the recently extinct Politburo members.

Entrance to Petrovka is through a narrow gate where each entrant must show his identification or invitation. The line moves slowly now because the guards who knew everyone by sight have been replaced, and many of the people who entered daily, some of them for decades, have themselves been told to seek other employment.

Twenty minutes after he had left Galina Panishkoya with the policeman named Tiomkin and ordered him to take her to her apartment to get her grandchildren, Porfiry Petrovich was waiting patiently outside Petrovka behind an assistant procurator named Lavertnikov.

"Madness," muttered Lavertnikov, who wore a heavy coat and a hat with earflaps that made him look like a small bespectacled boy.

Rostnikov nodded and grunted without looking up from the particularly grisly passage he was reading in his American detective paperback, an Ed McBain titled *Widows*, which he had read only twice before. His fingers were cold, and every few moments he shifted the book to the other hand and plunged the cold one into his pocket.

The assistant procurator's observation had seemed a reasonable one to Rostnikov in spite of its lack of a clear context.

The line was moving slowly.

Rostnikov closed the book and placed it gently in the wide pocket of his coat. "How well do you remember the house in which you lived as a boy?" he asked.

The assistant procurator adjusted his spectacles and looked at Rostnikov. "I . . . we lived in an apartment," he answered, clutching his brown briefcase protectively to his side.

Rostnikov nodded. "What good is the past if we cannot remember it?" he said. "A woman named Galina Panishkoya reminded me of that earlier."

"Galina . . . ?"

"We remember only the shared past we are taught," Rostnikov went on, "the history of czars and commissars, premiers, generals, scientists, and presidents. We can be reasonably sure that at some point in our lives even that will be revised."

They had moved another few paces closer to the guard window. The assistant procurator was looking decidedly uncomfortable. "History is . . ." he began, and then paused.

". . . elusive," concluded Rostnikov. "Nostalgia, the history of our own lives, is too often demeaned as trivia. And that demeans each of us."

"Indeed," agreed Lavertnikov as he turned to show his identification card.

"It's not madness," said Rostnikov. "It is chaos. And they are not quite the same thing."

The guard waved the assistant procurator in and turned to Rostnikov, who held up his photo identification card. The young man in uniform looked at it, then at Rostnikov, then back at the card before nodding him on.

Beyond the gate Petrovka 38 is modern, utilitarian, and very busy. Police officers wearing the gray uniforms with red braid and investigators of the MVD, the Ministry of Internal Affairs, in their blue suits stream in and out of the building throughout the day and night. All are wondering if they will be uniformed at the same hour next week, which leads to a sense of irritability spoken of only behind closed doors and only among friends.

Just inside the inner doors at the top of the wide steps in each wing of Petrovka 38 stand uniformed officers armed with automatic weapons. Where there were two, there are now six. They have been told to watch not for disgruntled Arabs or separatists as in the past, but for old-guard Communists who might go mad like those postal clerks in America who seem to run amok every month or two because they've lost their routes, jobs, or bonuses.

Rostnikov moved up the steps past the armed guards and into the overwhelming warmth of the building. Since the fall of the union someone had decided that Petrovka needed more heat. It was probably impossible to determine who made this decision, but the building had become soporific.

On the top floor of Petrovka, in the right tower facing the narrow street, is the office of the director of special projects, Colonel Aleksandr Snitkonoy. On this morning three men sat at the oak conference table in the office of Colonel Snitkonoy, their backs to the door, as the colonel paced in front of them and spoke in the commanding deep voice that had made him a favorite speaker at factory openings and funerals of military and party leaders.

The three men watched the colonel, known throughout the MVD as the Gray Wolfhound. The colonel was tall and slender, with distinguished-looking gray hair at his temples. He wore a brown uniform, perfectly pressed. His many medals and ribbons of honor were neatly aligned on his chest. One of the ribbons commemorated his legendary speech in Prague in 1968 when he turned a rabble crowd of irate young Czechs with promises that were never delivered upon. The speech had been spoken in perfect Czech. The colonel's latest ribbon had come when his men had thwarted an assassination attempt on President Gorbachev.

During the days of confusion when Yeltsin had barricaded himself in the Parliament Building, Colonel Snitkonoy had found himself torn between two apparently conflicting orders, one from Major General Gurov himself commanding him and his men to support the loyal militia preparing to storm the parliament, and one from a KGB source whose name was indecipherably signed at the bottom of a hand-delivered directive ordering the Department of Special Projects to resist all efforts to undermine the revolution.

The colonel, confused but dignified, had assembled his small staff, manned all phones twenty-four hours a day for the entire week of conflict, and reassured all callers, and there were few, that his office would follow only the orders of those legally empowered to issue them. The result was that he and his staff followed no orders at all until it was quite clear who was in charge.

The result of this position was inaction with the appearance of great activity.

In appreciation of the work and loyalty of the Special Section during the days of tension, the colonel had been given responsibility for "various matters of a delicate investigatory nature as they arise in the newly independent Republic of Russia."

The colonel was vaguely aware that his mission prior to

the new directive had been almost entirely ceremonial, but all that had changed. The Gray Wolfhound and his men now had the official responsibility for politically sensitive cases that no other branch would touch. In short, the Gray Wolfhound's Special Section was now the unofficial scapegoat of the new and not yet clearly defined criminal justice system.

Colonel Snitkonoy, hands folded behind his back, head held high, continued his regular early-morning meeting, a meeting he had called an hour earlier than usual. "The union for which our fathers fought and died has come asunder. The revolution is over and the images of Lenin are crushed. As Marx said, 'The task I have set myself is to sweep away the stumbling block which people under the guise of Marxism are offering as order but which is something incredibly muddled, confused, and reactionary.' And therefore, comrades, we must make the present better so that our children and their children will have a past worth remembering."

Colonel Snitkonoy had no children and, in fact, had never married, as those who listened knew. He lived in a dacha just outside of Moscow beyond the Greater Ring Road with his former military aide and a woman who served as his cook-housekeeper. It was rumored that his monthly salary was now fifteen thousand rubles compared with the maximum four hundred and twenty rubles a month a uniformed policeman could earn.

The colonel paused at his favorite morning spot, where the sunlight, what there was of it, outlined him dramatically for those who sat before him. "And now, comrades, to our task."

He looked at the trio at the table and smiled enigmatically. He meant that sly smile to suggest that he was about to give them a philosophical puzzle that only the brightest of them might be able to solve.

The men were looking at the papers in front of them when

Rostnikov entered the room behind them. He removed his coat, placed it on an empty chair at the end of the table, and sat.

The colonel looked at the new arrival. Rostnikov looked back at him emotionlessly, then pulled a pad of paper in front of him, removed a Japanese-made Rolling Writer pen from his pocket and began to write.

"Events move quickly in troubled times," Snitkonoy announced. "A revolution can take place in a moment."

The three other men at the table looked at Rostnikov, who continued to write on his pad.

"Promptness is essential," continued the colonel.

Since Rostnikov continued to write without looking up, the colonel turned his attention to his assistant, Pankov, a very small man with thinning hair who held his job primarily because he was such a perfect foil for the colonel. Whereas the colonel, in emulation of the American General MacArthur, changed his clothes three times a day and always smelled fresh and ready for battle, Pankov had been a perspirer even in the days when Petrovka was kept frigid. He was always uncertain, his clothes were always rumpled, and his few strands of hair were unwilling to obey even the most determined attempts to tame them with oil. In appreciation of his assistant's total inadequacy the colonel never failed to treat Pankov as if he were a bewildered child.

"Pankov," the Wolfhound said gently but firmly. "Schedule."

Pankov shuddered as if someone had placed an ice chip from the Moscow River down his back.

"Formatov and Seekle," he began, "are to report this morning on the thieves who are attacking shoppers in the Cherymushinsky farm market, grabbing their shopping bags, cutting their *avoska*, their string bags, and—"

Pankov stopped suddenly. The colonel was bored. His

department was now beyond such pettiness. "We must continue to improve our efficiency," he concluded abruptly.

Though the statement made no sense under the circumstances, the Wolfhound nodded indulgently and turned to the man sitting to Pankov's left, Major Andrei Grigorovich, a blocky man in his mid-forties who had once offended a general without knowing why and, as punishment, had been assigned to the Gray Wolfhound. Considering the recent transfers and suicides (one by way of three bullets to the head) of many ranking members of the KGB and MVD, Major Grigorovich regarded his offense as a good career move. Now he nurtured a renewed spark of the ambition he had once held. With the recent elevation of the Special Section, the major believed it was only a matter of time until the new minister of the interior came to the same conclusion Major Grigorovich had about Colonel Snitkonoy's competence.

"The daughter of the Syrian oil minister is still missing," Grigorovich said. "Progress is slow. I suggest—"

"Who is on the case?" asked the colonel.

"Tkach and Timofeyeva," replied Grigorovich with a touch of scorn in his voice. Sasha Tkach and Elena Timofeyeva were not among those in the Special Section aligned with the major. They, like Emil Karpo, the tall specter to Grigorovich's right, were known allies of his painfully unambitious rival, Porfiry Petrovich Rostnikov, who sat at the end of the table. Grigorovich noted that Rostnikov had not looked up from his notes since being seated.

"Bring me their reports when they return," said Colonel Snitkonoy. He turned his gray eyes on Karpo. Colonel Snitkonoy did not like being eye to eye with Investigator Emil Karpo, the unblinking Tatar with thinning hair. Karpo was called "the Vampire" behind his back. To Snitkonoy he looked more like the man who played the somnambulist in *The Cabinet of Dr. Caligari*, a German silent film he had seen at the Moscow Film Festival of 1984, where the colonel had served as official government host.

"Comrade . . ." he began, and then corrected himself. "Citizen Karpo."

"Written reports on the telephone exchange suicide, the woman who claims her dead husband is not dead and is trying to kill her, and the—"

"Old business," the colonel interrupted. "You must put old business aside. Do you know how many unsolved crimes we have in the records room for the past five years alone?"

"Four thousand three hundred and six as of Monday," Karpo replied seriously.

"Four thousand three hundred and six," the Wolfhound repeated, as if Karpo had just come up with the correct answer, which the colonel knew as well as he knew his own military ribbons.

"Anything else, Karpo?" he asked indulgently.

"It was Lenin," said Karpo.

"Lenin?" repeated Colonel Snitkonoy.

"Lenin, not Marx, who said, 'Namely, the task I set myself . . .' "

"Yes." The colonel sighed. "It was Lenin, not Marx. You did not fall into my little trap. Porfiry Petrovich," he now said, "you are to put aside whatever you are working on and take up an emergency case. It involves *Prahvahslahvnahyah tsehrkaf*, the Orthodox Church."

It had long been believed by all who attended these morning meetings that the man known as the Washtub missed not a word, not a nuance. However, for the past few minutes, Rostnikov had been paying little attention to the Gray Wolfhound. He had been trying to remember precisely the small one-bedroom apartment in which he had grown up on Leningrad Prospekt. After his conversation with Galina Panishkoya that morning it seemed a very important task. The house was long gone, replaced by a poured-concrete Stalinist high rise with frightened oblong window eyes.

His bed had been right by the window in his parents' room. He had drawn the bed carefully with his pencil, right down to the remembered pattern of faded flowers on the quilt. But what about the sofa, the walls, the chairs? Had there been three? He could remember only two vividly, but a third chair, with a high back and a carving . . .

"Porfiry Petrovich," the Wolfhound repeated, and with a sigh Inspector Rostnikov put down his pen and looked up at the waiting colonel.

The colonel continued, "A case has come to us regarding an important church matter which will soon be brought to the attention of the public." He paused, prepared to stun his staff with the name of the infamous priest.

"Merhum," said Rostnikov. "Father Vasili Merhum. He was murdered yesterday in the woods of Arkush. Ax blows to the front and to the back of the head. He managed to crawl to his nearby cottage. There he muttered a few words to his housekeeper, an old nun."

The meeting was on the verge of becoming a disaster, but with military genius the Gray Wolfhound smiled. He had perfect strong teeth. "And do you know what those words were?" he asked. He did not know the words himself, nor had he known that words had been muttered, but he had been assured by his superiors that the death of the priest had been kept quiet, that the town of Arkush had been effectively sealed, that—

"Sister, Oleg must forgive me," said Karpo.

Major Grigorovich placed his pencil neatly atop the pad before him. The battle with Rostnikov was definitely lost for the day. It was time to lay down his arms and prepare for another tomorrow. He would quietly explore the mystery of how Rostnikov and his men had learned of the murder.

He suspected that the information had come to Karpo from

Kosnitsov, the forensic scientist who worked in the bowels of Petrovka. Kosnitsov would have already examined samples of the victim's hair and blood and bits of his clothing. He would have relayed his findings to Karpo and Rostnikov.

"Sister Oleg," said the colonel.

"His housekeeper was a nun," explained Rostnikov. "It was into her arms that he crawled and in her arms he died."

"Her name is Oleg?" Pankov asked incredulously.

The colonel gave his assistant an imperious look of pity and ignored his question. "You will go to Arkush immediately," he said to Rostnikov. "You and Investigator Karpo. Father Merhum was, as you all know, well known for his frankness. It is particularly awkward at this crucial moment in our history that such a tragedy should take place. Father Merhum was scheduled to make a highly critical speech here in Moscow. The speech, which attacks those at the highest level, is in the hands of the foreign press. President Yeltsin himself will tomorrow issue the following statement. . . ."

Snitkonoy looked at Rostnikov to see if he also knew this, but Profiry Petrovich's face betrayed nothing.

The colonel went to his desk, lifted a spotless manila folder, removed a typed sheet and read: " 'The death of this innocent, revered citizen is a tragedy we must all feel. We shall spare no effort in finding the person or persons responsible for killing this respected figure.'

"The honor of this investigation, the confidence of the president himself, has been granted to us," said the Wolfhound, gently returning the sheet to the folder and placing the folder even more gently back on his dark well-polished desk.

Which means, thought Rostnikov, that if the killer is not found, it will be considered a government cover-up. If the killer *is* found, it will be accepted as a frame-up. The situation was a familiar one. A change of flags did not change a national psyche.

"Pankov has a complete file for you," the colonel said. "You may take a car. Do you have any questions? Do you have any ideas with which to begin?"

"Oleg," said Inspector Rostnikov, looking down at the drawing he had made of his family's house.

The colonel was seated, his hands flat on the surface of his desk. He said, "It is likely the priest was simply babbling. However, he may well have been identifying his attacker. Perhaps, in his confusion, someone named Oleg. Perhaps the sister of someone named Oleg."

Rostnikov stood, steadying himself with both hands on the desk to keep his too-long-motionless leg from betraying him. "Very likely," he agreed. "Under the circumstances it is probably best that I take immediate action."

The colonel looked at Rostnikov, as did Major Grigorovich and Pankov. Only Emil Karpo, who also rose silently, did not look at him.

Major Grigorovich reached for the pencil he had set down only moments earlier. The battle, it seemed, was not completely lost. It was possible that Rostnikov's mission would result in total disaster.

THREE

THREE MILES AWAY FROM PETROVKA, NEAR THE ARBAT pedestrian mall, Special Section investigators Sasha Tkach and Elena Timofeyeva were waiting in line.

Lines are a way of life in Russia. There are housewives and house husbands, babushkas and grandfathers, who spend their lives in lines. People go mad in lines, come to the major decisions of their lives in lines, get their principal education and entertainment from the books they read in lines, and make lifelong friends and enemies in lines.

In this particular line there were eight people ahead of Sasha to buy pizza from the big white truck. Though few could afford it, pizza had replaced McDonald's burgers as the new rage in Moscow.

Sasha's ears were cold and he didn't particularly want to try pizza, though Elena, who had spent two years studying English and English history in Boston, said it was "passable" pizza, nothing like in the state-run shops, where it tasted like baked pencil shavings. Nor was it anything like the pizza in the Pizza Hut across from the Intourist Hotel. But, she insisted, it was not bad.

Sasha did not really care about the quality of the pizza. He could afford neither pizza nor anything else on the Arbat now that the price of everything had gone up with Yeltsin's free-market insanity. He had a wife, a child, another on the way, a mother. Elena had no one to support but herself and she lived with her aunt, who had, no doubt, a comfortable government pension. Elena could afford pizzas.

Now that they were approaching the open window from which the pizzas were dispensed, Sasha could smell the dough and the cheese. It was a warm smell of something in the past and it made him even more irritable. "We should be at the Nikolai," he grumbled, without looking at his new partner.

They had already been to one restaurant and a rock-and-roll club. No one remembered the Arab girl at the restaurant. No one had been at the rock-and-roll club so early in the morning. The Nikolai Café looked like their best chance, if something was to be accomplished today.

Sasha shifted his weight and decided that there were many reasons to be miserable. For one thing he would be thirty years old in three days, which did not please him. Nor did the prospect of the birthday party Rostnikov and his wife were preparing. He did not want to be thirty. He did not look or feel thirty. He looked no different than he had for the past six or seven years, and most people took him for no more than twenty-three. He was, he knew, reasonably good-looking, if a bit thin. His straight blond hair frequently fell over his eyes and he had an engaging habit of throwing his head back to clear his vision. He also had a large space between his front upper teeth, which seemed to bring out the maternal instinct in most women. Another thing that contributed to Sasha's misery was that the woman who stood with him seemed not only immune to his boyish charm but indifferent to almost everything about him. She was a year or two older than he, granted, but he was the one with experience.

He had been shot at and had shot back. He had even killed criminals. He had seen death, corruption, and misery. Now with a mother, a wife, a child, and another one on the way, he looked forward only to financial disaster, a greater loss of privacy, and increased responsibilities. And now he had this inexperienced woman acting as if she were the one in charge.

"Why do you look so angry?" Elena asked.

"Because I am angry," Sasha replied. "When I am angry, it shows on my face, if I choose to allow it to show."

"And you have reasons for this anger?"

"I have reasons," he said, plunging his hands into his pockets.

"Which you do not wish to share."

"Which I do not wish to share."

"Try a slice this time," she said, looking over his shoulder at the well-dressed businessman directly in front of them who was shifting his shopping bag from one hand to the other.

"I think I'll eat two slices," Sasha said casually.

Elena shrugged.

Sasha wasn't even hungry. He had eaten some bread and kasha with tea before he left home. He had made breakfast for his pregnant wife, Maya. Sasha's mother, Lydia, had been in the living room, the only other room in the apartment, when Sasha had brought his wife breakfast in her bed. The doctor, Sarah Rostnikov's cousin, had insisted that Maya move as little as possible until the pains started or her water broke.

The irony of this was that Sasha, Maya, and their daughter, Pulcharia, had recently moved in order to have some privacy from Lydia, whom Sasha loved dearly, as one should love a mother, but who, he admitted, was difficult enough to drive a monk to suicide. She was close to deaf and would do nothing about it. She was uncompromising on food preparation, etiquette, child care, and hygiene. Maya had urged Sasha to use his position as a policeman to find a way to exchange their old apartment for a small one for them and another small one for Lydia, and he had done so with guilt but with little regret. Now, only weeks after the separation, Lydia, with a leave of absence from her government job, was back in their apartment to help take care of Maya and Pulcharia, who was now almost two. There was no sign that his mother ever contemplated moving out when the baby came.

Maya had told him to be patient and he had tried to be. This morning he asked Lydia if she had seen his *tooflyee*, his shoes, and she answered, "Like your father. He was thirty when he started to say crazy things." Then she looked at her son and said, in a tone obviously meant only for a demented child, "Why are you looking for a *tighgah*?"

"I am not looking for a rain forest," Sasha had answered, without raising his voice, as Lydia looked at Pulcharia for confirmation of what Sasha had *really* said.

Now, to add to his misery, he was spending his days with Elena Timofeyeva instead of Zelach, his usual partner. Zelach was recovering from the near loss of his eye, an injury he might never have sustained if Sasha had been doing his job instead of being seduced by a suspect. Zelach was an amiable, if exasperatingly slow, hulk of a man. There was no doubt of who was in charge when he and Zelach were on an assignment.

Sasha wanted to put his hands over his ears to warm them, but he looked at Elena, who was hatless, and decided to suffer.

"You look cold," she said. Her thigh-length cloth coat was not even buttoned. "It will warm up later."

"I'm fine," Sasha said, though he now feared that he might be coming down with a cold.

"If you want to go stand in the metro entrance, I'll bring the pizzas," she said.

"I am not the least bit cold," Sasha said emphatically.

Elena shrugged and looked at the man with the shopping bag. The man tried to ignore the scrutiny by feigning a great interest in a lumber truck parked in front of a government food shop.

"You see the man ahead of us?" Sasha suddenly said in a whisper that could be heard for at least half a block.

The man couldn't help turning his head slightly in their direction. Elena looked at the man with sympathy, which seemed to increase his discomfort.

As the line moved forward a flurry of automobile horns signaled a battle over a few feet of space on Kalinin Street.

Sasha looked at Elena. She was a bit hefty for his taste, but he had to admit that her face was pleasant, her skin clear, her eyes blue, and her teeth, though a bit large, remarkably even and cleaner looking than most Russians'. Her dark hair was just long enough to be pulled back and tied behind her head with a rubber band. At that moment of unnecessary embarrassment Sasha was glad that he did not find her particularly attractive. He loved his wife, her voice, her laugh, her face, but all too often he had been betrayed by his flesh.

"What about the man?" Elena asked.

"It's Semykin," he said. "Gregor Semykin, the one who was arrested with Folyoskov last year, the glass-tumbler case."

Elena looked at the man, who was now studying the fascinating head of the woman in front of him. The line moved forward. "It is not Semykin," she whispered. "The man looks nothing like Semykin. Semykin is in jail. Semykin is short."

"Perhaps it's his brother," Sasha replied. "The similarity—"

The man in front of them suddenly looked at his watch, gave the impression that he had forgotten an important meeting, and left the line hurriedly.

Sasha urged Elena forward in the line.

"That was unnecessary," she said.

"We're in a hurry. You said we're in a hurry. Besides, the man was guilty of something or he wouldn't have run."

The warmth of the truck made a difference now that they were only two customers away from being served.

"Everyone is guilty of something," Elena said. "It makes—"

"And it is our task to find out what it is," Sasha said, standing on his toes so he could get a better view of the interior of the pizza truck.

"Only if they are guilty of a crime," Elena said.

"There are so many crimes," he said with a shrug. "And there'll soon be new crimes. Crimes against the rights of individuals, women, crimes against dignity. This is too serious and I am hungry."

They stood in front of the truck window now. The line behind them numbered about forty.

"No more," said the man in the window. "We're out of pizzas."

He was a heavy man in need of a shave. Perched on his head of unruly black hair was a white cap designed to protect the food. His smile revealed teeth in need of emergency dentistry.

"We're the police," Sasha said.

The man shouted over their heads, "You see, there is no more cheese. I'm not a magician who can make cheese appear where there is no cheese. And I do not make pizzas without cheese. So, no more pizza today."

The line held for a moment and then, amid groans and threats, it broke up. The man with the white cap and bad teeth started to close the doors.

"We are the police," Sasha repeated.

"Once that meant something," the man said, leaning forward, "but read the papers, turn on the television. Look at the political paintings being sold on the walls of this very street. The police can't threaten. Boris Yeltsin will not tolerate it. We are becoming a democracy. A democracy with no cheese. If you were cows and could give me cheese, we would have something to talk about."

"You are not humorous," Sasha Tkach said, looking at Elena. She did not seem to be enjoying the scene.

"Then do me a favor. Don't hire me as a comedian."

Sasha felt Elena's hand on his shoulder and turned to shrug it off so he could carry on his debate with the pizza man, who now had one of the doors almost closed. Elena stepped in front of Sasha and gave the pizza man her best smile. The man returned a frown.

"No more cheese. I'll say it slowly one last time, and then I'll say good-bye. No . . . more . . . cheese. Now arrest me for not having cheese."

Sasha's hand went out past Elena and grabbed the second door as the man started to close it.

"Tkach," Elena said. "It doesn't—"

"You wanted pizza," he said. "You will have pizza. I will taste pizza. I will eat it and imagine what it must be like to live in Naples or Boston and eat pizza."

Sasha pulled the door from the man's hand. It shot out with a clatter against the side of the truck. A few people in the line who had not decided on a breakfast alternative looked up.

"Are you crazy?" the pizza man said, losing his cap. "Boris, help."

A voice from inside the truck, dark and deep, called, "What are you doing, Kornei? Close the damned door and let's get out of here."

As the voice came from within, Sasha grabbed the sleeve of the pizza man and pulled him forward. The man hit the partly closed door, popping it open with a bang.

"No, no, what are you doing?" screamed the pizza man, grabbing the open door to keep from falling to the street.

Sasha felt an arm on his shoulder again and dimly heard a woman's voice behind him, but it was too late. There were too many lines, too little cheese and money, too many mothers, children, eyes, birthdays, people demanding.

Over the rear end of the pizza man named Kornei appeared a huge round face with a very flat nose. This second pizza man, Boris, wore a white cheese-and-sauce-stained apron and a look of total bewilderment. "Call the police," he shouted at Elena as he grabbed Kornei to keep him from being pulled to the street by Sasha.

"They are the police," cried Kornei.

Whereupon the man inside the truck let go of his partner, and Kornei tumbled onto the sidewalk.

"Tkach," Elena said, moving past him to help the panicked pizza man, who rubbed his shoulder as he inched his way backward on his behind till his back was against the truck.

Sasha looked up at Boris, and what Boris saw in the young man's eyes made him say, "We were saving one for ourselves. It's yours. Don't touch him. Wait. Wait."

"Help," Kornei called out to the growing crowd.

The cry for help started an immediate debate.

"Help him," called a woman.

"What?" said a man. "I'm going to fight with the police, get my head broken over a pizza?"

"He must have done something wrong if the police are beating him," said another man. "Maybe he's selling tainted pizza."

Some of the crowd—Elena was sure it was the ones who were eating pizzas they had luckily or unluckily purchased before the madness began—began to grumble and move forward.

The big man appeared at the window, holding a pizza covered with cheese and a red sauce. "Here," he said, holding it out.

Sasha took the pizza and handed it to Elena. "How much?" he asked.

"You're paying?" asked Boris, leaning over to see if his partner was still alive.

"We are not thieves," said Sasha.

"Ten rubles," said the man.

Sasha opened his wallet, found five rubles, half his monthly rent, and handed them to the man.

"Kornei has a wife and four children," said Boris softly through the window.

"Yes," Kornei agreed, "I have a wife and four children."

"One generally has a wife if he has four children," Sasha countered madly. "If one does not have a wife, one usually cannot tell how many children he has."

Sasha took the pizza from Elena and stalked away. He handed her a slice as they moved through the crowd.

"And he looks like such a child," said a woman, whose voice sounded uncomfortably like his mother's.

They walked swiftly down the Arbat, eating just-slightly-warmer-than-cold pizza.

"Do you go insane frequently?" Elena asked.

"No," he said. "Not enough."

"And it feels . . . ?"

"Fine, just fine," he said, gobbling down pizza. It had no taste and its consistency was that of a tennis shoe.

They were standing in the Sobachaya Ploshadka, Dog Square.

"You know what was here two hundred years ago?" Sasha asked, stopping to look around, waving a floppy slice of pizza.

Elena shrugged.

"Dog kennels, the kennels of the czar. The dogs were treated better than people," he said to a fat little woman who waddled quickly by. "I hate this pizza."

Elena took it from him and began to munch on it.

At that moment Sasha decided to bang his fist down on top of an illegally parked white Lada.

"I live with my aunt, you know," Elena said. They were next to one of the sidewalk stands that sold marioshki dolls and enameled boxes. A year ago the Gorbachev doll was the large outside one in which all the others nested. He had been replaced by Yeltsin, into whom Gorbachev now fit snugly.

"That is not relevant," Sasha said. "I don't want to talk about your aunt. I want to stay angry. If you hadn't insisted on the stupid pizza—"

"You know my aunt?" Elena asked, still munching on the pizza.

Sasha stood in the middle of the sidewalk, his hands in his pockets. "Yes," he said. "I was with the procurator general's office when she was a director."

He looked down the Arbat, hoping for trouble, but none was coming. He longed for a pair of young men with punk American clothes and weirdly cut hair who would look at him with a challenge or dare to say a word. He would even settle for a vendor he could catch taking American dollars.

"You want some of this pizza back?" she asked. "I don't need to get any fatter."

"You are not fat," he said, considering another assault on the innocent Lada.

"My aunt had four heart attacks," Elena said. "That's why she retired."

"I know," said Sasha.

Later, he decided, he would go home, stare his mother down, stare his wife down, and grunt at Pulcharia if she was still awake. He would sit in the corner watching American music videos on the television all night without saying a word, and if they dared to speak to him . . .

"We live in a small apartment with her cat, Baku," Elena said.

A truck hit its horn somewhere in the direction of Kalinin Prospekt. There was a screeching of tires but no crash.

"It used to be," Sasha said, "that a policeman had respect, even fear. It used to be that a policeman could do his job. It used to be—''

''—that a policeman was a police man and not a police woman,'' Elena supplied. ''There will be more of us now.''

''Yes,'' he said defiantly, looking at her. ''I know.''

She nodded, wiped her hands together, and sucked some sauce off her left thumb. Sasha had a sudden mad urge to step over and suck her thumb.

''Do you want to go find a missing Arab girl?'' Elena asked, pushing away from the wall. ''Or do you want to hit more cars and beat up more people?''

''I didn't beat him up,'' Sasha said. He knew he was losing the anger, and he wanted to recover it.

''You should take up some hobby,'' she said, starting down the street toward Kalinin.

''I'm too busy for hobbies,'' he said. ''I work all day and half the night, and whatever time I have left I spend taking care of my daughter and trying to please my wife and my mother.''

Elena was about twenty yards away now. She stopped and turned to speak to him. ''That is a very sad story, Tkach,'' she said with mock sympathy. ''I'll tell you mine someday.''

Someone not long ago had said the same thing or something like it to Sasha. It felt as if it had been Elena in this same place.

''Damn,'' he shouted.

''What now?'' she called.

People were crossing the street, pretending to look for some address to avoid the insane couple.

He moved toward her, his hands still plunged in his pockets. Sasha threw his head back to clear the dangling hair from his eyes.

Elena said nothing as they walked side by side.

''My birthday is in three days. You want to know how old I'll be?''

"Thirty," she said.

"I look thirty?"

"You look fourteen," she said. "My aunt and I have been invited to the party for you. If you are reasonably sane by then, we may come."

"I'm sorry," he said.

"I think I like you better crazy than contrite," she said. "Or even better, something in between."

"I'll try," he said.

"Feel better?"

"Yes."

"Then . . ."

"Let's find an Arab girl."

FOUR

BEFORE HE LEFT PETROVKA, PORFIRY PETROVICH ROSTnikov called his wife. He knew she would be home. Sarah was recovering from surgery for a brain tumor. The operation had gone well, but the recovery was taking much longer than they had expected. They had gone on a vacation to Yalta, which had not been much of a rest, and some progress had been made, but Sarah still grew dizzy if she walked more than a few blocks and she needed at least ten hours of sleep each night.

"You're home," he said when she answered the phone.

"I was about to go through the door when you called," she said. "I'm trying out for the circus in an hour."

"Trapeze?" he asked.

"High wire. Only the Americans and the Brazilians still do trapeze. What's the bad news?"

He was doodling again, trying to find . . . "I've got to go to Arkush today. I may not be back tonight. A priest has been murdered. Father Merhum."

There was a silence on the line and then a sigh. "Iosef's play," she said.

Their son had been out of the army for almost six months, and a play he had written about his experiences in Afghanistan was scheduled to open that night.

"I'll try to come back," he said.

"Father Merhum," she said. "Isn't he the one . . . ?"

"Yes."

"Who would . . . ?"

"That's why I am going."

She laughed. Her laugh had not changed and it always broke his heart. He had known her since she was a young girl, and now he saw a few film frames of the young pale girl with the long red hair laughing in the park. It was a laugh filled with sadness.

"Try to get back for the play," she said.

"You'll be all right?"

"My cousin Gittel will be here this afternoon."

"Good," he said. "Sarah, you remember my family's apartment near the Arbat?"

"I was only in it twice," she said.

"Were there three chairs in the bedroom or two?"

"I don't know, Porfiry. Is it important?"

"Perhaps," he said. "I will be back tonight if I can. If not, I will call Iosef and tell him we will come tomorrow."

"They still murder priests," she said. "The Cossacks are back in the street."

Sarah's uncle, her father's brother Lev, had been a rabbi. Just before services on a Friday afternoon in the winter of 1940, before Rostnikov had met his future wife, her uncle had been taken by the police and never returned. And when Sarah had married a policeman, a gentile policeman, most of her family had ceased to speak to her.

There was a silence. Then Rostnikov said, "I must go."

"I think there were two chairs," she said. "And a sofa."

"Yes, perhaps. Rest."

And she hung up.

Rostnikov stood and massaged his leg in the privacy of his

tiny, unbearably hot, windowless office. He considered what he might need for his trip and decided he required his briefcase, which contained a clean shirt, a toothbrush, a book, and a change of underwear. He removed the briefcase from beneath his desk and walked into the next room, where Emil Karpo was hanging up the phone.

Rostnikov wondered if Karpo's call had been to Mathilde Verson. Mathilde was the prostitute Karpo now visited every Thursday evening. Today was Thursday. Though she was a prostitute, she was also a friend. For four years Karpo had lived under the illusion that no one knew of his relationship with Mathilde Verson. Karpo the emotionless, unsmiling vampire in black, devoted only to his work and the party, wanted no one to know of his human need.

But Rostnikov had discovered the relationship, and Karpo had learned to accept this exposure just as he had learned to accept the need. At first he had seen his relationship with Mathilde as a weakness. Over the past year, however, he had begun to recognize that his dependency on her went beyond the animal needs of his body.

Mathilde was a large woman of forty, with a handsome face and billowing red hair. She worked as a telephone operator during the day and as a prostitute at night and on weekends. Age and increased competition from young girls seeking survival had cut into her clientele and she had seriously begun to consider retirement.

"We are ready?"

"I am ready," said Karpo, picking up a black plastic briefcase.

"Then," said Rostnikov, "we are off to see the wizard."

"He was a priest," Karpo said. They walked along the aisle between desks where a few investigators were on the phones or talking to each other. Far off in the Petrovka 38 kennels dogs began barking.

"I think I have an assignment for you, Emil Karpo,"

Rostnikov said. Approaching the elevator, they passed a trio of uniformed officers guiding a very sullen and bruised little man. The little man glanced up at Karpo's face, turned white, and looked away, a bit less sullen than before. "Learn a joke and tell it to me."

"A joke?"

"Something that makes people laugh," said Rostnikov.

"What would be the function of my learning to tell you a joke?" Karpo asked as the elevator reached the sixth floor, its door opened, and out stepped a plainclothes officer and a group of civilians, all male, who hurried in the direction of the three policemen and the sullen little man they had passed.

"To broaden your emotional potential. To make you better company on train rides such as the one we are about to take," explained Rostnikov as both men stepped into the elevator.

"It will be a waste of our time," said Karpo. "Every minute I spend learning a functionless joke could be devoted to the investigation of a crime. A minute lost might hinder the successful conclusion of an investigation or the apprehension of a criminal who might need that minute to run or cover his trail."

"That is reasonable," Rostnikov agreed. "But if you develop a sense of humor, you will have greater insight into the workings of people's minds. This will make you more capable of understanding them, innocent and criminal alike."

They reached the main floor and the elevator doors opened.

"I will leave understanding to you, Inspector. I prefer procedure and no distraction. Understanding makes me uncomfortable."

The six uniformed and armed young men in the lobby glanced at the familiar figures of the Washtub and the Vampire and turned their eyes away to scan the faces of those who were entering.

There was a car waiting for them at the curb on Petrovka Street, a Moskovitch. Since the triumphant rescue of the kidnapped President Gorbachev and the alignment of the Special Projects office with the new government, the Gray Wolfhound's men had reasonable access to motor-pool vehicles and drivers. Rostnikov had not as yet been given one of the BMWs that were being added to the police transport pool, but a cramped Moskovitch might be better than no car at all. The assignment of a car and driver was, in fact, often no great saving in time, since the metro was much faster than a car even in the privileged center lanes of the larger streets. But the Wolfhound insisted that his staff drive whenever possible.

There was an additional problem. It was also well known that in the past drivers were often KGB informers within the MVD who reported on conversations within the supposed privacy of the assigned cars. This had led to long, silent, and boring automobile rides or conversations with the drivers about safe issues. Rostnikov was not yet sure that this situation would not return and so he chose to remain uncomfortable.

"A moment," said Rostnikov, moving past the car to a kvass cart a few yards down. There was no line, and like most Muscovites, Porfiry Petrovich Rostnikov could not resist the opportunity to buy something without having to wait in line.

"*Mahlyeneen'kooyoo pahzhah*, a small one," he told the old woman bundled in a coat, gloves, and babushka seated on a rickety wooden folding chair next to the cart. "You want one, Emil?"

"No."

"Ask the driver."

Karpo approached the car, leaned forward, conferred with the driver, then called out again, "No."

The old woman filled a plastic cup with the dark liquid and handed it to Rostnikov, who drank it without haste while Karpo stood patiently at his side.

"Good," said Rostnikov, dropping the empty cup in the tin can on top of the cart.

The old woman, whose face was very round and red, responded with the hint of a smile.

When they were seated in the rear of the car, Rostnikov said, "My father believed that kvass was like medicine, the mixture of black bread and yeast stimulated the body fluids."

"It's possible," said Karpo.

"There are fewer and fewer carts in the city," said Rostnikov with a sigh. "Do you remember the apartment in which you were a small boy?"

"Yes," said Karpo.

"In detail? Where the chairs, beds, tables, windows were?"

"Yes."

"About the joke. You don't have to learn one. I was joking."

"I see," said Karpo, looking straight ahead and making it quite clear that he saw nothing.

There were only two people Emil Karpo trusted, Porfiry Petrovich Rostnikov and Mathilde Verson. He did not always understand either of them, but he had come to the conclusion that not only could they be relied upon but that they had strong feelings for him. Since he was well aware that there was no humor or warmth within him, he found their feelings inexplicable and meaningful.

For more than forty years of his life all meaning had been contained in the Soviet state and the revolution. The function of Emil Karpo had been to obey his superiors and to locate and bring to justice all criminals, all enemies of the revolution.

The union was gone. The Soviet Socialist Republics were now a commonwealth of sovereign states. Leningrad was once again St. Petersburg. They had even gotten rid of the hammer and sickle and designed a flag that seemed no flag. Next, he thought, there would be a return to the two-headed eagle of the czars. The party was underground, crying in pain, dying. The revolution was gone and there was nothing ahead but a gray imitation of the Western democracies.

Meaning was disappearing, but what little there was he clung to. His faith and loyalty had lost their certainty and there were moments when panic threatened to break through, moments that were longer each time they came. And each time the moment was accompanied by the headaches, the headaches that he still welcomed, that still tested him as they had since he was a boy. There were still the headaches and he could still welcome them. There were still criminals and they could be identified. He wondered if Porfiry Petrovich was aware of these moments of doubt.

Rostnikov was looking out the window making a sound that might have been humming and might simply have been a sound. "Were your grandparents religious, Emil Karpo? Did they believe in a god?"

"They were members of the Orthodox Church," said Karpo. "They died long before I was born."

They drove the rest of the way to the train station in silence.

Through a curtained window slightly parted so that he could look out onto what had recently been Dzerzhinsky Square, Colonel Vladimir Lunacharski looked down at the group of tourists gathering for a guided tour of Lubyanka, the former headquarters of the Committee for State Security, the KGB. The tour guide was pointing to the empty pedestal in the center of the square where the statue of Iron Felix Dzerzhinsky, the founder of the Soviet Secret Police, had stood until the rabble had torn it down. There were rumors that Lubyanka, too, would either be torn down or turned into a government office building.

The tourists would pass by his office door sometime later that morning, whispering such rumors in foreign languages, looking at everything as if they were in some Byzantine church.

Cars circled the square, headed toward the heart of Moscow. A small group of people gathered in front of the toy store beyond the square.

The colonel suppressed a sigh. He had no great love for these changes, for this new Russia that brought Americans and jabbering Germans galloping past his office. Independence had resulted in a demotion for him. Well, they had not called it a demotion.

The fifth directorate, the directorate responsible for monitoring the activities of dissidents, the directorate in which Vladimir Ivanovich Lunacharski had served for thirty years, had been reorganized even before the collapse of the union. Its name had been changed first to Directorate Z, but now, for almost a year, it had been called the directorate for safeguarding the constitution. This reorganization, the tours of Lubyanka, had all come about after the KGB's power had been transferred from the Politburo to the Supreme Soviet, implying greater scrutiny over the KGB's activities. But that, too, had changed, and now every day there were new laws and new restrictions. Lunacharski did not even know with certainty from day to day what organization, if any, he worked for.

The KGB had, since its inception, been at the service of the Communist party. Now all security forces within the

Russian borders were under the direct control of the egomaniac Yeltsin and his young idealists.

But General Karsnikov had assured him that the collegium, the highest decision-making body of the KGB, would remain strong, that the nation needed the confidence and control of the security apparatus, whatever they chose to call it. Of this, General Karsnikov had no doubts. General Karsnikov had called Colonel Lunacharski into his office on the first floor less than a month ago to tell him all of this. The office, with large, modern furnishings, sturdy chairs, and a circular conference table for six, had not changed in twenty years, and the large photograph of Lenin still hung on the wall near the door.

Others had removed their Lenin photos and paintings and replaced them with nothing, but General Karsnikov had left his where it had always been, a sign that for him the change would not come simply, that too many lives had been invested in the institution to give it up with a whimper.

''Changes will have to be made,'' the general had said.

He was a heavy man who liked to wear uniforms but had ceased doing so a week before Russia declared its independence. Colonel Lunacharski had done the same.

Colonel Lunacharski was fifty-one years old. His weight, maintained by vigorous exercise and diet, was the same as it had been when he had entered the service at the age of twenty-one, the son of a hero of the revolution and the war against the Nazis. Lunacharski always stood erect and kept his still-dark hair cut military style. Lunacharski's one regret was that he was not quite five and a half feet tall. He was determined that this lack of height would not keep him from rising in the ranks, that no one would ever say that this man with the face of a peasant and size of a large Alsatian dog could not represent state security at its highest levels.

''So, there will be some cosmetic changes, little things,

temporary things,'' the general had said, sitting across from him at the round conference table. ''A few big ones.

''The truth,'' he had continued, lowering his voice in confidence, though no one else was with them, ''is that the KGB grew stronger, not weaker, with this perestroika. We withstood the attacks within our ranks, the attempts to cut our financial resources. We maintained more than two hundred and twenty thousand border guards, a volunteer militia of eighty thousand. Some of the army's best units, including two paratroop divisions, were transferred to the KGB. We had our own planes and ships, our own army, and do you know what we provided?''

''Stability,'' Colonel Lunacharski had answered, knowing that he was being prepared for some sacrifice.

''Stability,'' the general had agreed. ''It is we who will hold this confederacy of fighting chickens together, we who will provide hope, we to whom they will turn when they fear their Ukrainian and Georgian neighbors, we to whom they will turn when the world treats them like hulking trash. Lunacharski, these new leaders are no different from the old leaders, but they do not have the the mask of communism to hold in front of them. They will change the face on that mask. They will call it democracy. And they will need us. But some surface changes are needed, temporary. There will be battles for control, power. Civilian idiots will think they are giving us orders and we will make them think we are obeying. There are those of us who will not allow the Russians to slip back into the nineteenth century.''

It was then that the colonel had been told that he would head the Office of Internal Investigative Control for the Division of Moscow. This meant that he would monitor and, when necessary, manipulate investigations of Colonel Aleksandr Snitkonoy's special investigation unit. When the unit failed, General Karsnikov would step in, and Lunacharski, if all went well, would take over. The general made it clear that Lunacharski's mission was informal. Such a subversive directive could not officially exist.

That meeting with the general had taken place four months ago, and Lunacharski had discovered much since. The staff of his office was twelve men and two women. In his last command he had had three hundred men and women. He could call upon resources from related divisions when necessary. The problem in calling on related divisions, as he had learned in the fifth directorate, was that other ambitious officers would then share his information, a situation not to be desired, especially in these volatile times. So be it. He would do as he was told. He would work eighteen-hour days as he had always done. He might be able to turn this demotion into an opportunity. It was not too late, given a major success or two, to move up. In fact this new Russia might well provide him with his greatest opportunity.

And so Vladimir Lunacharski turned away from the window and walked to the desk in his small Spartan office. He sat, put on his glasses, opened the file before him, which he had read before, skimmed it, running his fingers over each line, and then removed his glasses to look at the man across from him, who had been sitting patiently for more than fifteen minutes.

The man, who was dressed in a dark suit and equally dark tie, was of average height and quite ugly. His lips and mouth were very large, as were his eyes, and his skin was marked by dark blemishes. His name was Illya Klamkin and he had, since boyhood, been known as the Frog.

''Go to Arkush in the morning,'' Colonel Lunacharski said.

Klamkin nodded.

''Use our resources there to keep track of the Wolfhound's investigation,'' he continued. ''Keep me informed. If any action must be taken, I want as much time as possible to consider it. You understand?''

Klamkin nodded again. "This Rostnikov," the colonel said, tapping the file in front of him with his glasses, "was a source of some concern for the KGB in the past."

Since this required no verbal confirmation, Klamkin nodded a third time.

"Read his file. Then watch, listen, and report, Lieutenant," the colonel said. "As their fortunes fall ours rise. There are only so many bones to gnaw in a hungry nation."

Klamkin rose quietly and nodded yet a fourth time. The colonel did not rise as the lieutenant left the room.

When Klamkin had gone, the colonel removed a second file from his desk. This file involved the search for a missing girl, an Arab whose father was oil minister of Syria. Like the Father Merhum investigation, it had been assigned to Snitkonoy's unit, which would be blamed if there was failure. If success were imminent, it was Lunacharski's responsibility to step in, file his own report, and take credit.

Fourteen more active files lay in the desk drawer, and Colonel Lunacharski knew he would go through each of them before the day was over, get reports on each case, either in person, which he preferred, or by phone. He would then review and revise, if necessary, each written report. It would be a long day, a long day in this small office with only a one-hour break for exercise in the gymnasium and a light lunch.

Footsteps tramped above his head. He was on the top floor of Lubyanka, and the roof above was where the prisoners had only months ago exercised twice each day. Now the sound signaled a stampede of tourists. The colonel shook his head and turned to his work.

There were no other distractions. His wife would not be looking for him. She had, years ago, resigned herself to a life alone, though she and her husband shared the same apartment with their two now-grown children, who at the earliest possible moment had married and moved as far from

Moscow as they could. Marina Lunacharski was accustomed to spending days or even weeks without seeing her husband, which suited both of them.

The tramping overhead was nearly deafening now, and the colonel could no longer ignore the fact that he had been given the worst office in the building.

FIVE

"An Arab girl?" the woman behind the bar asked as she dried a series of glasses.

They were in the Nikolai Café on Gorky Street, which was no longer officially Gorky Street. The city leaders had changed the name of one of the busiest streets in Moscow back to its prerevolutionary name of Teverskaya Street, the street that leads to the town of Tver. It wasn't that the leaders disliked Gorky but that Gorky had been Stalin's favorite author.

The decision to change the name had been made almost two years before, but few street signs reflected the change, and it would be difficult to locate a Muscovite who referred to it as anything but Gorky Street.

The woman had been answering the questions of the policewoman with questions of her own while the good-looking young policeman used the telephone in the corner.

"How many Arab girls do you get in here?" asked Elena Timofeyeva.

Tatyana, the woman behind the bar, was in her forties, wearing a bright yellow blouse with puffy sleeves and a blue skirt much too young for her. Her artificially blond hair was straight and her loose skin was overly made up, but her sultry look was enhanced by the dim light of the bar. When they entered, she had looked at Sasha with some interest, but it was clear that his thoughts were somewhere else.

"Lots of Arab girls come here. It's a mecca for Arabs," Tatyana said, smiling at her own joke.

"We're looking for this one," Elena said. She handed a photograph to the woman, who stopped cleaning glasses long enough to look at it.

"Pretty," she said, "but she looks like lots of girls who come in here. What did she do?"

"Nothing," said Elena. "She's missing."

"Arabs go other places besides here," the woman said. "The Mahal on Kalinin and across the river—"

"She came here," said Sasha Tkach, returning from his phone call.

"She told a few people that she liked to come here," said Elena. "She didn't mention the other places, but we will be checking them."

Tatyana shrugged. "I can't help you."

"Her name is Amira Durahaman," said Elena. "Her family is concerned."

"Her family is rich and important?" asked Tatyana.

"What makes you—" Elena began, but Sasha jumped in.

"The police would not be looking for some servant girl."

"Is there a reward for finding her?" asked Tatyana.

"I don't know," said Elena.

"There's a reward," said Sasha. "One thousand rubles."

"One thousand only? You can't buy two chickens for that. This is a hard-currency bar. Arabs come here, they spend a hundred American dollars a night."

"Perhaps we can get a thousand American dollars," Sasha said. "If she is definitely located."

"I'll ask around," said Tatyana. "No guarantees, but . . . you know. How do I reach you?"

Elena pulled out her notebook and wrote her name and

Petrovka telephone number on a sheet of paper, which she tore out. Tatyana dried her hands on a towel before taking it.

"Sasha Tkach," she said, reading the sheet. "That's not a policeman's name. That's a ballet dancer's name."

"He doesn't use his real name," Elena said. "He is Sasha Shevardnadze."

"You mean . . ."

"I mean nothing," Elena whispered. "If you find her, Sasha Tkach will be very pleased. You understand?"

"I am not a fool," said Tatyana.

Back on the street Elena and Sasha nearly bumped into a huge man with a black plastic bag in each hand.

When they had passed the man, Elena turned to Sasha. "A thousand American dollars? We can't pay her a thousand kopeks."

Sasha moved ahead. "The girl's father will pay," he said.

"And if he won't? If we are told not to ask him?"

"Then we lied."

"You lied, Tkach," Elena said angrily.

"I lied," he said. "If we find her . . ."

"*When* we find her . . ."

"When we find her," he amended, "you can include on the report that it was accomplished by my lying to a bar owner who is probably also a prostitute."

"A prostitute? You are a—" Elena began.

"—son of Shevardnadze," he finished. "We'll come back tonight and look for someone who knows her. Let's go."

"Go where?"

"To the apartment of Grisha Zalinsky near the university," he said, moving in the direction of Pushkin Square.

"Why? Slow down, Tkach," she said.

"Are you tired?"

"No," she answered. "I can probably outrun you in any distance over a kilometer, but I can't understand you when you move away and turn your back. Who is Grisha Zalinsky?"

Tkach stopped suddenly and turned to her. She almost ran into him. "Grisha Zalinsky was the Arab girl's boyfriend," he explained.

"Was? They are no longer friends?"

"Grisha Zalinsky no longer *is*."

"And how do you know all this?"

"When I called into Petrovka five minutes ago, I was told he had been beaten to death in his apartment early this morning. Letters from her were found. The investigating officer recognized her name from the missing persons list."

"You are not a pleasant man, Sasha Tkach," Elena said.

"I am having a particularly difficult decade."

"You don't like me, do you?"

Tkach considered the question seriously. "I don't think so. But today I do not particularly like anyone, not even myself, especially not myself."

He turned and headed toward the metro station.

The man with the two black plastic bags was named Leonid Dovnik. He had seen Sasha and Elena enter the bar and knew they were policemen. It was not a difficult thing to recognize. So instead of entering behind them, he had waited outside till they left.

Leonid did not know why these policemen had gone into the bar, but he was sure that when they came out, he had heard them discussing the young man he had beaten to death just a few hours before.

It had been no trouble finding the young Jew. He had simply looked at the photograph of Zalinsky and the Arab girl that had been given to him and waited at the university where he knew the young man was a student. He had waited for two days till he saw him this morning and followed him home.

Following the murder, Leonid had come to Gorky Street,

where he bypassed three state-owned grocery stores, not even bothering to look inside, since there were no lines. No lines meant no food.

He finally stopped at the Gastronon No. 1, the fourth state grocery store. It was crowded and warm even on a cool morning. Forty or fifty people were at the sausage counter waiting to buy kielbasa.

Leonid moved to the milk-products counter. Less than ten minutes later he had been through the line to pay and was back in the linc to pick up his cheese and milk. People pushed, shoved, cursed, but given Leonid's size and his lack of a neck, those who could avoid contact with him did so. Since the latest round of shortages and rockcting prices that were part of the so-called new freedom, people had grown even more rude than before. Leonid was never rude. He made a living being brutal, but he did it with courtesy when possible. It was a job that paid him well enough to eat and live comfortably, and since he had absolutely no moral sense, it was a job that suited him well. He could afford to be polite.

Since he had not brought a bag, Leonid stopped at a kiosk further down Gorky Street and bought two black plastic bags with gold drawings of Elvis Presley printed on them. Less than an hour later the bags were full, including a fresh loaf of bread that he had purchased for an American dollar from a black-market dealer. Leonid was pleased with his acquisitions.

When he was almost in front of the door of the Nikolai, he had seen the young policeman and -woman enter. He had stood patiently for ten minutes till thc pair had burst out of the door arguing. The young woman had chased the angry man down the street and Leonid had watched. They had paid no attention to him. When the name Grisha Zalinsky was mentioned, Leonid was perplexed. There was no way he could have been connected to the murder, certainly not so quickly.

Leonid waited till they were lost in the morning crowd before entering the Nikolai. He had done his job. He wanted no complications. He wanted to collect his pay, go home, have something to eat, and watch television.

Although he did not put the feeling into words, Leonid was sure that this turn of events, this appearance of two policemen, meant that he would probably have to kill someone else and quite soon. He hoped it was not the pretty Arab girl, but if it was, so be it. Tatyana would know.

A little over forty miles northwest of the Nikolai in the village of Arkush another murderer was reading a newspaper.

This murderer, unlike Leonid Dovnik, had a very strong moral sense. Killing the priest had been frightening, but necessary. It had marked a definite end. The killer's hand had shaken as he waited in the trees. He had been afraid his legs would not carry him into the open to strike, but they had, and he had done what had to be done, and now, a day later, he trembled again.

His mother had not believed in revenge. Oleg had told him that revenge would give him no satisfaction, and he had believed and put it aside. Then Father Merhum had given him the reason.

After the murder he had gone home calmly, cleaned the ax, put it away, and sat listening to himself breathe. He wanted to spend the day at his work, but the word of Father Merhum's death had spread quickly through the village and drawn him into the discussion, the lamenting.

He had watched television as much as he could, waiting for the news of his deed to appear on TSN. There were no special bulletins. "Vremya," the nine o'clock news program, did not mention it, and this disturbed him. He wanted the world to know. He wanted word of this death to reach every corner of the stupid new commonwealth.

This morning he had attended services for the fallen martyr. The four-domed church had been jammed. People had to stand outside, dozens of people, people from as far away as Moscow, weeping, angry people.

He had slipped away as quietly as possible to be at the train with the others to meet the policemen from Moscow. He was very curious about who they would send and what they would do. He did not fear being caught—at least not very much—but he was curious, and now he stood with the others and watched the train pull in.

People clambered out, more people than usual, curious, mourning stupid people who had never met the dead priest. And then the ones they were waiting for; a tall pale unblinking figure in black and a squat man who looked like a small refrigerator and walked with a limp.

He stepped forward with the others to welcome the men and was sure for an instant that the limping man had looked into his eyes and seen something. But the killer did not panic. He told himself that this was the way of a policeman, that the man had certainly looked into the eyes of each of them for that same brief time, looked into their eyes and touched a raw coil of guilt in each of them.

He smiled sadly and assumed the others around him were looking sad, too. He smiled sadly and did his best to hide his fear of these two men who had come to expose him for a crime that was even more unspeakable than they could imagine.

SIX

THE FOUR MEN WHO MET ROSTNIKOV AND KARPO ON the platform of the Arkush train station were a somber lot. The little man with a smile of pain on his face, which Rostnikov soon learned was perpetual, introduced himself as Dmitri Dmitriovich, the mayor of Arkush. His white hair was parted in the middle and he wore a heavy, ancient dark gray wool suit that appeared to be at least a size too big. When Rostnikov took the extended hand, he felt a slight tremor, the first stages of some palsy or a reaction to the events of the past two days.

Next to introduce himself was Misha Gonsk, who had been the local MVD directorate. He was an overweight man in his late forties who wore a brown uniform and struggled to hold in his ample stomach. Evidently unsure whether he should shake hands or salute, he settled for standing at attention, closing his eyes for an instant, and bowing his head almost imperceptibly to the two visitors.

As the other two men stepped forward to be introduced, Emil Karpo made notes in his black book. The mayor was disconcerted.

"Why . . . I know it is not my place to ask . . . but why are you taking our names? We are not . . . this is . . ."

When Karpo did not so much as pause in his note taking, the mayor shrugged, touched his hair to be sure that it was still symmetrical, and looked at the two remaining members of the delegation. One of them, a tall man of about fifty, had the strong arms and slouched shoulders of a farmer.

"My name is Petrov, Vadim Petrov. I was Communist party representative of the Arkush council. Now . . . who knows?" He faced both policemen squarely and shook hands with a firmness that impressed Rostnikov. "Our mayor is understandably nervous," Petrov explained. "Crime is unknown in our community."

"Not exactly unknown, Petrov," the policeman, Gonsk, asserted. "In the twenty years I have had the responsibility of enforcing the law in Arkush, there have been many crimes, all of which have been immediately investigated and reported to Moscow. Only last week—and our mayor will confirm this—there was a theft in the marketplace—tomatoes. And last month the toilet seats were taken from the party hall. Two seats."

"Grave offenses," Petrov said dryly. "But now we have a murder. Let me finish the introductions and take you for some tea. This is Peotor Merhum, the son of Father Merhum."

Peotor Merhum, solid and handsome with blond hair and a fair complexion, was a sullen young man who did not offer his hand. He barely nodded.

Petrov, who had clearly taken over leadership of the small band from the bewildered mayor, led the group past the brick ticket booth of the train station to a sidewalk. "There is no point in taking a car," he said. "Arkush is too small. Tea is waiting for us at the party hall."

"From which," Peotor Merhum added bitterly, "the infamous and important toilet seats were taken. Perhaps in your spare time you can help our town protector"—he glanced at Misha Gonsk—"to find the culprit."

"Peotor is our town cynic," Petrov explained.

"He is distraught about his father's—" the mayor began, but Peotor Merhum cut him off.

"I am not distraught. Father Vasili Merhum was father to everyone but his son. It is no secret that I was less than dutiful. Why should we present a lie which the police will recognize the moment they talk to any man, woman, or child in Arkush?"

They were moving slowly because of Rostnikov's leg, but Peotor kept stepping out ahead. The ample-bellied Gonsk kept pace with Rostnikov. Karpo dropped back a bit to follow and observe. All of the passengers who had gotten off the train had moved ahead of them.

"They are going to the church," the mayor explained. "Services for Father Merhum this afternoon. A bishop is in Arkush to conduct the service. A bishop."

They passed small ancient houses of wood and stone along the cobbled street. It struck Rostnikov that he had gotten off the train and stepped into the past. The street curved to the right and into the town's main square where the buildings were no more than two stories high. Behind the buildings to his right was a small forest of brown-and-gray treetops over which he could see the four golden towers of the church.

In the center of the square stood a pedestal. There was nothing on it.

"Lenin," said Vadim Petrov, the party chairman. "Vandals knocked it over during the first days of madness."

"A crime our protector of toilets failed to mention," Peotor Merhum said derisively.

"I was going to; it was in my report," Misha Gonsk said quickly, looking back at Karpo to see if he had noted this omission.

"He isn't sure of your politics yet," Peotor Merhum said. "Our Misha is a survivor. He puts both hands in his mouth and holds up all ten fingers to decide which way the wind is blowing."

"We are a close-knit and supportive community," said Petrov, "a big family, as you can see."

Peotor shrugged.

"How old are you, Peotor Merhum?" Rostnikov asked.

Since these were the policeman's first words, the four men of the village studied him carefully to determine the meaning of this question.

"That is of no . . ." Peotor began, looked at Petrov, shrugged, and continued, "thirty-one. Why? What difference does that make?"

"In the presence of their fathers or the ghosts of their fathers, many men are forever children," Rostnikov said.

"Is that an insult?" Peotor said.

They had stopped in front of a three-story, gray wooden building, evidently the party hall.

"An observation," said Rostnikov. "Would you like another one?"

"No," said Peotor.

"Go ahead, Inspector," said Petrov the farmer, his eyes on Peotor Merhum.

"I have frequently seen grief expressed as guilt and anger. It is my experience that it should be recognized, acknowledged, and tolerated to the extent that it does not interfere with the life that must go on."

"He's telling you to stop behaving like a child, Peotor," Petrov explained.

"I understood, I'm not a fool," Peotor Merhum shot back.

"Gentlemen, gentlemen," the mayor said nervously. "We are on the street. People can . . . Let's go inside, inside."

They made their way through the first door to an overly warm room furnished with a table and seven chairs. The room looked and smelled like Communist party meeting halls Rostnikov had been in from Yalta to Siberia.

Everyone but Emil Karpo hung his coat on a rack just inside the door. On the table, the kind that folds in the middle and has black painted legs, were cups and a plate of large *pyeechyeh'yah*, cookies. They all sat down, and an old woman and a boy who must have been watching from another room came hurrying in with boiling pots of tea.

The walk from the station had not been terribly long, but after the train ride in which Rostnikov had moved very little, the distance had taken a toll on his leg. He resisted the urge to massage it.

Rostnikov looked at the blond boy who served the tea. Normally children and adults found it difficult to keep from looking at Emil Karpo. This boy, however, was watching Peotor Merhum with a mixture of emotions that Rostnikov had difficulty reading—fear, concern, grief. Peotor Merhum did not look up.

"We have prepared rooms for you here in the hall," Petrov said. "I'm certain you will find them comfortable. There is no hotel in town. It is said that Trotsky spent two nights here."

"A comforting thought," said Rostnikov, accepting a cookie from the plate offered to him by Misha Gonsk, who then took three for himself.

"Given the madness of our times," said Petrov, "it may well be that Trotsky will soon be reinstated as a hero of the early revolution, his picture on walls. We are in need of new gods now that the old ones have been broken."

"I've had nothing to eat all day," Gonsk jumped in. "Much too busy with the . . . I'll take you to the scene of the . . . whenever you like."

"Inspector Karpo will be remaining here overnight. I must get back to Moscow. You will take him to the location of the crime and I will remain here and talk to each of you individually."

The cookies were good, and Rostnikov had two more. The conversation ceased for a few minutes, except for requests to pass the teapot, until it was revived by Rostnikov.

"There are a few others I would also like to talk to. Is there another priest in town?"

"Not on a regular basis," Misha Gonsk said quickly, "but since Father Merhum was so well known, many priests, especially young ones, came from time to time. There are quite a few here now, for the funeral services. And the bishop. Did we mention the bishop?"

"I mentioned the bishop," the mayor said with obvious irritation.

"Yes," said Rostnikov.

"And there are newspaper reporters. *Pravda* itself," Gonsk said.

"And," the mayor added with undisguised pride, "a television crew from the nine o'clock news, 'Vremya.' "

Karpo, who had taken neither tea nor cookies, was taking notes.

"Perhaps we will talk to one or two of them later. And the nun, Sister . . . ?"

"Nina," said the mayor, who started to cross himself, looked around the table, and stopped with his hand almost to his heart. The hand went quickly to his lap.

"I should like to see her. And anyone in the town named Oleg."

"Yes," said Gonsk, coming to life. "I anticipated this request. We have seven Olegs. One of them is four months old. Another is six. Six years. His father . . . but that is not important. That leaves five, including Oleg Boshisi, who is possibly the oldest—no, the second oldest person in town. Oleg is ninety-one. Illyana Gremonovaya is ninety-four. The other three are Oleg Brotsch, the baker. He baked these cookies—"

"Very tasty," said Rostnikov.

"Uh, and then," Gonsk went on, squinting at a crumpled piece of paper he had extracted from his pocket. The paper looked like the torn corner of a newspaper. "Then, let me see. . . ."

"Oleg Brotsch's son, who is also Oleg. He is fifteen," said Petrov, his hands folded on the table.

"Sixteen," Gonsk countered.

"Sixteen," Petrov responded. "I am corrected. He is sixteen and feebleminded. He needs his mother's help to fart."

"Oleg Grogaiganov is some kind of businessman. He travels."

"Is he in Arkush now?"

"Yes."

"And the last Oleg?" Rostnikov added.

"Oleg Pninov," said Misha Gonsk, returning the paper to his pocket.

"Pninov is the last of a proud line," Peotor Merhum said. "Town drunks running back for generations. We have several town drunks and a trio of village idiots, though some would say we have even more. Inbreeding does it."

"We will talk to them all," said Rostnikov, without looking at Peotor Merhum.

"Even the baby and the child?" asked Gonsk.

"Their parents."

"The father, the baby's father, is in Siberia. He's an engineer working on—" Gonsk said.

"Use your good judgment, comrade," Rostnikov said. "And one more request, please turn the heat down in this room. Now, if we are finished with this welcome refreshment, I would like to talk to Inspector Karpo privately for a few moments."

The murderer rose with the others, looked at Rostnikov, and started for the door. It had gone reasonably well. He could think of no error he had made that would give him away. He had played his part with the skill bred of years of practice.

He would watch, listen, and be prepared to act if the two

from Moscow began to approach the truth. How he would act was not yet certain, but he had killed once. It could be no harder a second time.

It is illegal to beg in Moscow, but in the subway stations one frequently encounters ragged Gypsy children with their heads almost shorn and their hands out in supplication. They furrow their young brows in transparent mock agony, which covers a bravado beneath which is the real layer of agony.

The Gypsy children, usually carrying even smaller Gypsy children, made Sasha Tkach uneasy. Most Muscovites simply pretended they were not there, though occasionally an older man or woman would scold the begging children. Sasha vacillated between giving them a few kopeks and striding past them as if they did not exist. It depended on his mood. Today his mood was running wild. He handed a little girl a ten-kopek coin and plunged his hands into his pockets.

"We'll take the purple line to the Dzerzhinsky station and then the red line to Universitet," he said.

"The green line to Marx Prospekt is faster," Elena said, "more direct."

"You are not in charge," he said as people flowed around them. "I am in charge. I am the senior officer." He tapped his chest and looked in her eyes.

"The green line is faster," Elena said. "But suit yourself."

Sasha looked at the people flowing by, a pair of sailors, shoppers with half-full bags, a mother and child, hand in hand, each eating something that might have been a cucumber. "All right, the green line," he said softly. "It is a small issue. When a big one comes, we do as I say."

Elena shook her head. This was her fifth day with this madman. She was not sure she could tolerate another, but what recourse did she have? To complain about her partner after less than a week? It was difficult enough being one of the few women in investigation without being one who immediately complained. Short of physical abuse, she would have to tolerate this sexist.

It was midafternoon when they reached the fifteen-story apartment building on Lomonosov Prospekt behind Moscow State University. A police van was parked outside with its light flashing. No one was inside the van and there was no large crowd of the curious, though passersby did glance toward the nearby doorway and into the empty cab of the van.

Sasha Tkach was familiar with the area. On three occasions he had posed as a university student, twice to uncover black marketeers and once to help find a murderer. Now he wondered if he could still get away with such a masquerade, a thirty-year-old man with a wife and, soon, two children.

The building was reasonably maintained, which meant that there were no major holes in the walls, and the stairs—there was no elevator—were a year or two from actual decay. Graffiti on the walls had been almost, but not completely, washed away. LET'S ASK ALBANIA FOR FOREIGN AID would remain until the wall was repainted.

"What floor?" Elena asked as they reached the first-floor landing.

"I don't know," Sasha said. "They didn't tell me."

Footsteps thundered down the stairwell, echoing voices of girls or young women. Sasha and Elena paused as two young women appeared above them. One of the women was dark-haired with very red lips and a little blue beret. The other was tall, thin, and breastless. The women wore identical dark blue coats. Both carried books and both looked at Sasha with interest.

"Grisha Zalinsky," Elena asked. "You know where his apartment is?"

The girls stopped. The dark-haired one looked at Sasha. "Zalinsky," she repeated. "Zalinsky."

"The Jew on eight," the tall girl said. "The one who had parties."

"Which apartment on eight?" Elena asked.

"I don't—" the dark-haired girl said.

"Eight-ten or eight-twelve," said the tall girl. "Are you with the police? Are they here because of Zalinsky?"

"Yes," said Elena, moving past the girls and up the stairs. Sasha moved up behind her.

"What has he done?" the dark-haired girl asked. "Black market? Drugs. I'll bet it's drugs. There are drugs in this building."

Neither Sasha nor Elena answered as they continued up and out of sight of the girls.

"The policeman's pretty," one of the girls whispered below them.

"He's married," said the other.

"How do you know?"

"He looks married."

The girls laughed and hurried down the stairwell.

I look married, Sasha thought.

Elena hadn't thought of Sasha as "pretty," but now that the girl had said it, she thought the description fit him better than "handsome."

They had no trouble finding the apartment when they reached the eighth floor. The door was partly open. Elena stepped back to allow Sasha to enter first.

They entered a chilly room where two young uniformed officers sat smoking. The corpse of Grisha Zalinsky lay on the floor in front of them. Books were strewn everywhere.

"What do you want?" one of the officers said. "This is a crime area. Are you friends of the victim?"

"I am Deputy Inspector Tkach and this is Deputy Inspector Timofeyeva, and you are contaminating the scene of a murder."

The two men stood up, one more slowly than the other.

"Stop smoking," Sasha said. "Put your butts in your pocket. Did you open the window?"

"Yes," said one of the two, looking toward the window. "The smell . . ."

"You don't open windows. You don't smoke. You don't touch anything," Sasha said.

Elena had moved forward and was kneeling next to the body. The face of the young man was badly mauled and bloody. The nose was a flattened mess. His legs were bent back under him.

The two young policemen said nothing.

"Why isn't someone from medical here?" Sasha demanded.

"We don't know," said one officer sullenly. "We called. They said they'd send someone when they could. We've been here an hour. That's why we opened the window."

"You called on that phone?" Sasha asked.

"Yes."

"Have you touched anything else?"

The two young men looked at each other.

"No," they both said, and Sasha read the lie.

"Who reported the crime?"

"Neighbor," said one of the men. "Heard noises early this morning, about six, told the building supervisor, who checked the apartment and found him."

"Go knock on doors," Sasha said. "Ask if anyone saw or heard anything. See if anyone knows any names or can describe people who visited Zalinsky."

The two policemen hurried away. Sasha expected nothing from their inquiries. Muscovites were unlikely to volunteer any information that might mean they would have to spend time with the police or, worse, appear in court. But once in a while . . .

"Have you seen a corpse before?" Sasha asked.

Elena looked up from where she knelt and said, "Cadavers at the institute, an accident victim when I was about twelve, my father. This man was beaten methodically. He was beaten even after he was dead. The bruises on his stomach . . . Several of his ribs are broken.''

She got up. ''I'll look around.''

The phone was on the table next to the chair in which one of the policemen had been sitting. A phone in a student apartment was unusual. Sasha wondered how Grisha Zalinsky had obtained such a luxury.

Since the two officers had already used the telephone, Sasha didn't bother going elsewhere to make his call. He dialed the medical investigation office. The dispatcher answered.

''This is Deputy Inspector Tkach. I'm at the apartment of the Zalinsky victim on Lomonosov. When is a doctor coming?''

''Lomonosov? We've got no call for Lomonosov,'' the woman answered.

It was not uncommon. Out of every five or six calls one got lost. And it was getting worse every day. It was a routine Sasha knew well, but the two young uniformed officers obviously did not. Had Sasha and Elena not arrived, the policemen would probably have been sitting and smoking till their twelve-hour shift ended.

Sasha gave the woman on the phone the address and apartment number and told her how long it had been since the corpse had been discovered. The woman said a medical inspector would be there ''soon.''

Sasha hung up the phone and looked around the room. The furniture was all modern, steel and black plastic. He did not care for it. He preferred heavy, brown sofas and chairs. Soft, comfortable furniture.

Along one wall of the one-room apartment were bookcases. A few books still remained on the shelves, but most were on the floor. Two of them rested on the corpse. The titles showed a wide range of interest from history to mathematics. Sasha saw no fiction.

To his right, along the other wall, stood a dresser, also black, with its drawers closed, and a desk, white, from which a single drawer had been removed and turned upside down on the floor. Elena was carefully examining papers, clothes, drawers.

"Anything?" Sasha asked.

"A woman or girl spent time here recently. The drawers smell of perfume. A few pieces of clothing. The woman had expensive clothes. See."

She held up a pair of black panties. "Paris," she said. "Not a fake label."

Elena dropped the panties back into the drawer and moved to the overturned contents of the desk. Sasha looked at the corpse again. He could not have been more than twenty-four or twenty-five.

"Photograph," Elena said, holding up a square picture that she had extracted from the debris.

Sasha stepped forward to look at it.

"Our princess," Elena said, holding up the photo of Amira Durahaman and a handsome boy with curly hair. "Zalinsky?"

They both looked at the battered corpse.

"Probably," Sasha said, tapping the photograph with his finger. "Place look familiar?"

The photograph showed the couple at a table, heads together, smiling, drinks in front of them, people at tables behind them.

"The Nikolai," she said.

"The Nikolai," he repeated. "Did the killer find what he was looking for?"

Elena looked at him and smiled. "Yes."

"And how do you know?"

"The dresser," she said. "He threw down the books and

dumped the desk drawer but didn't touch the dresser. He found what he was looking for before he got to the dresser."

"Or someone wants us to think they were looking for something."

"Back to the Nikolai?" she asked.

"Tonight," he said. "Where do you think we should go now?"

"If we can get authorization, to the girl's father. With the photograph of Zalinsky and his daughter."

"If we seek authorization to approach a foreign diplomat, we may never get it. I suggest we naively assume the right to approach him in an effort to keep him informed of the progress of our investigation. The possibility exists that someone else may be looking for her, someone who has committed a murder."

"And in fact?" asked Elena.

"What do you think?" asked Sasha.

"He's a Syrian," she said. "An Arab official worried about his daughter who may have run away with a Jew. The Syrian is a murder suspect."

"And so is the daughter," Sasha added.

"So is the daughter," Elena agreed.

She was, Sasha admitted to himself, not at all bad for less than a week on the job.

SEVEN

IN HIS OFFICE IN LUBYANKA COLONEL LUNACHARSKI shifted the telephone from his right to his left ear. The right ear was moist. What he really needed was his old phone, on which you could simply talk into the box while sitting back or examining a file. The inconvenience of having to hold a sticky plastic receiver reminded him of the distance he would have to travel to redeem himself.

The first call, from Arkush, came late in the afternoon. The report was complete. Colonel Lunacharski took notes.

"They arrived slightly after two, had tea at the Communist party hall, and prepared a list of those they wished to interview," Klamkin reported. "Would you like the entire list over the phone?"

"Yes."

They went through the list, name by name, detail by detail.

"I want backgrounds on all of them," Lunacharski said.

"How deep?"

"To birth or before, if records permit. What else?"

"Rostnikov is returning to Moscow for the night," the agent reported. "The other one, Karpo, will remain."

"Where will Rostnikov's investigation take place?"

"Party hall."

"Do you have equipment to monitor?"

"One of the new directionals would be useful."

"We cannot get one," the colonel said, hiding his bitterness. In his previous position at the fifth directorate Lunacharski would simply issue an order and any technology would be available instantly. Now . . . "Use the standard plants. They will be adequate."

"Yes," said Klamkin.

"Then drive back here to report. I don't care what time it is. I'll be in my office."

By six o'clock three more reports had come in. The colonel had access to the pool of typists, but like a good officer, he distrusted the pool. The departmental assistant who had been assigned to him could type, but Lunacharski distrusted him, too. He had requested his own assistant from the fifth, but the request had been denied without explanation.

He would prepare his own reports for General Karsnikov until he could identify someone within his structure whose loyalty he could depend on. Klamkin was good, but there was a difference between "good" and "loyal."

The last call came in before seven and was the most distressing of all.

"Tkach and Timofeyeva are at the Syrian embassy," the agent reported. "They went there directly upon leaving the Zalinsky apartment."

The caller waited for a response from the colonel but heard only a pause, during which Lunacharski savored the likelihood that Tkach and Timofeyeva had gone well beyond their authority in approaching the Syrian embassy.

"Continue to monitor their activity," he told the agent. "Give me a report when they go home for the night. I will be here at all times."

It was almost eleven at night when Colonel Lunacharski decided to call his wife. "I'll not be home tonight," he said.

"All right," she answered.

"I will stop by in the morning, early, to shower and shave

and change my clothes. I may have to work all night tomorrow, too."

"When will you sleep?"

"When I can. On the couch here."

"Good night, then," she said.

"Good night," he answered, and hung up the phone.

He had known she would be up, that she had within the hour returned home from the apartment of her lover, a low-ranking member of the State Commission on International Trade. The lover traveled frequently. Lunacharski kept track of the man's schedule through an agent who was told that the man was a security risk.

Lunacharski was neither vengeful nor angry nor jealous. He was, in fact, pleased that this man kept his wife distracted, kept her from draining his energy with domestic battles. His work required Lunacharski's full attention and it was work to which he now returned.

When Leonid Dovnik entered the Nikolai Café that morning, Tatyana was just hanging up the phone.

"So?" she asked.

"So," he answered, setting his packages on the bar. "He is dead."

Once Tatyana would have shuddered or at least shrugged with resignation. She had known the young man, Grisha Zalinsky, had seen him in the Nikolai many times, heard him laugh, watched him touch the Arab girl gently, tried to remember what it felt like to be touched like that by a man.

Leonid went into his pocket and came out with a crumpled package of letters tied together with string. He handed them to her and she walked behind the counter.

"I found these under his socks," he said.

Leonid watched as she took out a lighter, lit a cigarette, and pulled out the first letter.

She read it slowly and looked at him. "I wonder who

would pay more for these love letters from an Arab girl to a Jew, the father or the daughter? If they are all as descriptive as the first . . . You want to read them?"

"No."

"Find her," Tatyana said, opening the second letter. "Do not bring her back here. Do not let her know that you have found her. Just find her."

Leonid moved toward the door without a question, which was one of the reasons Tatyana liked using him. He had absolutely no curiosity. He ate, drank, enjoyed having money, though he did not seem to spend very much of it, and he seemed to have no sexual appetite. Tatyana had twice attempted to take him on the cot in the storeroom. The first time was after she had been rejected by a customer, a woman. The woman, not much of a prize, had almost sneered. She had tried to take Leonid Dovnik in anger more than lust, but he had simply said that he wasn't interested in such things.

The second time had been more calculating. It was after he had begun doing "jobs" for her and she thought that sex might bind him, at least that is what she told herself. She did not wish to be rejected by this dull hulk again, and if it happened, she did not want it to be because he found her unappealing. Once again he rejected her.

"I don't like doing that," he said.

She hadn't bothered to ask him why he didn't like sex, but she could tell this time that it was the truth. He was not rejecting Tatyana the individual. He would have rejected any woman. She asked him, gently because he had killed at least seven people with no apparent remorse, if he liked men.

"You mean homosexual? No."

And that had ended it. Since that second attempt their relationship had been all business. He spent much of his time seated at a table in the rear of the café drinking beer in the shadows. Tatyana had no trouble ignoring him until he was needed to eject a drunk or do a chore for which a favored customer had paid in hard currency.

"I just saw two people, a man and woman, come out of here," he said. "They were arguing."

"Police," Tatyana answered, considering whether she wanted a drink. Both the good and bad thing about running a bar was that you could drink whatever and whenever you wished. Leonid Dovnik did not drink anything harder than beer. Leonid Dovnik did not smoke. Leonid Dovnik did not like women. Leonid Dovnik did not like men. Leonid Dovnik did not even like to do what he did best, kill. "Do you want to know why they were here?"

Leonid looked at her blankly.

"They are looking for the girl," she said, leaning toward him over the counter.

"We are looking for the girl," he said.

"We will be paid well by her father if we find her first," she said.

"It would be easier if I just killed her," he said. He looked into his bag to be sure everything he had bought was there. A piece of meat would have been good. He could make a kind of casserole or meat pie. But he had no meat.

"Our goal is to make money," Tatyana said, lighting another cigarette to help her think. She leaned forward, elbows on the bar, head in her cupped hands. "When you find her, don't do anything. I told you. Just let me know."

The door to the café opened and Yuri, the cleanup man, shambled in. He looked at Leonid and Tatyana and scurried away to the storeroom to fill the wash pail with water.

"Perhaps we can have them bid against each other, those people who want her found and those who do not," Tatyana said. "I'll work on it. First, we must find her."

Leonid stood up. "Can you put my groceries in your refrigerator?"

"Yes," she said. "Of course."

* * *

The Syrian embassy in Moscow is located at number 4 Mansurovsky Street. It is open from 9:00 A.M. to 2:30 P.M. Monday through Friday. It is a relatively busy embassy compared with those of, say, Thailand or Australia. It is busy because the interests of the commonwealth states and Syria are often similar enough to make frequent intercourse worthwhile. The foremost of these interests is oil, an interest grown all the more vital since the disastrous loss of supplies from Iraq and the collapse of the ruble. The People's Oil Industrial Investment Euro-Asian Corporation was promising new Siberian oil wells and improved transportation systems, but oil production had begun to fall even before the demise of the old Soviet Union and was expected to continue to fall by at least ten percent a year, perhaps till the end of the century.

As they sat in the small waiting room of the embassy, Sasha Tkach and Elena Timofeyeva were not aware of the depth of the relationship of their country and Syria, but they knew that an Arab oil minister was to be treated with sensitivity and courtesy.

There was nothing to look at in the room except a large photograph of Syria's President Assad, staring to his right in the general direction of Poland.

The room was almost unbearably hot. Both Sasha and Elena had removed their coats and rested them on their laps. Now they awaited the return of the man with the thick dark hair and bushy mustache who had led them into this room.

"*Kahk dyeelah?* How are you?" Elena asked.

Sasha was staring at the president of Syria.

"How are you?" Elena repeated.

"I am growing sullen again," he said.

"Have I told you you are a difficult man to work with?" Elena said.

"Yes, but I am not always difficult."

"One hundred percent of the time in my experience," she said.

"And that experience, you must admit, is very, very limited."

"If you—" Elena began, but stopped abruptly when Sasha put his finger to his lips and motioned over his shoulder with his thumb.

At first she sensed rather than saw or heard the man who had entered the room. Tkach had not even looked in the direction of the man behind him, but he had known he was there.

Elena's eyes met Sasha's with a question, her mouth opening slightly. Sasha smiled enigmatically, stood, and turned. Elena stood and turned also.

"I am Hassam Durahaman," the man said in a deep voice that betrayed no accent.

He was tall and trim and wore an unwrinkled blue suit. His skin was dark in sharp contrast with his white hair and thin white mustache. He stepped forward and held out his hand to Tkach. Tkach responded and found the grip firm and powerful. Durahaman nodded, almost a bow, in Elena's direction.

"Coffee?" he asked, turning his back and motioning for them to follow. The man who had ushered them in entered the room.

"Yes," said Tkach.

The second man took Sasha and Elena's coats and the oil minister said something in Arabic. The man bowed and disappeared behind them as they entered a large office with a desk to their right. To their left a quartet of armchairs covered in a silky, muted red material circled a round table inlaid with what seemed to be thousands of black and white stones in an elaborate design. There was a large, ornate, rectangular rug. The background of the rug was a dull cream yellow.

The foreground was a variety of colors, primarily red, in a labyrinthian pattern.

Durahaman moved to the table, held his palm out to Tkach to take a seat, and pulled out another chair for Elena. As she sat he pushed the chair in for her.

"Thank you," she said.

When they were seated, the minister adjusted his trousers adroitly to keep them from wrinkling, rested his arms on the arms of the chair, and looked at them. "You have come to report on your efforts to find my daughter," he said. "I can see by your faces that you have not located her. Am I correct?"

Elena waited for Sasha to answer, but he said nothing. "Correct," she said. "But we have some ideas. We know where she spent much of her time and with whom. We would like to know if you have any information on where she might have gone or the people she associated with."

Tkach pulled the photograph of Amira and Grisha Zalinsky from his pocket and held it forward for the oil minister to see.

Durahaman barely glanced at it. "Ah, the Jew who was murdered this morning," he said as the door through which they had come opened. "Our coffee."

The dark-haired man set a silver tray on the mosaic table. On the tray was a brass coffeepot with an ornate handle. The coffee cups were also brass with matching handles.

"How did you know about Zalinsky?" asked Elena.

"Sugar?" Durahaman asked.

"Two, please," said Elena.

"None," said Tkach, though he normally took three cubes at least if he could get them.

Durahaman poured and then waited while Sasha reached over to pick up the cup. The brass handle was painfully hot. He put the cup down gently and said, "I've changed my mind. I would like sugar. Three lumps."

Durahaman nodded, dropped three cubes into his cup, and handed Sasha a spoon.

Elena reached for her cup, picked it up, and barely got it back into the saucer. A few drops spilled on the table. "I'm sorry," she said, leaning over to wipe the spots with a napkin.

Durahaman lifted his own steaming cup to his lips with a forgiving smile in her direction and sipped slowly.

"This table has withstood two revolutions," he said. "A man died on this table. That was in Egypt many years ago. It took me four days to clean the blood from between the small tiles."

"A steady hand and great patience," said Tkach.

Elena tried to pick up her coffee again. It was too hot. Sasha had already picked his up and was drinking. She was damned, she decided, if she was going to play this game. She left the cup where it was.

Durahaman said, "Observe the carpet beneath our feet. It was made by hand more than three hundred years ago. I am told it took a year. The artist worked with infinite patience more than ten hours a day. The rug is priceless, but it is of no value unless it is seen and appreciated."

"Like your daughter?" asked Tkach.

The minister did not answer.

"How did you know about the death of Grisha Zalinsky?" Elena asked again.

"A grateful friend in the law kindly informed me," he said. "You are not drinking? Too strong?"

"Too hot," she said.

"And is it too hot for you, Inspector?" he asked Tkach.

"No," said Tkach. "I am a deputy inspector."

"Yes," said Durahaman. "You are both young. Experience with coffee and life are very helpful when one wishes to stay unburned and alive."

"Your daughter is still missing," said Tkach. "But we will find her."

"It is your job to say that, Deputy Inspector," Durahaman said, reaching out for the coffeepot. "You'd like a bit more? Not too strong, is it?"

Tkach accepted the coffee without putting the cup back in the saucer. Hassam Durahaman smiled at Elena. His teeth were white. She found him very charming.

"I have sent my limited staff in search of Amira," he said. "I have a few humble resources."

"Like your friend in the law?" asked Tkach.

"Yes, like my friend in the law. In my country young men are taught to be polite to those in positions of power and authority."

"I am sure," said Tkach, putting down his cup and rising, "that our superiors and your friends will keep you informed about our efforts to find your daughter. Now, we must get back to work."

"The young lady has not had her coffee," Durahaman said calmly, "and I have something to tell you."

Tkach stood awkwardly for a moment. His fingers, he knew, were burned, probably blistering. He looked at Elena and sat again, arms out on the arms of the chair as were those of his host. Elena tested the handle of the cup. It was still hot but manageable. She brought it to her lips.

"A woman called me several hours ago," Durahaman said. "She said that she was sure she could locate my daughter. She wanted confirmation of the reward which the police had indicated I would pay. I asked her what police and she described a handsome young man with unruly hair and a very lovely young woman."

Durahaman smiled again and toasted Elena with his cup. "I confirmed the reward," he said, looking now at Tkach. "In fact, I increased the reward and told her she would be paid in hard currency, French francs not American dollars. Do you know this woman?"

"Yes," said Elena.

"I do not like people making offers on my behalf without my consent," said Durahaman. "I do not pay extortion. My country and my people have learned a great deal from our enemies."

"The Israelis," said Tkach.

"Yes," said Durahaman. "If this woman finds Amira, I do not intend to pay her. However, I expect you to meet her again, if necessary, tell her she will be paid, and get my daughter."

"You want us to lie," said Elena.

"As you already have in my name," he reminded her. "It is not my honor that is in question. It is yours. It is growing late."

As he rose slowly Elena hurriedly finished her coffee. "And," he continued, "you have work to do."

"There has been a murder," said Tkach. He stood up with Elena. "The murder of a young man who knew your daughter well. She may be in danger. She may be dead."

"I hope no one is foolish enough to harm her," Durahaman said, holding out his hand to guide them toward the door. The meeting was definitely over.

"We will find the murderer," said Tkach as they walked.

"The murder of the Jew is of no interest to me," Durahaman said gently.

"No interest?" asked Tkach. "A Jew was your daughter's . . . friend and you are—"

"—not interested," said Durahaman. "Understand me. It is not Jews as a race I despise. It is Israel. I am a Semite, as are the Jews. My quarrel and that of my country is a political, not a racial, issue. Perhaps we shall speak again soon."

The man who had served the coffee was standing outside

the office door when Durahaman opened it. The man handed the police officers their coats and Durahaman stepped back inside the office and closed the doors without another word.

Tkach's burned fingers tingled with electric pain as he put on his coat. The dark-haired man helped Elena on with hers and led them toward the front door.

"Your oil minister is descended from royalty?" asked Elena.

"Hassam Durahaman was born the fifth son of a street cleaner in Damascus," the man said. "He did not learn to read or write until he was twenty-three. He has fought often, in many countries, has been severely wounded five times, and has lost his left lung."

"Fascinating," Sasha Tkach said sourly.

"He and his only surviving brother are known to have personally assassinated three traitors to Syrian liberty," the man said, opening the front door for them. "He is a man of respect in my country, a man who is known for his determination and his successes."

"And," said Elena, stepping out onto the sidewalk, "what would he think of your telling us all of this about him?"

"He ordered me to tell you," said the man. "And he ordered me to tell you that I had been so ordered." With that the Syrian closed the door of the embassy.

"He lied," said Tkach.

"About what?"

"His daughter and her Jewish lover," he said. "He cares."

"So what now?" asked Elena with a sigh. "Back to the Nikolai?"

"Now," replied Tkach, "I go home and eat. I will meet you in front of the Nikolai at ten."

"You think she is dead?" Elena said.

"Dead, kidnapped, on her way to Australia, who knows?" he said, rubbing his eyes. "We do what we must do. We look."

"If she is still in Moscow and alive, I think it would be best for her if we are the ones to find her."

"Or," said Tkach, "if no one finds her."

The night was growing cold, and Sasha was feeling the chill, but it did not seem to bother Elena.

"Go home and meet me at ten," Sasha said, wanting to take care of the tingling pain in his fingers. He turned abruptly, shoved his hands in his pockets, and strode away.

EIGHT

ALEKSANDR WAS FRIGHTENED WHEN THE POLICEMAN with the bad leg asked him to sit down. "I must get to the church for my grandfather's funeral," the boy said. "I have to help the new priest."

"Have you had any of these cookies?"

The boy shook his head no.

"Would you like one?"

The boy shook his head yes. Rostnikov handed him a cookie, which the boy took warily.

"You can go now," Rostinikov said.

The boy stood up and started toward the kitchen door. Then he stopped and turned toward the policeman.

"Yes?" asked Rostnikov, who had stood and was now putting on his coat, which Aleksandr had brought him.

"Have you ever eaten a hamburger at the McDonald's?"

"Yes," said Rostnikov. "I waited in line with my wife for four hours when it first opened. Now the lines are shorter because no one but Americans and Japanese can afford it. We had cheeseburgers called Big Macs and french fries."

"Were they good?"

"Very good," said Rostnikov.

"Did they cost a lot of money?"

"Nine rubles," said Rostnikov, limping toward the door. "I just thought of two questions for you."

"Yes?" asked the boy.

"Did you love your grandfather?"

To his surprise Aleksandr found himself about to say no. No one had ever asked him this question and he had never directly thought of it. His grandfather was his grandfather, Father Merhum. His father had not encouraged him to love the priest, but people he met every day respected him as the grandson of Father Merhum.

"Yes," Aleksandr said, and he was surprised to discover that he meant it.

"One other question. Did your grandfather ever talk about someone named Oleg?"

"You mean Oleg the baker who lives—"

"A special Oleg," said Rostnikov.

"No," said the boy. "I'm late."

"Do you ever think of what you want to be, Aleksandr, when you grow up?"

"No."

"No? My son was a soldier and now he writes plays about soldiers. He wants to be a policeman like me."

"I want . . ." the boy began, "I want to be a pilot."

"Perhaps when you are old enough to be a pilot, there will be fuel for airplanes," said Rostnikov. "I must go to my train. You must go to your grandfather's funeral. We'll talk again, Aleksandr. I'll tell you what the McDonald's looks like. Maybe I can bring a picture of it for you."

"You won't tell anyone I want to be a pilot," the boy said.

"Policemen and priests must keep secrets," said Rostnikov, buttoning his coat. "Do you have another secret you would like me to keep?"

"There is another Oleg."

"Another Oleg," repeated Rostnikov.

"I heard my grandfather talk about Oleg to Sister Nina," said the boy.

"And you are sure it was not one of the Olegs of Arkush?"

"I am sure. They . . . it was like he was talking about someone . . . I don't know, someone dead."

"Thank you Aleksandr," said the policeman.

Aleksandr nodded and dashed through the door into the kitchen. As he hurried past the old woman he was suddenly afraid again, afraid that the policeman would discover that it was not from the mouth of his father or Sister Nina that he had learned of Oleg.

"Dust thou art and to dust thou shalt return, until the day of the Resurrection."

The words were sung by a choir of six in the crowded church of Arkush, where the funeral of Father Merhum was under way.

The decision had been made for Emil Karpo to attend the funeral alone. "Watch, listen, report," Rostnikov had said. "I'll be going back to Moscow after I talk to the boy."

"The boy?"

"His eyes, Emil Karpo. Look at the boy's eyes. He holds a secret and it troubles him. I'll return in the morning."

Karpo understood why Rostnikov could not attend the funeral. The congregation would stand during the entire two-hour service, and Rostnikov's leg could not bear weight that long. As an outsider, he could have asked for, and would have been given, a chair. But the congregation, the people with whom he and Karpo would have to deal, would see this Moscow policeman sitting apart from them, an outsider.

It would be better for Karpo to serve as Rostnikov's eyes and ears.

"Look for those who weep too much," he said to Karpo, who had moved to the door of the meeting hall. "And look for those who do not weep, or pretend to weep."

Karpo had nodded and left the hall.

Now he stood in the church among the weeping and the silent. Those in the crowd did their best to ignore the specter, which all but those closest could do. Among the mourners were several children. One of them, a girl of about four with corn-gold hair, kept turning from the coffin to look at the policeman.

The coffin contained Father Merhum in full white vestments. A cotton burial shroud was laid over the body as the choir sang of resurrection. Karpo's eyes moved to the third level of icons on the iconostasis behind the priest. Each icon was a painting that depicted an event in the life of Christ. Karpo found the icon depicting the Resurrection.

Peotor and Aleksandr Merhum stood to the right of the coffin along with a plump woman with a pretty round face and an ancient nun whose eyes never left the coffin. In the crowd, close to the front of the congregation, stood two more of the men who had met Karpo and Rostnikov at the train station. Vadim Petrov, the burly farmer, stood on the right of the mayor, who tried not to fidget. A woman, who seemed to be the mayor's twin and was probably his wife, kept nudging him to stand erect.

The thin, bearded priest who conducted the ritual appeared to be no more than forty. He incensed the body, sang prayers, and placed a paper and candle in the dead hands. Then, amid a great deal of weeping, Father Merhum's family, even the boy, and the ancient nun kissed the hands and forehead of the dead man.

Peotor Merhum, however, did not weep, nor did he smile or pretend. His face was solemn, but he seemed to be thinking of a chore that had to be done somewhere far away.

When the family was finished, the congregants and visitors lined up to kiss the corpse. The little girl with corn-gold hair was held up by a woman who could have been her mother or grandmother. The girl looked at the dead priest and then at Emil Karpo as if there must be some connection between these two frightening pale figures.

When the line of mourners ended, two men stepped forward. The candle was removed from the hands of the corpse and the two men laid the coffin lid over the body and hammered in the nails. The echo of their hammers brought a new round of wailing.

When the priest who had conducted the ceremony disappeared, the old nun moved through the crowd, touching hands, kissing, and consoling. When she reached Emil Karpo, who had not moved during the entire ceremony, she said, "Policeman?" Though she was old, her skin was barely wrinkled. Her back was straight and her voice steady. Her black habit made her face look round.

"Yes," he said.

"I am Sister Nina. Come with me."

She turned and walked to the entrance of the church. Karpo caught up to her and walked at her side. Behind them the mourners continued to hover around the coffin.

"I watched you," she said.

Karpo had not seen her lift her eyes from the coffin, but he did not doubt her, especially when she added, "Something touched you."

He did not answer as they moved down the steps, through the people gathered outside the church, waiting to see the coffin. Something had happened to Karpo during the funeral. Perhaps it was the heat of the small church, but in the midst of a prayer sung by the congregation he had felt an impulse either to weep or to join the song. It had passed quickly, but it had been there and it had been like nothing he could remember.

No, wait. He had felt like this before. When?

"You are trying to remember something," the nun said as they reached the street and headed toward the woods.

Karpo said nothing as they passed small houses and a few shops that were closed in mourning.

"You wonder how I know," she said. "You are not used to people understanding you. It makes you uncomfortable."

"Uncomfortable? No. Curious perhaps."

"Come this way." She stepped onto a paved pathway between two houses spaced further apart than the others they had passed. "The house is this way, just beyond those trees."

As they moved along the path an animal scuttled through the bushes.

"I have spent a lifetime watching people during services. Almost all nuns have an intuition. You are a particularly difficult person to feel."

Karpo followed the woman silently. They walked for about ten minutes through the woods until they came to an old house.

"Here," she said.

He followed her through the gate.

"It was there he died in my arms," she said, pointing to the path just inside the gate.

Karpo looked at the path and saw nothing. He followed her through the unlocked door into the house.

"I'll make us tea. Wait here, please," she said, and moved into the next room.

The walls of the room in which he stood were covered with icons. One depicted a man in a striped prison uniform. The man was gaunt and pale, more pale than Karpo, but similar enough to be his brother.

"You are looking at the icon of Saint Maximilian Kolbe," the nun called from the other room. "Everyone who comes here is drawn to it. The Catholic pope canonized him four years ago."

Her voice was closer. Karpo turned to watch her enter the room and gesture at one of the five chairs that circled the room. The chairs, all wooden, straight-backed, and armless, faced a plain wooden table in the center of the room. On it stood a brass candle holder.

The austerity of the room suited Karpo and he felt comfortable as he sat facing the nun.

"The tea will be ready soon," she said.

"Maximilian Kolbe," Karpo said.

"Ah," said the nun with a smile. "One of Father Merhum's favorites. He was a Polish Catholic priest who exchanged places with a Jewish prisoner at Auschwitz during the war. The prisoner escaped, dressed as a priest, and Father Kolbe perished."

Sister Nina smiled, and Karpo suddenly remembered when he had felt the way he did in the church. When he was a boy of ten, he had gone to his first party meeting in the gymnasium near his house. The massive banners with the red star and hammer and sickle had draped the wall behind the makeshift stage flanked by massive paintings, Lenin on the right and Stalin on the left. The room had been crowded and his father had been excited and had looked down at him with pride. People had smoked and talked until a trio of speakers had stepped forward. There was wild applause.

Then the three had spoken. With conviction and power they had spoken of the revolution, of the new world to come, of sacrifices and discipline. Emil Karpo had not understood it all, but he had been seized by it, by the cheers, the deep voices, the paintings, the banners. It had given his life meaning, a dedication to the party that had been torn from him in the past months.

"You remembered," she said.

"I remembered," he admitted.

A hissing came from the kitchen and the nun rose. "A moment," she said.

Karpo willed the memory to go away, but it would not obey. He remembered vividly the worn pants of his father, and the man who stood to their right at that meeting, a cigarette dangling from his lips, his few teeth showing. The cap upon his head. He even remembered that his own palms had grown moist and that he had known that everyone in the hall felt as he did. He had been certain they were all of a single mind, a family united by communism.

The old nun returned with two cups and handed one to Karpo. The cups were brown, simple and large. The nun settled back in her chair across from the policeman.

"I wish to ask you some questions," he said.

"What would you like to know?"

"Father Merhum, who might want to kill him? Who is Oleg?"

"Yes," she said. "His last words to me. It was none of the Olegs who live in Arkush."

"You are sure?"

"Yes," she said.

"How can you be sure?"

"The Oleg from whom Father Merhum sought forgiveness is with our Lord. I can say no more."

Karpo took one sip of the strong, hot tea and put the saucer and cup on the floor. "How long did you work with Father Merhum?"

"I have served him and our Lord for the past fifteen years," she said. She had not drunk her tea, though she continued to look into it from time to time and to touch the rim of the cup with a tentative fingertip.

"And before you came?"

"Father Merhum's life was inseparable from the history of our church. Have you time?"

"I have time," he said.

"In 1917, when I was two years old," she began as if she were a Gypsy reading the images that appeared in the steaming cup she cradled in her hands, "before your revolution, there were over a thousand monasteries and nunneries in Russia. There were also more than eighty thousand Orthodox churches. Today there are seventy-five hundred.

"By the fall of the following year special commissions began to eliminate the churches. The procedure was simple.

The GPU, which was soon replaced by the NVD and later by the KGB, would arrest a priest for being a 'counterrevolutionary,' shoot him, or send him to Siberia. His church would be torn down or turned into government offices. Before your revolution half a million people worked in churches the same number of people who were in your Bolshevik party.

"Through the next years nuns smuggled the Eucharist to arrested priests in loaves of bread and apples. When they were caught, they, too, were imprisoned or executed.

"And the people, so many of them believed that the Church was in league with the fascists. Before the end of the war with the Germans the Church was in ruins. There were less than one hundred active churches. The few surviving priests were broken, frightened, hiding. Thousands, thousands of priests were murdered. The truth lies hidden behind the doors of Lubyanka in Moscow. It was just before the war that Father Merhum, the older Father Merhum, came to Arkush from the west with his wife and his son. They came on foot. During the war, in spite of the horrors the government had visited on our holy church, Metropolitan Sergei and the Orthodox Church rallied believers to battle the invading Nazis. And the Church donated millions of rubles to the struggle."

Sister Nina looked up from her tea as if a trance had been broken. "There is more, much more," she said, "but all you need to know is that there were those who never lost their faith. They never stopped giving their love to priests like Father Merhum. There are tens of millions of us. Our faith in our priests cannot be shaken. Your tea will get cold."

Karpo reached down and picked up the cup and saucer. As he drank he watched the old woman over the rim of his cup. She smiled at him warmly. He was not accustomed to people smiling at him.

"Something amuses you?" he asked.

"Something pleases me," she said. "A priest dies and a

convert comes. A death is followed by a birth. It is God's grace."

Karpo stood and placed his cup and saucer on the table next to the candlestick. "You have misread me," he said, looking down at her.

"You are a true believer," she answered. "A true believer needs a cause or he will wither. It is known in the lives of the saints that a man is twice blessed who embraced the devil before he embraces God. I see it in your eyes. During the service for Father Merhum the Holy Mother found you."

"Do you have any idea who killed Father Merhum?" Karpo asked evenly.

"You change the subject," she said.

"I cannot believe in your religion simply because the revolution has failed."

"I do not expect you to," she said. "But it will come. It has already begun."

"Do you have any idea who murdered Father Merhum?" he repeated.

"He was killed on the morning of the day he was to denounce those for whom the day of retribution had come," she said.

"Party members," said Karpo.

"Father Merhum's list was not limited to the secular. He was not beloved by the hierarchy of the Church." She stood and placed her cup next to Karpo's on the table. "There are Orthodox leaders who spoke for the government, supported government claims that freedom of worship was welcome. The Church donated millions of rubles to the Soviet Peace Committee. All religious activity was regulated through the Council for Religious Affairs."

"You believe that the Church ordered Father Merhum murdered because—"

"—he was about to denounce the Church," she finished. "There are those who believe this. There are a few in the

Church who are not true Christians, and it is they who have risen as tyrants rose."

"You are a revolutionary," Karpo said.

"And you are in need of a new revolution."

"I must go," he said.

"Perhaps we can talk again." She walked him to the door. On the way they paused to look at the icon of the pale saint in prison clothes.

Karpo said, "When we do talk again, perhaps you can tell me who Oleg is."

"You did not believe me?" asked Sister Nina.

"No."

"There are things that are best left buried," she said.

"Like the records of murdered priests inside Lubyanka?" Karpo asked.

"Father Merhum believed that such records are long dead," she said.

"But you believe in resurrection."

"You are clever and I am an old woman," she said. "But my faith is strong and yours weak. Do you wish to arrest me for refusing to answer your questions?"

Karpo opened the front door. A wind was blowing through the woods and there was suddenly the smell of cold rain in the gray winter air. He stepped out while the nun held the door open. "No."

"Good," she said into the wind. "I'm too old for threats. We will talk again. God bless you."

After she closed the door, Karpo stood for a moment. This had not been the afternoon he expected. He felt as if a migraine was coming, but he had none of the aura that usually accompanied it, no strange odors, no unbidden sexual impulses. He had to admit as he headed for the town that something about the nun and the service for the dead priest had shaken him. It reminded him of that day from his childhood, but it could not be what Sister Nina had said.

* * *

The murderer of Father Vasili Merhum stood back in the woods watching the tall pale policeman move slowly along the path to Arkush.

Moments ago the killer had stood next to the window of the dead priest's house and heard Sister Nina avoid the question about Oleg. Then he had heard the policeman say that he did not believe her.

The murderer was shaken. At the moment he could see no alternatives. He wanted to see an alternative, a way out, but there didn't appear to be one. She knew and someday she might tell the policeman or another priest or nun. He could not live with such a fear. It was not just he who would suffer, he told himself. Other lives would be ruined.

Besides, she was old. She believed in an afterlife. If there was an afterlife, he accepted his own damnation. If there was no afterlife and no damnation, then the nun had devoted her life to a lie.

The wind stirred as the policeman disappeared into the trees. The murderer let the next gust push him toward the small house.

Tears welled in his eyes as he reached the door of the house. He could take no time to think about it. If he took time, he would change his mind and Sister Nina would have an opportunity to tell the policeman.

No one locked doors in Arkush, especially a nun. He entered the house and found the old woman in the kitchen cleaning teacups. She looked over her shoulder when she heard his footsteps.

He was trembling, his hands at his sides, but he was determined to act. Sister Nina dried her hands on a small clean rag on a rod over the sink. She crossed herself and turned to face him.

"This is not the way," she said softly.

"I can think of no other," he cried. "God help me. I can think of no other. I have become a monster."

"Then," she said, "we will both suffer. I for a moment and you for eternity."

NINE

ELENA TIMOFEYEVA AND HER AUNT ANNA LIVED WITH Anna's cat, Baku, in a one-room apartment not far from the Moscow River. The apartment building was an old one-story plaster-and-wood box with a concrete courtyard of concrete benches. It was one of the apartment buildings constructed as temporary shelter after the war against fascism. The plan was to tear it down within a few years of its construction. That had been more than forty years ago. Until Elena came three months ago Anna had lived alone in the same apartment for more than half of her fifty-two years.

Elena had the bedroom. Anna had the living room/kitchen. It was hardly *lyuks*, luxury, but Elena had little choice. New to Moscow, Elena had been lucky to have an aunt who not only took her in but used her influence to get her on the Special Section staff.

Anna's influence stemmed from her former status as deputy procurator. Three years ago, during her second ten-year term, she had suffered her third, and most serious, heart attack.

Anna had worked a lifetime of eighteen-hour days and six-and-a-half-day weeks, first as an assistant to a commissar of Leningrad in charge of shipping and manufacturing quotas, and then, as a result of her zeal and ability, as deputy procurator in Leningrad and Moscow. Because she came from sturdy peasant stock, she had felt free to neglect her health. But then, suddenly, she was idle. Rostnikov, her chief investigator, had brought his wife's cousin Alex, a doctor, to examine her after the state security doctors told her she was to lie in bed and prepare to die.

Alex had looked at her dumpy egg-shaped body and told her to get out and walk, walk, walk. She had gradually worked her way up to four miles every day, though she refused to wear the Czech jogging suit that her sister, Elena's mother, had sent her from Odessa.

Anna still retained the respect of the people in the apartment building, at least those who had not moved in the past three years. A few of them still called her Comrade Procurator.

Early in the evening when she returned from her afternoon walk, Anna had sat at her small table near the window overlooking the bleak courtyard. Below, four babushkas watched over their bundled grandchildren by the light of a few courtyard lamps and the lighted windows of nearby apartments. Two hours later Anna was still seated at the window. She held a book close to her eyes, and the fuzzy orange ball, Baku, was in her lap, when Elena entered. Anna took off her glasses and looked up.

"The man is insane," Elena said, dropping her bag on the table near the door.

"You want something to eat?" asked Anna. She placed her book on the window ledge and Baku on the floor.

Elena kicked off her shoes and moved to a second chair near the window. "No . . . yes. What do we have?"

Anna went to the kitchen alcove. "We have two eggs," she said. "*Keefeer*. Bread. A tomato."

"A tomato?"

Anna reached into her cupboard and pulled out a slightly overripe tomato. "And," she added, "I made leek soup."

"Let me do it," Elena said.

Elena had learned to take over the preparation of meals whenever possible. Cooking was neither a talent nor an interest of Anna, whose true passions were crime and her cat.

"Who is insane?" asked Anna as Elena turned on the small electric stove that stood on the table in the kitchen corner.

Baku rubbed against Elena's legs and she motioned for him to join her. The cat leaped into her arms and she stroked its head as she smelled the leek soup and pushed the pot onto the burner.

"Tkach," she said. "He's like a madman. You prepared me for the madness in the streets, but not in the people with whom I must work."

"He is in the wrong business," Anna Timofeyeva said.

Elena put Baku down and carefully cut the soft tomato with a less-than-sharp knife.

"He isn't insane," said Anna.

"He rants, he threatens." Elena sighed. "He almost killed a man selling pizzas today."

Outside the window one of the babushkas had taken off her gloves and was paddling a small child with her bare hand. The other babushkas were watching silently. The child's wails penetrated the window.

"If I have children," Elena said, carefully slicing the loaf of bread with the same dull knife, "I will not allow them to be hit."

"Perhaps," said Anna. "Tkach has a child and another on the way. Do you think he strikes his child?"

"I don't care what he does to his child," Elena said, turning her head from the window to her aunt.

"He is young," said Anna.

"He is only two years younger than I," said Elena. She examined the uneven piece of bread she had just cut.

"In years," said Anna. "In experience perhaps he is older, but in emotions, no. I've known him since he was twenty-three or twenty-four. What he wanted yesterday, he no longer wants today, and what he wants today will be forgotten tomorrow in the self-pity of not knowing what he wants. But he is a good policeman. I bought him a scarf from one of the old ladies. We'll give it to him at the birthday party."

"Fine," said Elena.

The cat had taken the chair at the window and was curled up in front of Anna's book.

"The Arab girl . . . ?" asked Anna.

"Amira Durahaman."

"You haven't found her."

"No. That's where we're going tonight. To look for her. Her boyfriend was murdered this morning, a young Jew."

Anna watched as her niece moved to the window and looked out, then leaned forward to scratch Baku's head and reach for the book.

"What are you reading?" Elena asked.

"Minds," said Anna Timofeyeva. "Today I am reading minds, your mind. He is a good-looking young man."

"Who?" asked Elena, examining the book.

"Who? Chairman Mao. You know who," said Anna. She went over to the table and tried to place the cup of *keefeer* on the plate next to the bread and tomato in an appealing arrangement. "Let's eat."

Elena put the book down, scratched Baku's head once more, and took her place at the table. Anna poured the soup and placed a plate of food in front of her. They ate in silence for a few minutes.

"I can't work with him," Elena said.

"He is a good investigator," replied Anna. "Smart. But too passionate."

"You said that."

"I suffer from lapses of short-term memory and the belief that the young are inattentive," Anna said.

Anna Timofeyeva knew that there was a highly classified

file on Sasha Tkach's indiscretions, a file of which he was not aware. There were thousands of such files—on members of the MVD, on government officials—files that Anna Timofeyeva had once had access to, and could still examine if she wished to do so. She wondered what the new zealots would do with this information.

"I don't think he will ever be able to control his passions," Anna said, "which is why I think he should not make a career as a policeman."

"A minute ago you said he was a good policeman," said Elena. "You see I am listening."

"A person can be a fine butcher and hate the sight of blood."

"It is unlikely that if he hated the sight of blood he would become a butcher," countered Elena.

"Destiny often hands us a sword too heavy to carry."

"You are being cryptic," said Elena, tearing off a piece of bread from the loaf. "You are reading too much Freud."

"I've been reading too much Gogol," said Anna with a sigh. "All right. I'll be direct. Better for you if Tkach was *byeezahbrahnay*, ugly. The food is all right?"

"It's fine," said Elena.

"It's soggy, the tomato, the bread," said Anna. She put her half-finished plate on the floor, and Baku leaped from the chair to eat. "And the soup is hot water with three onions."

"He might get me hurt, even killed," said Elena.

"Let us hope you survive at least your second week. Your mother would never forgive me."

"I must get back to work."

"Trust his instincts and experience, question his passions," Anna said, reaching down to pet Baku, whose head was bent over the cup of *keefeer*.

"Can I ask you a question?" asked Elena, rolling a crumb of bread in her fingers.

Anna had carried her niece's plate to the sink in the corner. "You mean, may you ask a question which might make me feel uncomfortable? Since I am curious, ask."

"Are you bitter?"

"Bitter? About . . . ?"

"The system you worked for is gone. The Soviet Union has gone. The memory of Lenin is dying. The law—"

"—remains the law," said Anna, turning to her niece. "I did not dedicate my life to a cause. I dedicated my life to the law. The goal was to improve the law and to seek justice within it. There was nothing wrong with Soviet law. The problem was in its corruption."

"You are being philosophical today," said Elena.

"Philosophy is the perfect exercise for a woman with nothing to do but walk and read about hysteria."

Elena moved back to the chair by the window, sat, and put on her shoes. Then she went to the battered wooden wardrobe in the corner, opened it, selected a clean blouse, and moved to the small bathroom to examine herself in the mirror. "I'm getting fat," she said.

"It is your genetic burden," said Anna. "Along with intelligence and determination. Your mother is heavy. I am heavy. But you are also pretty. You won't be truly fat like us for ten years, twenty if you are careful."

"Thank you," Elena said as she came out of the bathroom, buttoning her blouse. "You are very reassuring."

"I am very practical," said Anna. "You want lies? Read *Izvestia*."

"I suppose I want the truth cushioned," Elena said, putting on her coat.

"It is still the truth. Besides, I don't know how to do that." Anna leaned over to pick up Baku's clean plate. "It is a skill, like cooking, which I never learned."

"I don't know what time I will be back," said Elena.

"Baku, Freud, Gogol, and I will be here," said Anna

Timofeyeva, moving back toward the chair near the window. "Maybe we'll watch some television. 'Wheel of Fortune.' Who knows? The night is still young."

"Aunt Anna," Elena said.

"You look fine," her aunt replied. "You look modern, efficient, pretty, determined. If I am sitting here with my eyes closed when you return, be sure I'm alive and then let me sleep."

Elena kissed her aunt's head and left the apartment.

Anna Timofeyeva folded her hands on the book in her lap and looked into the darkness of the courtyard. The babushkas and children were gone. There was nothing to see but the lights in the windows.

"Well, Baku, what will it be, Gogol, Freud, or 'Wheel of Fortune'?"

Baku looked up at her and blinked his eyes.

"So?" Lydia said, placing a bowl of borscht in front of her son.

"So?" repeated Sasha Tkach, looking down at the dark red liquid filled with beets and a very small white touch of what may have been sour cream.

Lydia Tkach was a proud woman of sixty-six who was almost deaf and quite unwilling to admit it. She continued to work, as she had for more than forty years, in the Ministry of Information Building, filing papers and telling anyone who would listen that her son was a high-ranking government official, a key adviser to the minister of the interior.

Sasha knew that his mother was no more popular in the Ministry of Information than she was at home. People avoided her because she drew attention to herself with her loud conversation. This tended to make her more lonely and crotchety with those who could not avoid her, particularly her son and daughter-in-law.

Maya had insisted on getting up to sit across from her

husband while he ate a hurried meal. Pulcharia sat on her father's lap. Maya's lap had slowly disappeared as the baby grew within her.

"So?" Lydia repeated to her son.

Sasha looked at his wife, who smiled in sympathy. Maya's stomach was large, low, and very round, but her usually beautiful round face was pale and thin, which made Sasha angry, which was easier than being frightened. He did not want her to be sick. He wanted her to be vital, well, warm, and supportive.

"*Shchyee*," said Pulcharia, putting her fingers in her father's bowl of borscht.

Sasha had no worry that his almost-two-year-old daughter would burn her finger in the soup. He had been drinking his mother's soup for almost thirty years and knew that she believed in tepid soup and room-temperature meat and chicken. What troubled Sasha at the moment was the strange thing in his borscht that looked like an animal claw.

"What is this?" he asked, picking up the object, which was definitely a claw.

"Don't change the subject," Lydia shouted, sitting down. "You'll frighten the baby."

"Why should changing the subject frighten . . . what is this?"

Lydia glanced at his spoon. "Meat," she said. "Gives flavor to the soup."

"That looks like the claw of a—"

"*Kroolyek*," said Maya.

Her voice, with its touch of the Ukraine, usually pleased and soothed Sasha, but there was a rage in him. He had awakened with it and had come through the door this evening determined to hide it. "The foot of a rabbit, yes," he said.

Pulcharia reached for his spoon. Sasha moved it out of her reach.

"Times are hard," said Lydia loudly as she poured herself

a bowl of soup from the pot she had placed on the table. "Lines are long."

"You may have the foot of the rabbit," Sasha said, leaning over to drop it in his mother's bowl. "The Americans think it is good luck."

Maya looked at her husband with mild disapproval, but he ignored her.

"So?" Lydia said, looking down at the dark red liquid in which the foot of the rabbit had disappeared.

"You are not eating," Sasha said to his wife.

"I am not hungry," Maya said softly.

"The baby inside of you is hungry," he said.

"Answer my question," Lydia insisted. She reached over the table to hand Pulcharia a piece of bread. "Without rabbit tricks."

" 'So?' is not a question I can answer," Sasha said, brushing the wild patch of hair from his eyes. He knew he would not drink this borscht, could not drink this borscht. He had a full hour before he had to meet Elena Timofeyeva, but he knew he would soon say he had to leave. Though they were hard-pressed for money, Sasha knew he would buy himself something on the way, possibly even a *pahshtyehtah*, a meat pie with little or no meat, if he could find someplace to buy one. A woman in a white apron had set up a table inside the Journalists Union Building two days before. She might be there again.

He had bought two pies and asked the woman what kind of meat she had used. The pained smile she had given him made him regret his question. Still, it had not tasted at all bad.

"Eat and answer," Lydia went on.

Sasha took a piece of bread and pretended to dip it in the soup. Pulcharia dipped her bread in the soup and dripped over her father's pants and her own dress as she brought it to her mouth.

"She's gotten you dirty," Maya said, handing her husband a cloth napkin.

"It's nothing," he said. "I have to leave."

He put Pulcharia on the chair next to him and got up.

"So?" Lydia asked again. "How is she? The baby Rostnikov makes you work with while he runs to his son's play?"

Sasha looked down at his best trousers. The stain was evident. He tried to blot it but had little success. "She is older than I am, and Porfiry Petrovich is on a very important case. He deserves a few hours to see his son's . . . why am I arguing about this with you?"

"Good. Don't argue. Tell us all about her, about this Timofeyeva."

"Her name is Elena," he said. "I told you yesterday, and the day before and—"

"So?"

"So, she is fine," said Tkach. "She doesn't know anything. She talks too much. She gets in the way. She asks too many questions. She may well get me killed, but she is fine. Does that answer all your questions about her?"

"Is she pretty?" asked Lydia. Maya found the question interesting enough to raise her eyes toward her husband.

"She is fat," said Tkach.

"She can be pretty and fat," said Lydia.

"I am fat," said Maya.

"You are temporarily overweight from a natural condition which will soon end," said Sasha, moving across the room toward the door. "You are not pretty. You are beautiful."

Pulcharia was trying to find something in the borscht with her fingers.

"Ida Ivanova Portov, remember her? Married to your father's partner, Boris. She was fat, but she was pretty. I remember the way your father looked at—"

"Ben," Sasha interrupted, putting on his coat. "Father's partner's name was Ben not Boris."

"You are changing the subject," Maya said. "Your mother asked if Anna Timofeyeva's niece was pretty."

"Is Comrade Anna pretty?" he asked.

"Can you answer a question with an answer instead of a question?" asked Maya in a louder voice.

"You are upsetting your wife," Lydia said.

Pulcharia began to cry.

"She is beautiful," said Sasha. "She is ravishing. She is a painting by . . . Rubens. I want to make passionate love to her. We are supposed to go to the Nikolai Café on Gorky Street looking for a missing Arab girl tonight, but the hell with it. We'll go make love in the snow."

"What are you talking about?" Lydia cried. "It's not even snowing."

"You've made the baby cry," said Maya. Pulcharia climbed onto her mother's stomach and stuck her thumb in her mouth.

Sasha stood at the door, facing three generations of women who determined the course of his life, a life that was moving much faster than he wanted it to move. He wished that Maya would lose the child she was carrying. No, no. He wished no such thing. Instead he suddenly ached for a son.

"Your wife needs calm," Lydia shouted.

"All right," he said, opening the door. "I'll give her a night of calm. I won't come home tonight. I'll sleep at my desk."

"Sasha," Maya said, shaking her head as she patted Pulcharia's head and comforted her. "Don't be . . ."

But he was in the hall and slamming the door before she could say more.

"What's wrong with him?" asked Lydia.

"He will be thirty in two days and he doesn't want to grow up," said Maya, running her finger along her daughter's nose.

"But he can speak French," said Lydia. "And he did not finish his borscht."

There was nothing to say to either comment by her mother-in-law, so Maya simply shrugged in resignation. She was reasonably sure her husband would be back, would climb into bed next to her, would hold her, would apologize even if he was sure she did not hear him. And if once he did spend the night at his desk, it would not be such a bad thing for him, though it would mean that Maya would have to face Lydia alone in the morning.

"I'm very tired," said Maya. "I'll help with the dishes, put Pulcharia to bed, and then go to bed myself."

"I'll do the dishes," said Lydia, reaching for the borscht no one had eaten. "You put my precious child of the summer into bed. I have to go out tonight, anyway."

Maya stopped herself from asking where her mother-in-law might be going. An evening with no talk would be a luxury she dared not hope for. Lydia had, in fact, been very helpful since Maya had been ordered to stay at home in bed, but the price that had to be paid for such aid was almost more than Maya could bear.

Nonetheless she did wonder where Lydia had suddenly decided to go.

Going to a play or a movie was a problem for Porfiry Petrovich, which was why he seldom went to either, though he enjoyed them both. During a movie he could at least stand, move about a bit, coax his leg back to life. It was difficult to stand during a play, or even to shift about to find a less painful position. The audience would be disturbed and his movements, even if he were in the rear of the theater, would distract the actors.

But this was a play written by his son, and Rostnikov was determined to attend the first performance, even though he didn't take seriously Iosef's remark that there might not be a second performance.

The train from Arkush had been late arriving in Moscow

and Rostnikov had decided to take a taxi home, which had been a mistake. Traffic was heavy, the fare insane.

When he entered the apartment on Krasikov Street after climbing the six flights of stairs, he reluctantly admitted to himself that he was tired.

Sarah was seated at the table near the window, drinking a glass of tea and watching the news on their little television. The room was cold, but something was cooking that he did not immediately identify because he was absorbed by the sight of his wife. She was wearing her orange dress, and her red hair was long enough, four months after surgery, to wear swept up. In her ears were the dangling blue earrings he had given her for her last birthday. Her face was made up and her eyes were bright with anticipation. She looked like the Sarah of a year ago, before the disappointments, the pain, the tumor. Rostnikov, in spite of his weariness, felt a definite physical undulation of desire.

"You look beautiful," he said.

"Flattery?"

"No," he said. "No. Had we time and you the inclination, I could prove what I say."

"Thank you, Porfiry Petrovich."

How long had it been since he has seen such an open smile on Sarah's face? She had worried through Iosef's tour in the army, his time in Afghanistan, and the threat of assigning him to duty near Chernobyl, which was a direct result of Rostnikov's too-frequent clashes with the KGB. She had been depressed when he failed to get the government to allow them to emigrate. She had abandoned her determination, put on a few pounds, and lost her job in the music shop. For almost a year, before the tumor, she worked only now and then, selling pots and pans for one of her cousins.

But Iosef was back now. Iosef was safe, a playwright, an actor. And Sarah was growing healthy and was not gaining back the weight she had lost after surgery.

Her determination had even begun to return and she had decided that when she felt completely well, in a month or so, she would again bring up to Porfiry Petrovich the possibility of leaving Russia. The borders were open. Perhaps even a policeman could now leave.

"Aren't you going to tell me I'm late?" he asked, heading toward the bedroom door.

"You know you are late, but not too late to eat if you hurry."

"What is that smell?" he asked from the bedroom. "Is that . . . ?" He stepped back into the room with his shirt off, a hairy barrel of a man with a smile on his face and a sweatshirt and towel in his right hand.

"I could only get half a chicken," Sarah said. "And as for the prune sauce, I had to improvise and use—"

"Chicken tabaka," he said. It was his favorite dish, chicken fried under a heavy metal plate weighted down by a hand iron. Sarah served it with a special prune sauce and pickled cabbage.

When she served this dish, it usually meant that she wanted something. Rostnikov decided that whatever it was, he would certainly try to give it to her.

On the television a man said something about the death of Father Merhum while in the corner of the screen a woman within a circle used sign language to translate for the deaf.

"Is sign language the same all over the world?" he asked. "Can deaf Chinese understand deaf Latvians?"

Sarah reached over and turned the set off.

"You went shopping?" he asked.

"With Sophie."

Rostnikov moved to the cupboard in the corner of the room and looked at his wife.

"I have time?" he asked.

"Would I be able to tolerate you tonight if you didn't?" she asked.

"Ten minutes," he said. "Maybe twelve. No more."

"Twelve will be fine," she said.

"You are beautiful."

"And you look like a small bear. You are fortunate that I have always loved small bears."

"I am fortunate," he agreed. He opened the cupboard and removed the rolled-up mat, the weights, and the bar. He took the blanket off the weight bench in the corner and began to set up for his routine. "Any calls?" he asked.

"Nuretskov on the fourth floor. Toilet is making noise."

"Toilets are a challenge," Rostnikov admitted.

"And Lydia Tkach."

Rostnikov sighed deeply.

"No message," said Sarah.

"Twelve minutes," Rostnikov said, reaching for a cassette.

For many years Rostnikov had done his routine to the music of Bach or Rimsky-Korsakov, but lately, since Sarah's illness, he had found himself attracted to plaintive songs, melancholy arias from operas, laments by Edith Piaf, blues sung by American women, particularly one called Dinah Washington. Even though he was a policeman, Rostnikov had paid dearly for the cassettes, but the price was of no consequence when it came to one of his few indulgences.

He inserted his latest acquisition, a Dinah Washington, and pushed the button.

Neither Porfiry Petrovich nor Sarah spoke for the next ten minutes, because Rostnikov's routine was a form of meditation. It involved the patient shifting of weights after each exercise, because Rostnikov did not have enough weights to leave them on the bar after each set. He followed the same routine for each session so that it required no thought, so that he could lose himself in the distant realization of the music and the concentration on each pull of his muscles.

His clean and jerk was awkward because of his leg, though

he could manage almost two hundred and thirty pounds. He could do a dead lift of three hundred and forty pounds, but he did it with all the weight on his right leg. Even so, Rostnikov was sure that he could significantly increase that amount if there were room to store more weights in the cupboard. Since his weights were limited, he had to settle for increasing his repetitions, which led to a very long routine. This was the abbreviated sequence. He would rise early in the morning and lose himself in the longer, more satisfying routine.

The music penetrated him as he moved. A voice, high and sad, yet powerful, sang of love for sale and claimed that "nothing ever changes my love for you." Rostnikov counted without counting; his body told him when he had reached his limit. When his face turned red, his veins ridged high and purple along his arms and forehead, and his breath came in short puffs, then he would do two more.

It was at that moment of satisfaction that Sarah turned away, unable to watch the combination of pain and ecstasy on her husband's face.

"Finished," he said, wiping his forehead with his towel and reaching over to the cassette recorder. He let Dinah Washington finish her line and punched the button.

Eight minutes later, after Rostnikov had taken a very quick cold shower and shave and changed into his good suit, they ate and talked of the dead priest, and of Sarah's cousin Aaron who had just received permission to emigrate to Israel. She had not meant to talk of Aaron, but somehow it had come up.

"They will never let me go, Sarah," Rostnikov said, enjoying his food, though he could taste the missing ingredients in his mind. He appreciated what she must have gone through—the lines, the battles—to get half of a chicken. "Even with the new open emigration. They will never risk my telling their secrets."

"What is lost by trying?" she said.

"Perhaps nothing," he answered. "Perhaps our lives."

"Things are different now," she said gently.

"Faces in the Kremlin are different. The names of nations, cities, streets are different. People are the same. I know a seventy-year-old thief named Misha who changed his name to Yuri, got his teeth fixed, and began to wear decent clothes. People commented on how respectable he looked but—"

"But," Sarah concluded, "he continued to be a thief."

"I've told you about Misha before," he said, using his spoon to find the last sweet remnant of sauce.

"Several times," she said. "With a different point each time. This time you were unusually cynical."

"I'm sorry."

"You are and you are not," she countered with a smile. "You want me to be happy, but you have never wanted to leave Russia."

"Iosef—"

"—is a grown man," Sarah said. "We would ask him to join us."

"And if he said no?"

"You would persuade him to say yes."

He shrugged and ate. This could lead to dangerous words that could end the fragile mood of the evening. "We must go," he said, standing. "This was wonderful, amazing, delicious. We will clean it up later, but we must go."

There was no question of taking the metro. Traffic had thinned. No rain had fallen. The night was chilly and the sky clear. This was a special night, a night for cabs.

Pravda had said the play would start, as most plays started, at seven, but Iosef had asked them to come earlier. "Earlier," as it turned out, was five minutes before curtain time.

Iosef was standing on the street without a coat looking for them as the cab pulled up. "You are late," he said, helping his mother out of the cab.

Iosef stood a head taller than his father, and though he would one day fall victim to hereditary thickness, he was now, just a few months out of the army, lean and looking very much like his mother. There was a touch of makeup on his face, which Rostnikov found disconcerting for an instant.

"You look quite beautiful," Iosef said to his mother as Rostnikov stepped out of the cab after paying the driver.

"See," Rostnikov said. "I told you."

Sarah smiled and Iosef guided them past the ticket takers and to their seats in the crowded little theater. They were on the aisle to the right of the stage so Porfiry Petrovich's leg would have more room.

"I'll come back for you after the show," Iosef said.

The audience was of all ages, but mostly young.

Iosef had gone halfway up the aisle when he returned to say, "I think it still needs some work, mostly the opening. It may be a little slow. Be patient."

"Go, act," said Rostnikov, touching his son's arm.

A few moments later the audience grew silent as the houselights went down and the curtain parted.

On the stage were three young soldiers and an older man who looked like an Arab in a strange but familiar uniform. The Arab was tied to a chair.

In the first act of the play the three soldiers argued about how they should deal with the man in the chair, who was an Afghan rebel. One soldier wanted to kill him, recounting the brutality of the rebels. Another soldier, played by Iosef, wanted to torture him for information. The third soldier wanted to let the man go.

The Afghan, speaking in broken Russian, claimed that he was not a rebel, that he knew nothing.

At the end of the act the Afghan and the soldier who wanted to save him were alone on stage, and the Afghan admitted that he had killed Soviet soldiers and would, if he were not executed, do it again till his country was free.

The compassionate soldier said that the Afghan reminded him of his own father.

The dilemma for the compassionate soldier was evident as the curtain came down. On one hand, loyalty to his country and his fellow soldiers; on the other, sympathy for a man who reminded him of his father, a man who behaved out of principles far more clear than those of the Soviet soldiers. The compassionate soldier now had a terrible secret.

The audience applauded politely, then headed for the snack bar.

"Iosef is a good actor," said Sarah.

"The one playing Vasha, the compassionate soldier, is a fine actor," said Rostnikov. "You like the play?"

"Of course," said Sarah. "He's afraid you won't like it."

"I'll tell him the truth," Rostnikov said.

"If necessary, lie," said Sarah, and she kissed his cheek.

"So far I like it," he said as they moved up the aisle with the crowd.

When they reached the line for the snack bar, someone behind them said, "Don't you return telephone calls?"

Both Rostnikov and Sarah knew who they would see before they turned, and since Lydia Tkach had been so loud, many others turned with them. Lydia was wearing a green dress with a green necklace that was almost lost in the ruffles around her neck. In her right hand she carried a rather wrinkled coat.

"It is good to see you," Rostnikov lied. "You have met my wife, Sarah."

"Of course," shouted Lydia, taking Sarah's hand. "Jewish lady with the brain tumor. It is good to see you again."

Rostnikov looked at his wife and was relieved to see a smile.

"It was nice of you to come to our son's play," said Sarah. "Are you enjoying it?"

"I don't like plays about secrets," she said. "Everyone whispers. Movies are better."

"Perhaps we can suggest to Iosef that he write a movie, a loud movie," said Rostnikov. "May I buy you a coffee?"

"I didn't come to see the play," she said. "I came to talk to you."

"I considered that possibility," said Rostnikov. "Coffee?"

"Pepsi-Cola," Lydia said.

They were at the bar now and Rostnikov ordered three Pepsi-Colas. Then they stepped through the crowd, heading back toward the auditorium.

The intermission was ten minutes. Rostnikov knew there could not be more than five minutes left. He faced Lydia politely.

"She is going to get my son killed," said Lydia, loud enough to attract the attention of at least a dozen more people.

"She?" asked Rostnikov.

"The little girl you have him working with, the one who is trying to seduce him and get him killed. Sasha is a husband, a father. Soon he will have two children. I don't believe anyone in Russia today should have two children, but they did not ask me. I told them, anyway, but it was too late. He is behaving . . . Inspector, I think my son is afraid."

The shrill insistence in her voice had given way to anguish as she finished. Sarah touched her shoulder, and Lydia bit her lower lip to hold back the tears.

"He's out now with that girl in some bar called Nicholas looking for some Turkish woman," Lydia said in a considerably lower voice than before. She lifted her eyes to Rostnikov and then went on, "I've never seen him afraid like this before. He doesn't even know he is afraid. It's making him angry like his father."

It was time to go in for the second act and the crowd flowed toward the inner doors.

"We will talk to you after the next act," Sarah said, putting her arm around the older woman.

"I've got to go back to the apartment," said Lydia. "Maya and the baby need me. They don't like to be alone. Besides, I don't understand whispering plays. Your son is in the play, too? Which one?"

"The one who wanted to torture. . . . The tall one with the short brown hair," said Sarah.

"Tell him to speak up," she said, and turned to Rostnikov. "Will you do something for my son? You have one child. I have one child."

"I will do something," Rostnikov said.

"Does Porfiry Petrovich lie?" Lydia asked Sarah.

"When he must. But he is not lying now."

Lydia nodded, looked at Rostnikov, not fully convinced, and put on her coat.

"I will do something," Rostnikov said, touching Lydia's shoulder.

Everyone was inside by now but the three of them.

Lydia nodded once and then once again before she moved into the night.

"What will you do?" asked Sarah.

"Now? Now I am going to see an Afghan die and a very angry soldier who called for blood be blamed for it, though he is not responsible. The disillusioned, compassionate soldier will turn out to be the murderer. He will have murdered this man who is like his own father because he cannot bear to see him killed by someone who doesn't respect him."

"Iosef let you read the script?" she asked as they moved back into the darkening theater.

"No," he said, "but I am a policeman and he is my son."

"You could be very wrong," she said.

"I am probably wrong," he agreed. "But that is the play I would write."

"What will you do about Sasha Tkach?" whispered Sarah.

"Quiet," said someone behind them, so Porfiry Petrovich didn't have to answer.

TEN

SASHA STOOD WATCHING THE GIRLS WITH THEIR HAIR wild and waving, covering their eyes, teeth white or appearing to be white in the dull, dim light of the Nikolai Café. The girls danced with gaunt men, with each other, or alone. Bodies touched and parted and touched again. There was no single style, though at least three of the twenty girls wore tight skirts that looked like shorts and black stockings with flower patterns.

The light was supposed to be intimate. It was supposed to hide the eyes, fill the sockets with a deep yellow. The music blared like clanking metal, vibrating as if the charged strings of the instruments were forever trying to tune up and forever angry because they were unable to achieve the elusive sound they sought.

And the girls, some with yellow artificial hair swept up like old French or American movie stars, dressed in tight silken blouses that showed the size and shape of their breasts and skirts that hugged tight, swayed and smiled as if they had wonderful secrets.

"You see her?" asked Elena. She and Sasha sat at the end of the bar, trying not to drink their warm, dark beer.

"No," said Sasha.

"I admire the zeal with which you examine each face and

body,'' she said, ''on the chance that the Arab girl might be disguised as a Russian girl.''

''She is not here,'' said Sasha, looking away from the dance floor to the crowded tables where teenage boys in slick imitation leather made jokes they convinced themselves were funny and the girls laughed too loudly to mean it.

There was little room to move, and it was almost impossible to hear anything except the laughter and the music that tingled across the bar and beneath Sasha's feet.

The woman they had spoken to that morning, Tatyana, was not there. Two young men, who were not so young when one looked too closely, served drinks from behind the bar. Girls in white blouses, who were not as old as they appeared when one looked too closely, served the tables.

''Another beer?'' asked one of the not-so-young men behind the bar as if he knew just how bored Sasha must be with the people of the Nikolai.

Sasha looked at the man. His teeth were stained and crooked.

''We haven't finished these,'' said Elena, holding up her glass.

The bartender shrugged and moved off to a customer down the bar, a man of about forty with an artificial flower behind his right ear and an empty glass held high.

There was a door in the wall behind the small dance floor. The door was covered with strings of dangling mustard-colored beads. The beads parted and Tatyana entered the café and looked around with distaste. She paused to light a cigarette, then maneuvered her way through the crowd, touching a breast here, a buttock there, and exchanging an intimate smile with each girl she touched.

Tatyana's yellow hair was swept up in back so that her neck showed like smooth weathered marble.

Elena watched the woman make her way toward the bar. She was the same woman, yet changed. She wore much more makeup and her clothes were clinging but not immodest. She was twenty years older than anyone else on the floor, and Elena felt that the emotions the younger people feigned were so clearly felt by this woman that she had no need to act. Tatyana's eyes came up through the crowd and found Sasha and Elena.

"If she goes back through the beads, you follow her," Sasha said. "I'll go out the front and stop her at the rear entrance."

Elena said nothing. They had found the rear entrance, checked the low windows before they had entered the Nikolai. Then they had gone to the bar, where, since they were the only customers who did nothing to draw attention to themselves, many had glanced their way.

Elena put down her glass and watched Tatyana make her way through the crowd. Tatyana did not turn or look away. She continued to inch her way along the swaying young backsides. When she reached the man with the flower behind his ear, he looked up from his drink at the mirror above the bar, shouted "Tatyana," turned, and put his arm around her waist. Elena expected her to push the drunk away or sting him with a word. Instead she smiled, removed the cigarette from her overly red lips, and kissed the man, fully, deeply, with her mouth wide. People around them whooped and applauded. When she removed her open mouth from his, the drunk sank back, removed the flower from behind his ear, and stuck it in his mouth.

"You look like policemen," Tatyana said, moving to Elena's side. "You are bad for business. Customers here see a policeman and they find other places to go."

"You called the Syrian," said Elena, pulling back from the touch of Tatyana's shoulder against hers.

Tatyana shrugged and looked over Elena's shoulder at Sasha, who looked back at her. "You would be very appealing if you smiled," she said to him.

"I will probably smile when I order everyone to leave in about five minutes," he said. "You called the Syrian."

"I called the Syrian," Tatyana agreed. "Who do I look like?" She was looking in the mirror over the bar.

Elena followed her gaze and examined the image. Tatyana's eyes were half-closed, the cigarette in the corner of her wide mouth. "Dietrich," she said.

Tatyana looked at Elena and Sasha in the mirror and saw no recognition. "Marlene Dietrich," Tatyana said.

"Do you know where the girl is?" asked Sasha.

"Everyone is too young," Tatyana said, shaking her head. "You want a drink? I'll buy."

"We've got drinks," said Elena.

"You have water," Tatyana whispered into Elena's ear. The woman's breath was warm and sweet. Elena forced herself not to move.

"You called the Syrian," Sasha said again. "Do you know where the girl is? If you do not answer, we will take you to a very small holding cell in District Eleven where you can sit all night on a bench in a very bright little room with nothing to do while you try to remember."

Tatyana smiled. "You are a year too late, pretty policeman," she said. "You can't do such things anymore. People will run and tell on you and you will have to say five Hail Yeltsins in penance."

"You are drunk," said Elena.

"I am stoned," Tatyana corrected in English.

"What?" Elena asked. The woman's face was now inches from hers.

"Your partner is very pretty," she said. "And you are very, what are the words in French, *plantureuse et douce.*"

Elena looked puzzled.

"She says you are full-figured and sweet," said Sasha.

"*Est-ce que vous parlez français?*" said Tatyana, turning her attention to Sasha.

"*Oui, je le comprends,*" he said above the music. "You can answer in French or Russian, but you will answer. I will ask once more and then I will climb on this bar, break that mirror, and order everyone to leave."

"I have a better idea," said Tatyana, looking into Elena's eyes. "Why don't the three of us go in back, climb on top of the beer cases in the storeroom, and take off our clothes?"

"The girl," said Elena evenly.

Tatyana looked past her in triumph and said to Sasha, "Did you hear that? The little tremor in her voice? She is tempted, our *petite choute*."

A man to Sasha's right had his back turned. He was engaged in earnest conversation with a very young girl with long dark hair. Sasha pushed the man out of the way and climbed up on the bar.

Heads turned toward him, smiles crossed faces. A few people clapped, believing a young drunk had decided to make a dancing fool of himself. One of the four young-old men in the electric band saw him, pointed with his guitar, and the music went wild. Sasha looked down at Tatyana, who was whispering something to Elena.

"Quiet," shouted Tkach, pushing the hair from his eyes.

No one was quiet.

"Get down," said Tatyana. "You'll get yourself hurt."

"I am the police," Tkach shouted, reaching down for his half-full glass of warm beer.

"It is Sting," shouted a young male voice, and those nearby who heard roared with hollow laughter.

Sasha flung the glass at the mirror. Shards of glass sprayed the bartenders and patrons, who covered their heads and eyes.

"Get down, Tkach," Elena said, touching his leg. Around her was an ocean of faces beginning to realize that this might not be a drunken joke. The music stopped suddenly, except for one guitarist with spiked hair whose eyes were closed. Another guitarist poked the spike-haired one in the shoulder and the final guitar let out a thin *eeeel* and died.

Conversations died; all attention turned to the show at the bar.

"We are the police," Sasha shouted. "This bar is closed. Hard currency has been exchanged here." He pulled out his wallet and held it up with his red identification card and picture showing.

"Throw it here and give us a look," came a tough voice from the yellow-gray shadows.

"No, pull your trousers down and give us a look," came a woman's voice, which brought further howls.

Tatyana reached for Sasha's right leg and grabbed his trousers. "Get down," she cried. "You . . . get down. I'll talk to you."

"You'll talk to me when everyone leaves," shouted Tkach. "You had your chance."

"Leonid," Tatyana screamed, pulling at Tkach, but there was so much noise from the crowd that no one could hear her.

Elena grabbed Tatyana's wrist and wrenched it from Sasha's leg. Tatyana's free hand went between Elena's legs as one of the bartenders shoved Sasha from behind. He fell forward into the drunk with the flower in his mouth, and both went tumbling onto the floor. Something smelled foul and acrid as he tried to stand. A booted foot caught him in the chest. Sasha had the sense that people were trampling him, stampeding toward the door. He felt like a soccer ball rapidly losing air. Women screamed. Men cursed. Something hit him behind the ear.

"Smash the bastard," Tatyana's voice cried.

Somewhere in the mesh of voices a musical instrument hit something hard and echoed like a wind chime. Somewhere close by, a fist came down against Sasha's ear and he sank back onto the floor.

Another foot. Another fist. Sasha covered his face and tried to roll into a ball as he had been taught to do in situations like this. He had also been taught that situations like this should never be allowed to happen.

He told himself to keep from tightening his back muscles as he groped for his knee and felt something solid crash against the knuckles of his right hand. He waited for the next blow, not knowing where it would land, wondering if Elena was alive. No blow came. It was a trick. If he opened his eyes and rolled over, he was sure the bartender with the bad teeth would smash him in the face with a beer bottle.

Sasha forced himself to roll over and open his eyes, to search for Elena, to try to help her. Above him, horizontal and five feet off the ground, was a man with a surprised look on his face. The man was suspended as if he were part of a stage magician's act, and then, suddenly, the levitation stopped and the man flipped over past Sasha's huddled body and skidded into a table. Another man, this one larger than the one who had flown past, tripped over Tkach with a loss of air and tried to regain his balance, but he was moving too quickly and the bar caught his back with a snap.

"Are you badly hurt, Sasha Tkach?" Porfiry Petrovich Rostnikov said, reaching down to him.

Tkach took his hand and was lifted easily to his feet. "Elena?" he asked, and then he saw her.

Tatyana was bending over the bar as if she were trying to vomit on the other side. Elena was holding the woman's head down. Elena's hair was wild, a wispy curl coming down over her right eye. There was a sound near the beaded curtain at the rear of the stage. Sasha looked and discovered that only his right eye was open.

In front of the curtain stood a large man in a leather jacket. Leonid Dovnik's eyes met those of Rostnikov, who saw that the man was considering whether to advance or retreat. Even with one eye Sasha could see that in spite of what the Washtub had done, the man was not afraid. That frightened Sasha. Elena looked up in time to meet Dovnik's eyes, which had turned to her. He looked at her for a moment, fixing her in his memory. Then, in no hurry at all, he turned and went back through the curtain.

The two men Rostnikov had thrown across the room lay groaning, one with fingers trying to hold in the blood from a smashed nose, the other grasping his back and trying to stand erect.

"What are you doing here?" asked Tkach on wobbly legs.

"Your mother found me," said Rostnikov. "She was afraid you might be doing something foolish and dangerous, which, as we both know, is absurd."

He reached over to Tkach and touched his swollen eye. Tkach winced and pulled back. Rostnikov shook his head and moved to Elena at the bar. "You are unhurt, Elena Timofeyeva?"

"I am fine," Elena answered. Her voice was almost calm, though Rostnikov could hear the last faint note of excitement and fear.

"Let her up," he said, and Elena released Tatyana, who pushed herself up and looked about the café. Her makeup was smudged.

"You didn't have to do this," she said to Elena. "What have I done to you? I had some fun, told you you were attractive. Is that a reason you two should break up my café?"

"We are sorry," said Rostnikov, handing her a clean handkerchief from his jacket pocket. He never used a handkerchief himself, but he had discovered it was very useful to a policeman when dealing with a weeping suspect or witness. "My young colleague is about to become a father for the second time."

"Well, why didn't he say so?" said Tatyana, turning with

the handkerchief in hand to examine herself in the mirror. But there was no longer much of a mirror behind the bar.

"He has a lot on his mind," said Rostnikov. "May I sit?"

"If you can find an unbroken chair," said Tatyana.

"I have a bad leg," explained Rostnikov, finding a chair and sitting.

"I am sorry," said Tatyana, "but I can't pay for this damage. Mirrors, chairs. Do you know what they cost? If you can even find them."

Rostnikov looked around. The two injured men were now gone and there was quite a bit of damage.

"And the business I just lost," she said. "I'm not a wealthy woman."

"Where is the Arab girl? Amira Durahaman?" asked Elena. "Her father will give you the reward if you know."

"You didn't have to hurt me because I made you feel something you never felt before," Tatyana said.

"I made love to two women when I was in college," Elena said. "It was mildly interesting. You think too highly of yourself."

Sasha Tkach pulled out a chair and sat next to Sasha. Both men looked at the two women.

"I'll get the reward?" Tatyana asked.

"If there is a reward," said Elena.

"I would like," said Sasha, "a mineral water with no gas. Is that possible?"

Tatyana shrugged and moved behind the bar.

"Inspector," Elena said. "I would like your permission to find a basin and wash myself."

"Wash," said Rostnikov. Elena moved toward the beaded curtains.

"I'm sorry," said Tkach, feeling his tender ribs. "I made a serious mistake."

"Not if you wished to commit suicide in the line of duty. If that was your goal, then there was no mistake, just the accident of my arrival. It is very strange, Sasha Tkach. I have never seen a fight in a bar before. In all my years as a policeman, never a fight until tonight. It was like a John Wayne movie."

"*The Spoilers*," said Tatyana, coming around the bar. "Dietrich and John Wayne." She placed a glass of mineral water in front of Rostnikov.

"Thank you," he said. "Please sit. I gather from what I have heard that you may know where to find the Syrian girl."

"A reward would help pay for the damage your crazy policeman has caused," she said.

"We can talk to the girl's father about a reward," said Rostnikov. "I will suggest he not pay. I will suggest to you that your reward for telling us about the girl will be our departure. Life is hard and getting no easier. But there are exceptions, moments of, if not hope, at least relief. A child is born healthy. A book absorbs us. A friend laughs. Unwanted guests depart and never return."

"I know nothing of the girl," Tatyana said, folding her arms. "But if I—"

"Look at me," Rostnikov said. And she looked at the homely face of a man with large, very sympathetic brown eyes. "My son wrote a play. I saw it tonight. I did not like the play. Not because it was a bad play, but because I saw in it what others may not have seen. The pain of my only son." He looked at Sasha Tkach, who ran his hand through his hair and turned away. Against the far wall the rattle of beads announced Elena's return.

"In the play my son's character is killed. He rose when the curtain went down and then came out to greet us. A boy who knew the missing Syrian girl died this morning. He had a father and a mother. He will not rise and greet his parents. Amira Durahaman has a father. You will tell us where to find the girl. Otherwise I will take you with us, and you will, I am sorry to say, be very unhappy."

"The girl came in here sometimes," Tatyana said, looking around at the three policemen. "She came in with a young Jew, sometimes others. I don't know their names, so don't ask me. I don't know names. I give customers nicknames—the Barstool, Hands, the Siberian, Phil Collins. They like that."

"And the girl?" asked Sasha. "Did you have a name for her?"

"Bright Eyes," said Tatyana. "I know no more, but I'll try to—"

"Lock your doors and come with us," said Rostnikov.

"Please," Tatyana said, almost in tears.

"Officer Timofeyeva, will you please take—" he began, and the woman crumbled.

"No prison. People are getting lost in prisons. They're not being fed. Names. Names. I'll give you names if you promise no prison."

Porfiry Petrovich nodded at Elena, who took out her pen and notebook and began writing the names that came from Tatyana.

When she was finished, Rostnikov turned to Elena and said, "Go home, sleep."

Elena Timofeyeva opened her mouth to say something, glanced at Tatyana, who was not looking at her, and decided to say nothing.

"Sasha Tkach, we'll stop at the hospital, have you looked at, sewn, and patched before we send you home."

"I can clean up at home," Tkach said.

"If you go home looking like that," said Rostnikov, "you will frighten your wife and child and bring the wrath of your mother down on my head. No, my own peace depends on the ability of some tired nurse to put you in acceptable surface condition. On the way we can talk."

"Her," said Elena, nodding at Tatyana. "She might run away."

"She will not run," said Rostnikov. "She is a woman of property."

Tatyana looked around the wreck of a room. "I won't run," she answered, so softly that Elena wasn't sure she had heard her. "This street, this city, this café. I won't run."

Something vibrated through Tatyana and her voice suddenly rose. "I will survive," she said. "I will prosper."

Rostnikov stood, moved the toes of his left foot, and found them still functional. "It has been a busy day," he said. "And tomorrow promises to be no easier."

Colonel Lunacharski was not hungry, but he sat alone in the almost empty cafeteria at two in the morning drinking a glass of coffee into which he had stirred three spoons of sugar. Colonel Lunacharski was not hungry, but he was tired. Getting out of his office was essential, and there was no place to go at two in the morning but the small cafeteria for night-duty officers in Lubyanka.

Only weeks before he had been among the elite stationed at Yasenevo, the headquarters of the KGB's intelligence-and-espionage arm, outside the city. From his office on the twentieth floor, Lunacharski had been able to look down at a lush *les*, the forest that had given the headquarters the name by which it was known to him and the others who were insiders.

The dining room in Yasenevo had been one of the principal perks of power. But that was gone, at least for him, at least for now.

Since Lunacharski disliked coffee, which he drank to help him stay awake, he could tolerate it only with massive doses of sugar. He was well aware from experience that the sugar and coffee would charge him with energy now, but that the artificial charge would not last. In half an hour he would have to remove his coat and stand outside in the cold air till he felt revitalized enough to go back to his office and take a pill, which would get him through till late in the afternoon.

Vladimir Lunacharski made it a rule to exercise vigorously and never to take more than two pills a week. He was well aware of the dangers of addiction and confident that he could walk the line between his need for wakefulness and his dependency on the orange pills.

Colonel Lunacharski knew well why he disliked coffee. His father, a man of terrible temper, had drunk massive quantities of both tea and coffee. His father's long, fine fingers had been stained by his addiction to the beans themselves, which, when he could get them, he chewed like candy.

His father, an army sergeant, had died in 1968 of a stroke after a screaming rage over his wife's having overcooked a ham.

Vladimir thought he remembered when he was an infant and his mother's breasts gave him sour milk after his father, an army sergeant, had shouted, pounded, and threatened.

The four people in the cafeteria were all at least forty-five years old. Each of them was sitting alone. None of them acknowledged anyone else or looked around. One man near the door had a notebook on the table in front of him, which he thumbed through as he drank coffee. The other two simply put their heads down and ate, though the cafeteria food was no longer the best in Moscow.

Lunacharski had given himself ten minutes, and the ten minutes were almost over. He pushed back his chair and started to rise. Then he saw Klamkin the Frog enter the cafeteria, look around, and head toward him. The colonel was not surprised at the agent's appearance. He had left a note on the door indicating where he could be found. As Klamkin approached, Lunacharski sat down again, for the Frog was at least two inches taller than he.

"May I?" asked Klamkin, who had brushed back his hair

and recently shaved so that he could appear fresh for the meeting.

Lunacharski pointed to the chair across from him and Klamkin sat.

"Spokniokov and Glenin are still outside the Intourist Hotel waiting for the German," Klamkin said. "Our agent reports that Timofeyeva and Tkach went to the Nikolai Café, where Tkach started a riot. He was beaten but not too badly. Rostnikov arrived to help him."

"Rostnikov?" Lunacharski thought he might not have heard Klamkin correctly.

"Yes. He went to the theater with his wife, took her home, and then went immediately to the Nikolai."

"His son's play," said Lunacharski.

"Yes. The play was antimilitary but well done."

"Well done?" asked Lunacharski. "You watched it? Our agents are now doing theatrical reviews?"

Klamkin said nothing.

"And where are Rostnikov and the others now?"

"Home. In bed or at least in their apartments. If Rostnikov goes to Arkush, I will go with him. The only person not sleeping is the Syrian. The light in his apartment window is on and he is pacing. He has people looking for his daughter."

"Go home, Klamkin. Sleep. Be ready for tomorrow."

"It is too late to sleep and my apartment building is too noisy in the morning. With your permission, Colonel, I will sleep in the back of the car while Brodivov watches for Rostnikov."

"Fine," said Lunacharski. "But don't become careless. Pull Spokniokov and Glenin from the German before you go to sleep. Reassign them to the search for the Arab girl. I wish to find her before the Syrians or Snitkonoy's people. Do you drink coffee?"

"Yes," said Klamkin. "But I prefer tea."

"Stay here and have a cup before you make the calls," said Lunacharski. He stood and motioned for Klamkin to remain seated. Klamkin nodded.

As Colonel Lunacharski moved down the corridor he listened to his boot steps echoing through the emptiness. Reports were piled on his desk. What he wanted to do was go into the streets and look for the Arab girl or from the dark interior of an unmarked Zil watch her father pace the floor. What he wanted to do was take the train to Arkush to see for himself, but he had to remain here to monitor the operations. There was no time for indulgence. For him there were reports and pills and a wife he would not have to see for another day.

The world was changing quickly. General Karsnikov sought the possibilities for survival wherever they might be and one of the possibilities lay in the former MVD office of Aleksandr Snitkonoy. Lunacharski had worked out a plan, which he was now perfecting. He would try to be patient. He would watch the Wolfhound's operation, perhaps even infiltrate it, and demonstrate that while it served a useful function, it was inefficient, ineffective, run by a blustering ass, and peopled by eccentrics who had been unable to function in other security branches.

"The moment will come," the general had said, "when we can place the evidence before the new Russian administration and I will be able not only to strongly suggest but to present evidence that your department is far more capable of pursuing the special cases of a new government."

"I understand," Lunacharski had said.

"I can give you little for this operation, Colonel, but if you succeed, it can mean much for us, much for you. You understand?"

"Completely."

"We have lost a great deal," General Karsnikov had said,

lighting a foul-smelling Turkish cigarette. "We must work to build a new base of power."

Colonel Lunacharski had not asked who "we" were, because he knew. In a time when there was little to be pleased with, it was a comfort to be part of the unnamed and waiting army.

ELEVEN

When Sasha Tkach woke up at seven o'clock the next morning, he was unaware for a moment that he had a broken rib, a badly swollen eye, and a variety of abrasions. He had been given a very large injection at the hospital so he had slept. Now pain ran through him from face to stomach and he held back a groan. Maya stirred at his side. She was too heavy with the baby to sleep on her side or stomach, and though she was uncomfortable sleeping on her back, she had learned to accept the discomfort and was now gently snoring.

Sasha had arrived home well after everyone else was asleep. He had undressed, dropped his clothes on the couch, and climbed painfully into bed next to Maya. In her sleep, sensing him, she had reached out, and he had guided her hand into his to keep her from touching his face or his taped chest.

He slept later than he intended. His plan had been to awaken first and be gone before Maya or Lydia could see him. He still had a chance, and had the pain not been five times greater than he remembered from the night before, he probably could have hurried into his clothes and made it into the hall. Had he made it, he would have shaved with the spare often-used disposable English razor he kept in his desk at Petrovka. He knew he should have thrown it away long ago, but since his beard was so light, it would not be too painful to use the blade once more. He got his feet over the side of the bed and was wondering how he would make it through the day when the scream came. Pulcharia was sitting up in her crib in the corner, staring at the hunched-over creature with the horrible eye in her father and mother's bed. She screamed and Sasha did not bother to whisper, since she had surely awakened both his wife and mother.

"It's me, Pulcharushka," he said. "Don't be afraid."

As his wife stirred awake at his side and his mother's footsteps shuffled to the bedroom door, Sasha felt, for no reason that made sense to him, that it would be all right, that whatever he had gone through had passed, that what had happened in the Nikolai Café had helped him to this understanding. He turned with a small smile on his face to comfort his wife. He knew she would soon be weeping.

At seven that same morning Leonid Dovnik, who had slept soundly for five hours, stood in front of the door of an apartment on the fifth floor of a gray building on Vavilov Street.

He had started early with two apartments near Moscow State University not far from where he had beaten Grisha Zalinsky to death the day before. Leonid had started early because he wanted to be sure to catch people before they left for work or school. It had taken him less than three minutes in the first apartment to discover that the Arab girl had visited there in the past but had not been seen for some time and had never slept there. Leonid was sure that he had been told the truth because he was a very persuasive man with a very direct manner, which let it be known that unless he received honest answers, violence would follow. He was aided by the belief of the people in both apartments that he was with the police.

He had checked the name off in the address book he had taken from Grisha Zalinsky's apartment and added two more names and addresses given to him by the frightened girl in the first apartment he had entered. It was slow, tedious work, but he did not mind.

Near the university metro stop he bought a newspaper from a formerly state-run kiosk that was now a shining example of private enterprise, which meant high prices and few papers for sale, since paper was scarce. In general Leonid supported the new capitalism. After all, he told himself, he was an entrepreneur. Chaos and change tended to mean an increased need for his services. Yuri Pepp and his money changers had found too many new competitors around the big hotels dealing with American dollars. Leonid persuaded most of them to find new fields of interest. Sophia and Kolodny Seveyuskin had a pipeline for stealing emergency food supplies coming in from the United Nations. A bureaucrat in the Office of Consumer Supplies wanted to become a partner. Leonid convinced the man to ask for a transfer to a Siberian regional office. People with ambition often found other people in their way and needed someone who could maim or even destroy for a reasonable fee. Leonid did not consider himself particularly intelligent, but he knew he was relentless, honest, and without any moral sense.

Six months ago Leonid had bought a waffle filled with whipped cream in one of the cooperatives along the street, but there were neither waffles nor whipped cream now, and all the cooperatives were closed. He had money, plenty of it, French money, American dollars, but there was nothing to buy on the street. It almost put him in a bad mood.

If he did not find the Arab girl at the next apartment on his list, he would go to the Cherymushinsky farm market and pick up something sweet, maybe even a cup of caramel, though the last cup had given him a toothache.

Leonid got off of the metro and walked along the torn-up

tram tracks, the piles of gravel. A bus coughed dark smoke from its exhaust and forced Leonid Dovnik against the wall of an apartment building, which turned out to be the one he was seeking.

There was a sense of urgency to his search, which he did not wish to fully acknowledge. He was not one to panic. The sense of urgency came not from the knowledge that the Syrians and the police were also looking for the girl. It was from the sight he had witnessed when he had returned to the Nikolai last night to report on his lack of success.

He had heard the noise from the office behind the stage where he had just reported to Tatyana. He had heard the shouts, the scrambling of bodies, the curses, and the running feet. When he stepped through the beaded curtains, he had seen a man who looked like a refrigerator hurl another man of some bulk through the air into the bar. The Nikolai had been nearly empty at that moment. Tatyana had been leaning over the bar, held there by the same policewoman he had seen in front of the Nikolai that morning. Beside them stood the young policeman. He had been beaten, not as well as Leonid would have done it, but he had been beaten.

Leonid had considered stepping across the floor and smashing the big man, who took a limping step toward him. There was no fear in the man's eyes, nor was there any eagerness for battle. If anything, there was a look of curiosity, and Leonid had the sense that this man might well be capable of prying secrets from him.

So Leonid had turned and left, certain that Tatyana could take care of herself, as she always had. Even if she could not, he was confident that he could survive without her, especially if he could find the Arab girl.

He found the apartment and knocked at the door. No answer. He knocked again and then stood listening. He listened patiently for a long time, five or six minutes. A woman wearing a thin coat and carrying an empty shopping bag walked past. She kept her eyes fixed on the floor in front of her except to steal a glimpse of Leonid. Then she hurried away.

He was certain now that no one was hiding inside the apartment. He would have heard some sound. Leonid tried the door. He knew there were several locks; he could feel their resistance.

To keep any listening neighbors at bay, he did what he had done many times in the past. He shouted, "Police, open the door."

He paused for a second, then kicked the door. It flew open and came off at the top right hinge. He stepped into the apartment, propped the door back in the doorway, and looked around.

The place was large and messy, which displeased Leonid Dovnik, who was a neat man. "If one is forced to live in a pigsty, one must keep his own corner of it clean or he is no better than the pig and deserves to be eaten"; that is what Leonid Dovnik's mother had taught him. It was the way she had kept her home while Leonid's father tried to turn it into filthy hell. Leonid's own room was almost as clean as a surgery, a surgery where he sometimes imagined carving his father's carcass and showing it to his approving mother.

Now, this sty. Leonid despised whoever lived here. The name in the notebook for this address was Chesney. That sounded American or English to Leonid. Americans and English could be filthy pigs, but so could Russians. Besides, there were many Russians with odd names.

He thrashed through the rooms, not worrying about making noise. The living room was overcrowded with soft furniture covered with a pink-and-yellow-flowered fabric. The dark drapes that covered the windows kept out the morning light, and the smell of something sweet reminded him of burning sugar. His tooth ached at the smell.

He searched and quickly found what he had hoped to find.

In the single bedroom was a bed, whose twisted sheets smelled of sex and sweat. Leonid found the odor slightly repulsive. In the closet were the clothes of a man and a woman. He thought he recognized a dress as the one the Arab girl had been wearing the one time Tatyana had introduced him to her. This memory was confirmed by the photograph he found on the dresser. He had to move a pair of stained male undershorts to find the photograph, but there it was, and in it was the girl. The photo had been taken along the Moscow River. Leonid knew the place, right across from the old monastery.

The girl in the picture stood next to a man much taller and much older than she. He had his arm around her possessively, and there was a smile of triumph on his thin lips. The girl was smiling, too, but there was a faint hint of fear in that smile. The man was tall, with lots of white hair and a smile of white teeth. He wore a white shirt and white trousers. Leonid Dovnik did not like this man.

He tore the photograph from the frame, folded it, and stuffed it in his pocket. Then he began to search the apartment for a clue as to where they might have gone. He could simply have sat down and waited till they returned, but it might be hours, all day, late into the night. That did not bother him, but he knew that others were looking and that he had only the advantage of Grisha Zalinsky's address book.

He found nothing that could help him, so he left the apartment and replaced the door in its frame. He listened for a moment and then moved to the door across the hall. Someone was inside. He could hear a radio or television and voices. He knocked.

"Who is it?" came a woman's voice.

"Police," he shouted. "Open."

The door opened.

A young woman peered up at him in fear. She wore a purple robe and her hair was wild from washing.

"The man across the way, Chesney," he said. "Where does he work?"

"I don't know," said the woman.

"What's wrong?" came a voice behind her, and a young man appeared.

Leonid didn't bother to look at him. "I want to know where the man works who lives in that apartment," he said.

"Chesney?" asked the man.

Now Leonid looked up. The man looked even younger than the girl and was dressed in an identical purple robe.

"Chesney, yes."

"He's English," said the young man. "He's with a trade delegation from some heavy-machine company. He told me once."

"The name of this machine company," asked Leonid flatly.

The young woman's robe flapped open and she hurried to cover her breasts. Leonid was not interested.

"I don't remember," the young man said. "I think it was Robinson or Robertson, something like that."

"The girl?" Leonid asked.

"Girl?" asked the young woman. "He has—"

"The Arab girl," said the man.

"The Arab girl," agreed Leonid. "How long has she been here?"

"Two nights, maybe three," said the man. "But she has been here before."

"If they return," said Leonid, "you are not to tell him that the police were here. Tell them that you heard noises, if you must tell them anything. Let them think they have been robbed. Go steal something in there if you wish. You understand?"

"We don't have to—" the young woman began, but the young man interrupted her.

"We understand."

Leonid turned away and walked down the hall. Behind him the door closed and the lock turned.

A man named Chesney who works for an English heavy-machinery company called Robinson or Robertson. It would be difficult, but not impossible. There were directories, government agencies anxious to guide a Soviet businessman to a foreign investor. It might take a few hours, but it was possible, and Leonid Dovnik fully intended to do it.

At seven in the morning on that day, Porfiry Petrovich Rostnikov looked out the window of his apartment at the black Zil parked across the street. He considered going down and inviting the men in the car up for some hot buckwheat porridge with butter, but it was not a serious consideration even for a second. The men would not come in and the situation would be very awkward. Rostnikov did not want to make their lives more difficult than they already were.

"They are there?" asked Sarah, moving to his side and putting her arm around his waist.

Rostnikov nodded in the direction of the Zil.

"It looks like a cold morning and their engine isn't on," Sarah said.

"Fuel is expensive," Rostnikov said.

"Then why drive a great fat Zil?"

"Because that is the legacy of the KGB," he explained, moving from the window and adjusting his tie. Sarah and Porfiry Petrovich had made love this morning, just before dawn, for the first time in many months, since before Sarah's operation. Tentatively they had clung together and she had put his rough head against her breasts and then she had said, "Would you like to try?"

And he had answered, "I believe we can do more than try."

It had not been perfect, but it had not been bad either.

"I'm going to look for work," she said afterward. "The hospital says I am well enough. I am going to try a music store on Kalinin. I have experience. What do you think?"

"If you are well enough and wish to," he said.

"Iosef will meet me for lunch. We will spend the afternoon trying to find enough food for Sasha Tkach's birthday party. Will you be back tonight, do you think?"

"Possibly," he said. "But I may have to stay in Arkush."

He stood silently as she searched for her good shoes in the freestanding wooden closet in the corner. She found them and turned to him.

"What?" she asked.

"I may have to stay in Arkush tonight," he said again.

She sat down to put on her shoes.

"You feel . . . ?" he asked.

"Wash your bowl and then let's go out together," she said, standing and taking his hand. "My intuition tells me that this will be a good day."

At seven in the morning, after spending the night trying to straighten up the Nikolai so she might open that night, Tatyana gave up. She looked in what was left of the mirror over the bar and saw the face of a tired woman with puffy eyes and wild yellow hair.

"Mirror, mirror on the wall," she whispered. "Forget it." She got her coat from the back room, turned off the lights, and moved toward the door.

Two foreign-looking men stood before her, blocking the door. She had not heard them enter.

"Closed," she said. "Come back tonight."

The men said nothing.

"Closed," she said. "Can't you understand Russian?"

The men did not move.

It was at this point that Tatyana felt fear. "You are the police," she said, hoping that they were but knowing that they were not. These men were too well dressed, too foreign. "What do you want?"

Again they said nothing.

She considered turning and running, but the backdoor was too far away and the pathway to it strewn with bits of broken bottles, shattered mirror, and lost dreams. "It isn't fair," she said, brushing back her hair as the two men moved toward her. "It isn't fair."

At seven in the morning of that day the man who had murdered a priest and a nun stood in the center of Klochkov Street in the town of Arkush. The street was named in honor of Vasili Klochkov, who, bleeding profusely, had hurled himself with a grenade beneath a Nazi tank, after shouting "Russia is vast, but there's nowhere to retreat. Moscow is behind us." That act of heroism supposedly inspired the nearly defeated Russian army to hold their positions and, soon after, turn the tide of the war. But few people in town called the street Klochkov. Most called it Venyaminov, the name it had sixty years ago. Innokenty Venyaminov was a nineteenth-century missionary who carried the gospel of the Orthodox Church to the Aleutian Islands and Russian Alaska.

The man standing in the street knew a great deal of the history of Arkush. Within the past three days he had been responsible for what would certainly be a most important part of that history.

The scrawny rooster belonging to Old Loski cackled beyond the houses. The assassin turned his head, unsure of what to do. He could not go home, could not face the bed he had left, the dreams that were bad, and the thoughts that came in the wakeful darkness, thoughts that were even worse than dreams.

And so, body weary, he had dressed and wandered with the first light of dawn. He had smelled the morning bread of Tkonin the baker and heard the birds in the woods beyond the town where ghosts now walked.

He had done what he had to do, he told himself. He had done what must be done. To do otherwise would have been to betray his family, his name.

Someone called that name from a nearby second-story window. He waved without looking up and moved down the street, hands in his pockets, as if he had somewhere to go.

He would have to go to work soon, though he could not imagine going through the motions of his work. That which had given him respite, even pleasure, before now seemed a horrible, endless burden.

A thought. It had come to him last night when he went home, afraid he would lose his breath and not be able to catch it, afraid that his wife would sense his terror. He walked more quickly to make the thought go away.

The thought would not be stopped. He squeezed his nails into the palms of his hands.

He would probably have to kill again. If he did not, Sister Nina would have died for nothing, and he could not live with that. No, better to kill anyone who might bring shame to his family, make each victim a martyr to his secret. He did not know if anyone else in Arkush knew the shame of his mother and brother.

He knew he should eat, but he had no taste for food.

As he walked he remembered the first Easter service he had attended. Father Merhum had stood in front of the congregation and sung out, "*Christos Voskresye.*"

And the congregation had answered, "*Veyeastino Voskresye.*"

The sound of voices chanting in the dead of night, the heat

of the church, a hundred candles. And then the bells had rung and he had shuddered. The bells rang out the triumph of life over death while he thought of murder.

He had joined the congregation as they sang an Easter hymn; then he went outside and circled the church. He heard the chanting and the bells echoing into the woods, and then he went back into the church. It was even more crowded now, for some of those who had stood outside to wait for the procession had now entered with it. Icons of the saints looked down at him, and he looked away, not because he feared their eyes, but because he feared others seeing the defiance he might show.

And then the priest stood in front of the iconostasis and sang from the Gospel of St. John: "In the beginning was the Word, and the Word was with God, and the Word was God. He was in the beginning with God. All things were made through him and without him was not anything made that was made. In him was life, and the life was the light of men. The light shines in the darkness and the darkness has not overcome it."

The words were chanted in church Slavonic and in Russian, and he had been moved by the words, had looked them up, had committed them to memory, and recited them to himself to calm him in moments of rage.

"The light shines in the darkness and the darkness has not overcome it," he said softly to himself. "The question I must ask myself is: Am I the light that shines or the darkness that cannot be overcome?"

Shortly after seven in the morning Emil Karpo heard the door of the meeting hall open and footsteps move quickly across the floor in his direction.

He had been awake for two hours. His bed was made and in the small kitchen he had found a pot of cold tea and some bread, which he had eaten slowly while he finished his report.

He was reading a book on the Russian Orthodox Church when the door opened. Karpo put the book aside and stood.

"Are you awake, comrade? Tovarish Karpo, are you up?"

Karpo opened the door and found himself facing Misha Gonsk, the MVD officer, in need of a shave, uniform partly buttoned, trying to hold himself together.

"Dead, murder," said Gonsk, trying to catch his breath.

"Who is dead?"

"The nun," said Gonsk, pointing toward the next room as if the body were just beyond the door.

"Sister Nina?" asked Karpo.

"Sister Nina," Gonsk confirmed. "She . . . he . . . her body is . . . Come."

"Wait for me in the street," Karpo said. "I will be there in a moment."

Gonsk nodded and hurried off. When he was through the outer door and into the street, Emil Karpo stepped to the hook next to the door and reached for his dark coat. He put the coat on and moved across the small room into the cold outer room and crossed to the door to the street. It was only when his hand went out to turn the doorknob that he became aware that he was shaking.

A little past seven that same morning Peotor Merhum, son of Father Vasili Merhum, father of Aleksandr Merhum, husband of Sonia Merhum, keeper of a farm equipment shop, decided to run away.

"Decide" is, perhaps, too strong a word. He fled in mindless panic, fled without packing, fled without eating, fled without leaving a note.

The hardest part about flight was remaining calm as he ventured out into the street. Pulling his coat around his chest and covering his ears with his cap, he stepped into the morning and turned to his right. He encountered no one as he forced himself to walk north from Arkush in the general direction of nowhere in particular. After almost an hour of walking he stopped abruptly, looked up, and realized that this would never do. He would be found walking this road or hiding in an icy barn. Night would come and he would be lost in the woods and never found. Or worse, he would be found frozen, his body nibbled by mice, gnawed by rats, his . . .

Peotor turned and headed back toward Arkush, moving faster, ordering his mind to come up with a plan. But he could think of sanctuary or survival for only a few seconds. A snatch of a children's rhyme came to him:

Thousands of animals on Noah's boat,
Two of all, even two goat,
Wandering decks, watching the rain,
Nowhere to go, just staying afloat.

He repeated the rhyme, ordered it to go away, but it would not. It simply returned like a prayer, "Nowhere to go, just staying afloat."

At the same moment on that day a very large and ugly crow, with black wings and head and a gray body, perched on the window of the house of Father Vasili Merhum. He cawed four times and pecked at something that might have been a seed but turned out to be a small, bright stone. He dropped the stone, cawed again, and looked through the window at the bloody room and the mutilated body of the nun. Just inside the window a small bright object that resembled a human eye shone on top of a torn icon of St. Sebastian.

The bird contemplated the object, tapped the window with

his beak, and cocked his head at an angle to get a better look at the ax embedded in the wall.

Once again he cawed four times and was about to caw again when he heard the sound of humans coming through the woods.

The bird turned on the window ledge, flapped its black wings, and rose slowly toward the trees. He caught the wind and soared upward. Before he had cleared the first row of birches, he had forgotten the house and was thinking only of finding something to eat.

TWELVE

WHEN ROSTNIKOV ARRIVED IN ARKUSH A LITTLE BEfore nine, he could tell from the delegation that watched him get off the train that something had changed. The farmer Vadim Petrov stood next to the little mayor Dmitri Dmitriovich, beside whom stood the disheveled MVD officer Misha Gonsk, who had made some effort, though a poor one, to put himself in order, an effort that had resulted in his cutting his cheek while shaving. Peotor Merhum was missing, but Emil Karpo was standing next to Gonsk, his unblinking eyes focused not on Rostnikov but through him and well beyond.

Rostnikov had never seen this look on the face of Emil Karpo. It was the look of a dreamer or a person in shock. Though his words had sometimes betrayed a hint of emotion, Karpo's face had never, till this moment, revealed anything but a slight tension of the forehead that told Rostnikov that his colleague was in some stage of a migraine.

"Who is dead?" asked Rostnikov.

"Sister Nina," said Vadim Petrov, his voice tense. "Someone—" He stopped, trying to find the words. A trio of men coming off the train brushed past them, talking excitedly, and Rostnikov heard one of them say, "Murder."

"She has been mutilated," said Karpo. "Someone has hacked into her body fifteen or sixteen times. The killer left the weapon, an ax, embedded in the wall. It is possible that it is the same weapon that killed the priest.''

''Madmen,'' mumbled the mayor, looking around for agreement with his observation. ''A madman is loose, killing priests, nuns. Maybe he will start killing government officials.''

''Let's go somewhere where we can talk, Emil Karpo,'' Rostnikov said, stepping past the four men.

Emil Karpo nodded, his eyes fixed where Rostnikov had been standing a moment ago. Rostnikov repeated, ''Somewhere we can talk and I can have a glass of tea.''

''Yes,'' said Karpo, tearing himself from the vision only he could see. ''The meeting hall.''

''What would you like us to do, Inspector?'' asked Petrov. He removed his cap and rubbed his head with a flat, heavy palm.

''Try to keep people calm,'' said Rostnikov. ''Tell them that more police will soon be here, that they are safe, that we expect to find the killer very soon.''

''You do?'' asked the mayor.

''We always do,'' said Rostnikov. ''We will talk to you all later. Where is Merhum's son? Peotor?''

''I don't know,'' said Gonsk. ''He wasn't home. I stopped to . . . his wife said . . . I don't know. You want me to find him?''

''Yes,'' said Rostnikov. ''Find him and bring him to the meeting hall. Bring his son, Aleksandr, too. And the wife.''

The three men moved away. Only Gonsk moved quickly. Petrov, who towered over the mayor, walked at the little man's side, supporting him gently at the elbow.

Rostnikov and Karpo walked down the same street they had taken the day before. ''About fifty paces behind us walks a man who was on the train with me from Moscow,'' said Rostnikov. ''He looks a bit like a frog.''

''Klamkin,'' said Karpo. ''He was here yesterday also.

He followed me. He was in KGB Five with Colonel Lunacharski."

"Our Wolfhound will find that interesting."

They walked a few minutes in silence.

"I have a confession to make, Emil Karpo," Rostnikov said when they came to the town square. "I do not like to stay in small towns at night. During the day I enjoy the isolation. At night I like to feel that there are people around, beyond the walls, down the street. I like the sound of an automobile horn from somewhere far away. I am uneasy in towns like this."

Karpo said nothing as he opened the door of the party hall and stepped back so Rostnikov could enter. The lights were turned on, a necessity since the room was low and dark even in the daytime. Something was steaming in a pot on the table where they had sat the night before. Rostnikov took off his coat and moved to the table. He found an empty chair, dropped his coat, and sat.

"It smells of the country," he said, leaning over the pot. "But that may be an illusion. Would you like a cup?"

"No. The written report of my interrogations, including one of the nun, are in the room where I slept. If you like, I will get them for you now."

"Later," Rostnikov said, pouring a cup of tea for himself. He passed his hand over the top of the cup and felt the warmth of the steam on his palm. "Emil, please sit. It is difficult to enjoy a cup of tea with you hovering."

Karpo sat stiffly, a palm on each knee. His jaw, always firm, was rigid.

"You have something to tell me," Rostnikov said, after taking a sip.

Karpo reached into his jacket pocket and removed a book with a badly worn black leather cover. The book was slightly oversize and as thick as a Tolstoy novel. Karpo placed the book on the table and returned his hands to his knees. Rostnikov dried the palm of his hand on his pants, pulled the book in front of him, and opened it. It was some kind of ledger or diary. The handwriting was firm, slanted, and almost certainly that of a woman.

"I found it less than an hour ago in the room of Sister Nina," said Karpo. "It was hidden in a compartment in the headboard of her bed. The bed had to be moved to reach it. To make the entries she had to move a very heavy bed each night and then return it. I found it an effort. The nun was almost eighty."

"Had the killer tried to find it?" asked Rostnikov, thumbing through the pages before him.

"I don't believe so. The house was torn apart, religious icons were broken, the priest's belongings were mutilated in much the same way that the body of the woman was mutilated. Whoever killed her appeared to be looking for something of the priest's. There was, in fact, very little in her room: a small case of religious books, a simple wooden dresser, a bed, and a painting of Christ on the wall. The woman lived simply."

"And died violently," added Rostnikov, thinking that the dead nun's room sounded much like Emil Karpo's room in Moscow, which Rostnikov had entered only once, a room that looked like the cell of a monk or a Lubyanka prisoner. The major difference between the dead nun's room and that of Emil Karpo was that Karpo had no paintings or photographs. His books, several hundred of them, looked not unlike the one before Rostnikov, but they were filled with notes on unsolved crimes going back to Karpo's first days as an investigator in Moscow, closed cases that Karpo diligently investigated on his own time.

"Have you read this book?" asked Rostnikov.

"I have had little time, but I've read some of it and have examined the most recent entries. I have placed yellow tabs on two pages that I think may be of particular interest. But first, see here, right at the beginning."

Karpo leaned over the table, opened the book, and pointed to its first entry. Rostnikov looked at the page held open before him and read where Karpo's finger pointed: "On this day I begin my journal. Father Merhum keeps his journal with diligence and suggests that I do the same, that I share my soul with God and look back at my past, confess my sins, offer my gratitude to Him as Father Merhum does, and so I—"

"Father Merhum kept a journal," Rostnikov said, looking up. "Is that what you believe the killer was seeking?"

"It is possible."

Rostnikov drank more tea and poured a cup for Karpo. "Humor me, Emil Karpo," he said. "Have a cup of tea while I read."

Karpo took the cup and drank obediently.

Rostnikov opened the book to the yellow tab nearest the front of the diary. It was dated May 2, 1959. He read:

> The son is come this day to Father Merhum and it brings him no joy. He confides in me and not his wife, and he does so without guilt. He does so knowing that I will say nothing. He does so knowing that it is for our Lord to judge if there is judgment to be made. He does so knowing that I will not judge. He has the power through God and he shall see his son through all the days of the rest of his life and that will be the burden of his guilt. He will be forever reminded that the Lord who gloried in his son looks down about his minion and sees that he shall not know this glory on earth.

> *Hearken to me, you who know righteousness,*
> *the people in whose heart is my law;*
> *fear not the reproach of men. . . .*

For the moth shall eat them up like a garment,
and the work will eat them like wool;
but my deliverance will be forever,
and my salvation to all generations.

Rostnikov looked up at Karpo, who had finished his tea and sat watching.

"It is from the book of Isaiah," said Karpo.

Rostnikov tried to hide his surprise at his colleague's knowledge.

"She gave me a Bible last night," he said. "I found it with little difficulty. If you turn to the next yellow tab, you will find that her entry begins with another quote from Isaiah."

Rostnikov turned many pages and found the tab on an entry marked "July 6, 1970."

For he grew up before him like a young plant,
and like a root out of dry ground.
He had no form or comeliness that we should
look at him,
and no beauty that we should desire him.
He was despised and rejected by men;
a man of sorrows, and acquainted with grief,
and as one from whom men hide their faces
and was despised, and we esteemed him not.

The entry for the day continued with,

The Father is of the flesh and of the Spirit. He cannot deny the sins of flesh. That, he believes, is the curse which God has placed upon him, and so he devotes himself to the sins of others against all men. The saints learned that they must fall low before they might find true redemption.

And each day Father Merhum sees him and is reminded.

That was the end of the entry. Rostnikov looked up again. Emil Karpo was motionless. His jaws did not seem quite as rigid.

"You are getting a headache?" Rostnikov asked.

"I can function quite efficiently," responded Karpo.

"Emil Karpo, I must conclude that you do not wish to answer the question I have asked you."

"I have a headache," Karpo said.

Rostnikov was well aware that Karpo's migraines were massive and painful and that Karpo would not take the pills that had been prescribed for him unless directly ordered to do so. For Karpo, to acknowledge pain was a sign of weakness. "Take a pill, Emil," said Rostnikov.

"It is probably too late. The aura has passed. It cannot be halted."

"Like the tea, it is an order."

Karpo rose, reached into his pocket, extracted a small bottle, removed a large white pill, put it into his mouth, bit it several times, and swallowed without the aid of tea or water. Rostnikov was sure, for he had smelled the pill, that the taste must be quite vile. Karpo put the bottle back in his pocket and sat again.

"And what do you make of these entries?" asked Rostnikov.

"That Father Merhum had a deep dislike for his son, and that the son represented some act about which the father was guilty."

"It would seem so," agreed Rostnikov, considering whether to pour another cup of tea even though it had little taste. It was the recent memory of Karpo chewing the pill and the sudden empathy Rostnikov felt at that moment that decided him. "Emil, find me information on Father Merhum and his wife. Find me information on Merhum's son. Find me photographs. Find what you can find."

Emil Karpo nodded and rose. "There is one more entry with a yellow tab," he said. "At the end."

Rostnikov turned to that final entry of the previous day. It was very brief.

"And the voice of the Holy Mother has said that the son slew the father. The laws of men shout that I must speak, but these are the laws of the men who have put a hand of iron over the mouth of the Holy Church and held it in place for nearly my entire lifetime. It is not the province of such men to decide the law, but it is the province of God. I shall leave it to Him. As Father Merhum lived with his guilt, so shall his son. And if the son comes to me, I shall tell him to seek the ear of the Holy Mother, who knows compassion even for those who have fallen most low."

Once again Rostnikov looked up.

"The son killed him. And then he killed the nun," said Karpo.

"Emil," said Rostnikov, with a great sigh, trying to inch his leg into a less distressed position. "The 'voice of the Holy Mother' told her. Are you telling me you now believe in religious visitations?"

"No," said Karpo.

Rostnikov could see that his left eyebrow was definitely drooping slightly, a clear sign that the headache was mounting.

"But I spoke to the woman and believe that her judgment was sound, that her intuition was grounded not in faith but experience."

"You liked the nun," said Rostnikov.

"I respected her," said Karpo. "There is a difference."

Rostnikov said nothing. He continued to look at his deputy with no hint of a smile.

"I liked her," Karpo admitted.

"Work, Emil Karpo. Work."

Karpo, understanding that he was dismissed, went quickly out the door.

Rostnikov sat alone in the large room.

He flipped through more pages of the diary, pausing here and there but certain that Karpo had read it carefully in spite of the brief time it had been in his possession.

He stopped at the entry for Christmas 1962:

> Father Merhum and his son have returned from Pochaev. He was called to protest the closing of the monastery. The son insisted on joining him. Two years ago there were one hundred and fifty monks in Pochaev Monastery. Many were forced by the government to return to their native regions. Others were tried for breaking the passport laws. And some who protested were given medical examinations, judged insane, and placed in asylums.
>
> When Father Merhum reached Pochaev Monastery, there were thirty-seven monks still remaining, but a special commission of the USSR Council of Ministers came to the cloister and ordered the remaining monks to leave.
>
> Father Merhum and the monks protested to Patriarch Aleksii in Moscow and to Khrushchev. Nothing. Ten protesting priests have been imprisoned. Novice Grigorii Unku, God rest his soul, has been tortured to death.
>
> And then, just three days ago, the voluntary people's militia of the Ternopol region came in trucks to beat the few remaining monks and priests and nuns and any who tried to help them. Armed KGB agents tore down the doors with iron bars, dragged the monks out by their legs, threw them in trucks, and drove them away while the people of the town who had gathered were driven back by water from hoses.
>
> Father Merhum has been hurt, but he does not complain. He has ribs which are broken. Though he had vowed to observe only, the son, too, bears a scar from trying to

protect the father. His chest shall carry this stigmata, and I pray to our Lord that each time he looks in the mirror he will be reminded of this desecration of the birthday of our Redeemer.

"You want to see me?" came a voice.

Rostnikov had heard the boy enter, but had chosen not to look up. He had never heard of the Pochaev Monastery, though he knew many such incidents had taken place. He closed the book and put it to one side.

The boy, grandson of Father Merhum, son of Peotor, stood at near attention, his eyes blinking as if stung by onions. He wore rough pants and a blue sweater at least a size too large. His hair was uncombed.

"Please sit, Aleksandr Merhum," Rostnikov said.

The boy sat nervously. Rostnikov watched his eyes move to the book and then turn abruptly away, as if he had witnessed something forbidden.

"Do you know what happened?" Rostnikov asked.

"Sister Nina is dead."

Rostnikov did not have to ask what the boy thought of the murdered nun. It was there in his face, body, and the weakness of his voice. "And what do you think?" he asked, allowing his hand to rest on Sister Nina's journal.

The boy paused and then said, "It is not right. It is not fair. Whoever did it should have his eyes poked out with a twig."

"Life is not fair, Aleksandr Merhum. I discovered that fact when I was a soldier not much older than you are. You see I had built a long list of wrongs that remained to be righted. I carried these injustices with me night and day. They made me very heavy. And then I realized. Life is not fair. It was a great relief."

"Sister Nina says . . . said things like that."

"You want some tea?"

"No," the boy answered.

Rostnikov stirred sugar lumps into his tea and said, "Since yesterday I have been trying to remember the house in which I lived with my parents when I was your age. What it looked like, where my bed was, who I played with."

"Why?" asked the boy.

"If I lose yesterday," Rostnikov said with a smile, "I may lose today. And if I lose today, then what will tomorrow be worth?"

"You are a strange policeman," said the boy. "And I know what you are doing. You think my father killed Sister Nina. My father wouldn't kill her. He wouldn't hurt her."

"And what makes you think I believe he would hurt her?" asked Rostnikov, massaging his leg.

"You are looking for him. Tovarish Gonsk, the policeman, and the . . . other policeman with you, they are looking for him. They told my mother. They can't find him. They think he ran away."

"Did he?"

"I . . . no."

"Have you ever seen this book, Aleksandr?" Rostnikov held up Sister Nina's journal.

Alexander's mouth opened just a bit and then he closed it again. "No."

"Did your grandfather have a book like this, one he kept notes in?"

"I don't know."

"I can tell when people have secrets," Rostnikov said. "It's part of being a policeman. Secrets cry to be shared and policemen keep them well. If we didn't, people would never trust us."

"People don't tru—" the boy began, and then stopped himself.

"I'm a different kind of policeman, a strange policeman, remember?"

"Yes."

"Think about it."

"I—"

"Where is your mother?"

"Outside, waiting," the boy said.

"Go tell her to come in."

The boy got off the chair quickly and hurried to the door. He reached for the handle then turned back to the policeman. "You want me to come back with her?"

"No," said Rostnikov. "You can go to school."

"There is no school today. They closed the school because of my grandfather and Sister Nina. The streets are full of people from the city."

"Then play," said Rostnikov.

"My mother is very frightened," said the boy.

"I will be gentle."

"I'm going to the church," the boy said, and went through the door and into the street.

Rostnikov wanted to read more of the nun's journal, but he had no time. The wife of Peotor Merhum must, indeed, have been standing directly outside the door, for she came in only seconds after her son had left.

Sonia Merhum was not what Rostnikov had expected, but that did not disturb him, for he had learned long ago not to be caught short by his expectations.

The woman was somewhere between thirty and forty years old, certainly older than her husband, but her beauty made it impossible to determine to which decade she was closer. She was tall, and her blond hair was cut short. Her body was full and firm, and she wore a plain dress of blue with white flowers printed upon it. As she approached, Rostnikov could see that her skin was perfectly smooth and unblemished and her mouth full and wide. Though the boy had spoken of his mother's fear, Rostnikov could see none of it on her face as she moved to the chair across from him and sat like an uninvolved spectator at a trial.

"Sonia Merhum, wife of Peotor Merhum?" he asked.

The woman nodded.

"Would you like some tea? I am afraid it is no longer really hot."

"No, thank you."

Her flat tone of voice indicated that she was trying not to express her feelings or, perhaps, trying not to accept them. Or perhaps the woman had been numbed by all that had happened.

"You would like this to be quick," he said.

"Please," said the woman.

"I have only a few questions," he said. "How old are you?"

"Thirty-six."

"And your son?"

"Twelve."

"And your husband?"

"Thirty. But why—?"

"You have any other children?"

"No."

"Any brothers or sisters?"

"Yes, one. Katrina, who lives in—"

"Your husband?"

"My—"

"Does he have any brothers or sisters?"

"No."

"Your husband and his father did not get along," said Rostnikov.

"Peotor did not kill him," she said. "And Peotor loved Sister Nina. He would never hurt her."

"Where is he?"

"I . . . I don't know. He will be back. Perhaps he has gone away for the day. Sometimes he is like a child. This is

. . . I think the news of Sister Nina may have been too much."

"So, you don't think he has run away?"

"No," she said without conviction.

"What did you think of your father-in-law?"

"Father Merhum was a great man, a great social and spiritual leader," she said as if she were reading from a script. "He will become a saint."

"And your son will become a priest like his grandfather and his great-grandfather?"

"Never," said Sonia Merhum, suddenly standing as she strained to keep her voice under control.

"You are not a believer, I take it," Rostnikov said.

The woman said nothing. She turned her head to one side, and Rostnikov thought that she looked even more beautiful in profile. She reminded him of a cameo his mother had worn on a chain.

"And Sister Nina, what did you think of her?"

"Her faith was strong," said Sonia Merhum softly.

"Faith in . . . ?"

"Father Merhum and the Lord," she said, still not meeting his eyes.

"And so you liked her?"

"Everyone loved Sister Nina," she said, so softly that he could barely hear her.

"Perhaps not everyone," he said. "She has been murdered."

Sonia Merhum gently bit her ample lower lip and nodded in agreement.

"If—" he began, but was interrupted by a knock at the door. Vadim Petrov burst in, hurried across the room, and stood before Rostnikov. He looked down at Sonia Merhum, who did not look back at him. The farmer's huge right hand held a cap that was crumpled into a ball.

"People are exploding into town," he said. "We can't control it."

"People?" asked Rostnikov.

"I don't know. The curious, foreigners, another television crew in a truck from Moscow. Gonsk cannot handle it with the few volunteers we can get. I ask you to call for more police to keep order."

Rostnikov looked at the woman, and Petrov followed his eyes. She had pulled herself together, and her face was an emotionless mask.

"I believe that we have a near-perfect ratio of police to crowd," said Rostnikov, standing up to relieve the pain in his leg. "Too few police and you risk disorder. Too many and you risk reaction and even riot. I would rather err on the side of too little than too much."

"You wish to protect yourself," said Petrov.

"I wish to allow myself to profit from experience," replied Rostnikov.

"There is a madman in this town murdering priests and nuns," said Petrov.

"I don't think any more priests or nuns will die," said Rostnikov, tapping his hand on Sister Nina's journal.

"We don't have many left," said Petrov.

"Those few you have are probably safe."

"You truly believe there will be no more killing?" Petrov challenged.

"I believe," said Rostnikov, "there will be no more killing of nuns and priests."

"The people of Arkush expect me to do something," Petrov said. "Their priest is dead. The mayor needs support; he doesn't give it. I am not capable of representing the state. I don't know if I even have a function. The party is . . . I'm tired and I'm rambling. I'm sorry. I am a farmer. I was up at dawn trying to find wood to build a fence around my potatoes. People are starting to steal potatoes. I cannot deal with this madness."

"Madness," Sonia Merhum suddenly said. "The policeman thinks that Peotor killed his father and Sister Nina."

The two men looked at her again.

"No," said Vadim Petrov, his broad face turning to Rostnikov. "He wouldn't. He is not capable. You don't know him."

"He could have been enraged," said Rostnikov, pacing the floor slowly, coaxing his leg to life. "He could have lost control."

"He would never openly challenge his father," said Sonia, and Rostnikov was certain that he heard more than a touch of bitterness in her voice.

"He would never," Petrov agreed.

"Then," said Rostnikov, "we had best find him and give him the opportunity to make that as evident to me as it is to both of you. Now, if you will excuse me, I have some reports to read and a murderer to apprehend."

Rostnikov helped Sonia Merhum from her chair and guided her toward the door. Along the way he motioned for Petrov to join them. "Comrade Petrov will help you home," he said, opening the door.

Outside, a small crowd, perhaps twenty people, had gathered. Most of them pretended to be chatting by chance in the cold street. A few, and Rostnikov assumed they were the curious from Moscow and the foreigners, made no secret of their interest in the three people at the door.

Petrov looked as if he were about to say something, but Rostnikov nodded at Sonia Merhum. Petrov gave in, took Sonia's arm, and guided her down the street as Rostnikov closed the door.

As he moved toward the room where Karpo had slept, Porfiry Petrovich considered the things he would have to do. First, he would have to find a phone and report to the Gray

Wolfhound. Second, he would try to find Elena Timofeyeva and Sasha Tkach to get a progress report on their search for the Syrian girl. Third, he would read Karpo's report. Then he would settle down to Sister Nina's journal.

Rostnikov moved across the hall, stopped before Karpo's room, and ran his fingers along the rim of the wooden door from top to bottom. Almost instantly he felt a piece of thread firmly caught in the closed door. When the door opened, the thread would fall. The person opening the door would not notice. But Karpo, when he returned, would feel for the thread and know that the room had been entered. Rostnikov was sure that there was at least one more thread or sliver of paper, but it did not matter. He was not trying to keep Karpo from knowing that he had entered the room. He was simply checking to be sure that Karpo, who was obviously deeply moved by the death of the nun, had not lost the professionalism that kept him balanced.

Rostnikov entered the room and found the bed made and the reports piled neatly on top of it. He picked up the small pile, glanced at the evenly printed writing, and moved back into the large room. He decided that he would see if there was something to eat in the kitchen.

He was fairly certain now of what had happened in Arkush. He hoped that Karpo's reports, the nun's journal, and information he soon expected to have would make him absolutely sure.

THIRTEEN

COLONEL SNITKONOY WAS IN THE PROCESS OF DICTATING a particularly important spontaneous speech to be delivered to a delegation of commonwealth drug enforcement officials who were going to France, England, and the United States in the hope of convincing those governments to send drug enforcement advisors.

While the Gray Wolfhound, full of morning energy, paced the floor of his office Pankov hurriedly took notes. "World experts now believe all of humanity is on the edge of a new epidemic of drugs. Last year in the Soviet Union we destroyed more than one hundred thousand farms on which drug-bearing plants were being grown. No sooner do we tear them down than two of them spring up like a . . ."

"Hydra," Pankov offered.

The colonel shook his head indulgently. "Too obvious. Like bamboo."

"Yes," said Pankov enthusiastically as he wrote. "Bamboo."

"In Kazakhstan they triple. Afghan crude opium spreads through our open borders through Central Asia. And now there are those calling for the legalization of all narcotics. When the walls began to fall," the colonel said, pushing against an invisible wall with well-formed, extended fingers, "chaos flooded in and now threatens to drown us all."

The phone rang. Pankov looked at the colonel, who said, "Answer it. And give me a list of facts about narcotics. Get it from . . . you know where to get it."

Pankov got up from the conference table and quickly left the room, closing the door behind him gently.

"Special Investigations, office of the commander," Pankov said, lowering his voice in the hope of approaching an official alto. "Yes . . . yes, sir."

He put the phone down gently, went back to the door, and knocked.

"Come in," called the colonel. The Wolfhound was pacing, his hair glistening in the morning light through the window.

"Colonel Lunacharski of state security," said Pankov.

"Lunacharski?"

"I believe he has replaced Major Zhenya in the Department of Internal Affairs. Zhenya who had an . . . an accident last—"

"Put him through, Pankov," said Colonel Snitkonoy with a wry smile that would have suggested to any but those who knew him well that he was fully prepared for this call. Pankov hurried to his desk and put the call through. He wanted to listen. He would have given his annual vacation to listen. Well, not all of his vacation, but certainly a day or two if the devil suddenly arrived with the offer, if there *was* a devil, which there certainly was not.

Had he listened, he would have heard the following:

LUNACHARSKI: Colonel Snitkonoy, I have some information which may be of value to you on two cases your office is investigating.

WOLFHOUND: Good, Colonel, please forward it to me at once, or if you like, I will send someone—

LUNACHARSKI: I would prefer it if you would receive the information yourself and not in writing.

WOLFHOUND: Then, Colonel, please come to my office.

LUNACHARSKI: That is very kind of you, but it would be impossible to meet in your office. I hope you understand.

Colonel Snitkonoy understood very well. The former KGB officer had something to say that he did not wish to have recorded, and he assumed, quite correctly, that the Wolfhound would record the conversation, just as the Wolfhound assumed Lunacharski would have recorded the conversation in his office in Lubyanka. As it was, there was no assurance that both men would not record the conversation no matter where they met, but there were ways to make it more difficult.

"The Seventh Heaven Restaurant on the TV Tower. We can have a light meal and I will be near my afternoon appointment," said the Wolfhound. "If that is convenient for you."

The TV Tower in Ostankino was convenient to neither man, but the restaurant, over three hundred and twenty-eight meters high in the needlelike building, rotated once every forty minutes. It would be difficult to record the conversation by directional microphones.

"Six-thirty," confirmed Lunacharski.

Colonel Snitkonoy hung up first. Then Lunacharski hung up the phone, rose, and moved to the window. He would have to arrive at the restaurant very early to be sure he would be seated so that the tall, lean figure of the Gray Wolfhound, a figure almost every Muscovite recognized from hundreds of pictures in the newspapers and on television, would not tower over him. Lunacharski would be required only to rise partially from his chair.

It was the best he could do. The entire scene would take place in a location where the Wolfhound was comfortable. Major Lunacharski tried to think of a way to avoid this disadvantaged meeting, but there was none. He had decided on this direction and this direction it would be. He would allow himself to be humiliated, but he would gain control. Then he would sit back and monitor the results. The reports he would bring to General Karsnikov would mark the first step back toward respectability and possible promotion.

And if this failed, he would simply have to try again and again until he succeeded in discrediting Snitkonoy and his staff.

Lunacharski considered what to do with the remaining hours of the morning and afternoon. It was almost certain that at this hour his wife would not be home. She dreaded being home in the late morning. In addition, her lover was in town. Lunacharski would go home, get four hours of sleep, and then confront the Wolfhound.

He checked the buttons on his suit, adjusted his tie, and examined his reflection in the small mirror he kept in his drawer. Vladimir Lunacharski was not vain, nor did he think himself particularly handsome, but he would not risk a tuft of wild hair or a misbuttoned shirt.

"You should be home in bed," Elena Timofeyeva said to Sasha Tkach, who sat at his desk opposite her on the sixth floor of Petrovka.

Investigators, clerks, technicians glanced at him as they walked by. Sasha scowled them away until one man with a broad homely face and a satisfied smile leaned over and whispered something to him, then sauntered away laughing.

"What did he say?" Elena asked.

"He asked if you sat on my face last night," said Sasha, and she could see from the small normal part of his face that Tkach was telling the truth.

Then she told him again that he should be home in bed. He laughed.

"You think I will get rest at home? My mother will rant and scold. My daughter will pounce when I dare close my one good eye, and my wife will be quietly sympathetic, so sympathetic, and that will be the worst of all."

He looked up at her with a challenge in his good eye and Elena laughed. She had not meant to laugh, but he looked so pathetic and his self-pity was so sincere that she could not help herself. She laughed and tried to hold the laugh down, but it came out in a spit and a sputter.

Sasha tried to feel angry. Her laughter was the final blow. It proved that she was not suited to work with him, that he was right about his own misery. But instead of feeling angry he found himself smiling and then laughing, too, a laughter that hurt his ribs and stretched his swollen eye with stinging pain, but still he laughed.

Zelach was still on leave. Both Karpo and Rostnikov were in Arkush. No one would see him, no one but Elena, and she had begun the laughter. It was safe and he laughed. There was no reason to laugh, but he laughed and watched her laugh.

"I must stop," he said. "It is too painful."

"All right," said Elena, wiping her eyes. "All right. We will stop."

She did her best and it was almost good enough, but she couldn't stop. Finally they sank back and caught their breath. It was at this point that for the third time she said, "You should be home in bed."

"I will feel less pain and feel less stupid about my actions last night if I work," he said. "We will go gently."

"Gently," she agreed, and knew that they had broken through to some understanding. It would not be perfect from this point on, but it would be better. "I have the names Tatyana gave us. Some have no last names and will be impossible to find, but a few are not so bad. I think I found the right Katrina Velikanova. The others, either she had the last names wrong, or . . ."

"Or she lied," said Tkach.

"Or she lied," agreed Elena. "But Katrina Velikanova is listed in the directory. Amira Durahaman was seen by Tatyana with Velikanova."

"Plus some young man named Stillsovik, an American named Paul Harbing—"

"—who I cannot find—"

"—and," Sasha continued, "another Arab girl with an unpronounceable name and—"

"It is a place to start."

"It is a place to start," he agreed.

And they started. They called Katrina Velikanova to be sure she would remain at home till they got there. She claimed that she could not wait, but Elena had made it clear that this was not a request.

The ride took half an hour, and it was half an hour of pain for Tkach, who stood in a corner of the electric bus with his back half-turned to protect his taped ribs. The crowd was not bad at this hour.

Sasha did not want to talk. He held the pole, ignored Elena, and looked out the window at the disabled cars and sagging power lines. Billboards along the way promised foreign luxuries—Volvos, Sharp computers, Mars bars, 7UP, M&M's—few could afford.

As they passed the Bolshoi Opera House Sasha could see the scaffolding and boards that covered the giant sculpted horses atop the building. Work had begun on repairing the horses almost a year ago. Perhaps now it would never be completed. He had seen the horses two or three times a week for his entire life, but at the moment could not remember how many of them there were.

He considered asking Elena, but his attention was caught by the policeman in the corner *stokinglass*, the glass-enclosed traffic station on the corner. The man, bundled in his gray coat, was changing the light from red to green.

"Here," Elena said, touching his shoulder.

They got off the bus and emerged into the chill daylight. The dark 1905 Revolution sculpture was behind them. In front of them were the dark streets that hid the crumbling apartment buildings from the eyes of tourists.

Tkach found himself walking very slowly.

One block along they turned a corner and found themselves in a narrow dirty street with concrete-block buildings and cracked sidewalks. They stepped around a place where the sidewalk seemed to have erupted.

At the next corner a group of men and women shifted from one foot to another as a scrawny man badly in need of a shave played an out-of-tune accordion.

Sasha and Elena crossed the street and moved past a pile of dirty concrete blocks intended at one time for some now-forgotten project. They stopped just in front of the building beyond the dirty concrete. Katrina Velikanova lived in an eight-story apartment building very much like this.

Elena started to speak, but Sasha spoke first. "Do not say it. I am not going home."

She closed her eyes to show that she accepted and they moved on. Katrina Velikanova's apartment was on the eighth floor, and of course the apartment had no elevator.

"Does he feel like this every time he walks up stairs?" Sasha asked as they moved upward.

"He?"

"Porfiry Petrovich. His leg."

When they reached the top floor and found the right door, the young woman who opened it insisted on carefully inspecting their identification. "You look nothing like your picture," she said, examining Sasha's battered face.

"I've been ill," he said.

She was pretty and looked no older than sixteen. She was also very frightened but determined to hide it. "What happened to you?" she asked, letting them in.

"Encounter with a reluctant witness," said Elena.

The apartment was incredibly tiny, a cell papered in bright yellow with orange flowers.

"You want to sit?" Katrina Velikanova asked, removing her hands from her hips and folding them in front of her.

"No," Sasha said.

"What do you want?" she said. On a table in the corner sat about twenty porcelain dogs of various sizes and breeds. She picked up a terrier and rubbed it with her thumb.

"Do you work?" asked Elena.

"Of course," she said. "I told you when you called that I had to get to work."

"Where?" asked Sasha.

"The House of Friendship with People of Other Countries," she said. "I can speak Romanian and Czech. My mother was Romanian. You don't believe me?"

"We believe you," said Elena. She realized that the girl was not terribly bright.

"You are here about Amira," the girl said.

Elena and Sasha glanced at each other.

"What makes you—" Elena began, but Katrina put down the dog and said, "The other one sent you. You are the follow-up and I—"

"The other one?" asked Elena.

"The cop," she said. "This morning. I've seen the movies. My boyfriend has a television."

"Did he show you his identification, this other policeman?" asked Sasha.

"No, I just . . . that's why I wanted to see yours. He wasn't—"

"What did he look like?" asked Elena, taking out her notebook.

"He wasn't a policeman?"

"What did he look like?" Elena repeated.

"Big. Like this." She formed a large rectangle with her hands. "Nose was flat like that actor."

"Tabakov?"

"No, the Frenchman. It doesn't matter," she said, picking up another dog. "He was wearing a leather jacket like the Frenchman wears."

Elena remembered the man in the Nikolai. When he came through the beaded curtains, he had looked as if he were going to charge at Inspector Rostnikov. He had looked directly into Elena's eyes.

"What did he want?" asked Sasha.

"He wanted to know if I knew where Amira was. I told him I didn't know. He asked if I knew any of her friends. He said she might be in trouble and he wanted to help her."

"So?" asked Elena.

"I told him what I know. It's not much. I only saw her at the Nikolai a few times. With Grisha Zalinsky and with the Englishman."

"American," Sasha said.

"No, Englishman. I hear enough English and Americans trying to speak Russian. This was an Englishman."

"Paul Harbing," said Elena.

"Paul Harbing?" said the girl, looking up at her. "I don't know any Paul Harbing. His name was—wait, he only said it once when we were introduced, but I have a good memory. I need it in my work. I took the memory course at the . . . Chesney, Peter. Peter Chesney."

"You are sure?" asked Elena.

"I am sure. Peter Chesney."

"You know where Peter Chesney lives?" asked Sasha.

"No, why should I know that? What's wrong with Amira?"

"Nothing," said Elena.

"Nothing. That's why people keep knocking down my door and threatening me."

"Thank you, Comrade Velikanova," said Elena.

"Now I am Comrade Velikanova," said the girl. "I'm

glad someone knows what we can call each other now. My mother has gone back to 'gospodin,' friend. My boss still says 'tovarish.' Can Comrade Velikanova ask you to call her boss and tell him why she is late?"

"Yes," said Sasha. "On one condition."

"One condition," said the girl, hands back on her hips.

"Our names," he said. "What are our names? We identified ourselves to you when we came through the door."

"You are Sasha Tkach. She is Elena Timofeyeva."

"And you are right," said Sasha. "Where is your phone?"

"Phone? Do I look like I can afford a phone?"

When they got back to the street, Elena said, "Tatyana purposely gave us a false name?"

"Perhaps. Probably."

"Because she thinks Chesney knows where the girl is. But someone was bound to tell us about him. Tatyana knew that someone—"

Sasha said, "Then she could claim that she got the Englishman's name wrong."

"And she gains—"

"—time," Sasha concluded.

"We should find an Englishman named Peter Chesney quickly."

"We should," Tkach agreed.

"You want me to give you some help?" asked Elena. She reached out to take his arm as a quartet of arguing women hurried by on their way toward the trolley stop.

"Get a cab," he said. "Porfiry Petrovich will approve the fare."

Through a window of the Byelorussian railway station Leonid Dovnik had a clear view of Mayakovsky Square and the heavy traffic coming across the bridge on what he still thought of as Leningrad Prospekt. He had noted when he entered the station almost an hour earlier that the clock above the entrance was broken, but his cherished American Timex told him it was almost noon.

He had found the Englishman Chesney with no difficulty. He had simply called the British embassy, identified himself as a Russian businessman, and expressed interest in talking to a Peter Chesney about a possible import arrangement. He willingly gave a number where he could be reached and said his business was rather urgent and that he would soon have to leave for the German embassy. The British had no reason to doubt him. If Dovnik were MVD or any other branch, he would not have needed the embassy.

The British woman had called back within ten minutes and told him the phone number and address of the trade office where Chesney could be found.

He had called the office to be sure that Chesney was in and then had gone to wait for him, the photograph he had taken from Chesney's room safely in the pocket of his near-leather jacket. Chesney had emerged from the office building, briefcase in hand, just before eleven.

Leonid had followed him on the green line of the metro, looking for an opportunity to get the man alone. None had arisen, and now he stood patiently watching the traffic go by. Through breaks in the traffic he could see the Englishman standing below the statue of the poet Mayakovsky, who, with his left hand in his pocket, looked silently down at the automobiles.

Chesney waited on the open, treeless concrete island for no more than five minutes before two men appeared. Leonid Dovnik reached into his pocket, pulled out his glasses, and put them on to get a better view.

The two men wore dark tailored suits. They stood close to Chesney and glanced around as they spoke. One of them looked directly across at Leonid, who stepped back from the window.

The conversation among the three took no more than three

minutes and then the two men shook hands with Chesney and walked away.

Chesney looked around, then headed across the busy street toward the metro station. Leonid decided to make his move. He would hurry ahead of the Englishman and encounter him before he went down the escalator. Using his knife, he would guide him to a delivery entrance of the Sofia Restaurant, where they could be alone. Then Leonid Dovnik would persuade Chesney to tell him where the girl could be found.

He hurried toward the exit, trying to keep track of Chesney through the steamy windows. He did not see the man who stepped in front of him till they almost collided.

"Out of the way," Dovnik said, putting up a hand to push the man aside.

Another man appeared to block the way. Leonid stopped and looked at the two men before him. They resembled the two who had just met with Chesney. Leonid's quarry, meanwhile, was getting away.

"We would like to discuss a business proposition with you," one of the men said. He had a thick accent.

It was one of the busiest railway stations in Moscow, and people were streaming past them. Leonid was about to throw the men aside and make a path for himself when he realized that the two men who had been across the square moments ago were a dozen yards away and moving toward him. Leonid put both hands in his jacket pockets and found his switchblade. He had purchased it for more rubles than it was worth, but it had been a prize he could not resist.

"Will you please accompany us?" one of the men said, pulling his hand out of his pocket just enough to reveal a pistol.

"You won't shoot that here," Leonid said.

"You have three seconds to walk with us," the man said. "If you are not walking, I shall shoot you."

And Leonid knew that it was so. "A proposition?" he asked.

"A proposition," the man with the pistol agreed.

Leonid shrugged and removed his hand from his pocket. The knife eased down comfortably against his ribs.

People were watching them. A family of four stopped arguing to glance at them, then resumed their quarrel. There were conspiracies being hatched in bars and public buildings and on the streets throughout the city these days, and the people who moved past them had their own thoughts and needs.

When they were outside on the Garden Ring Road, a large black car pulled up to the curb. The car's windows were dark. The backdoor swung open, and as Leonid Dovnik was guided in he wondered whether he should fight and run. The desire to fight, however, was overcome by his curiosity. He got in without a word and the car sped into the noon traffic with a blast of the horn.

Rostnikov heard a noise outside the party hall and the door sprang open. Four men entered. Two of them were ancient, and one of them—who could have been any age from sixteen to thirty—was obviously retarded. The fourth man was sullen and bewildered. They were followed by Officer Misha Gonsk.

"Here they are," Gonsk announced triumphantly.

"I see," said Rostnikov, rising and putting Karpo's report down on the table. "Who are they?"

"The Olegs," Gonsk announced. "All the Olegs in Arkush, except the children."

"You have done a wondrous job, tovarish," said Rostnikov. Karpo had told him of the nun's assurance that it was not an Oleg who had killed the priest and that none of the Olegs in Arkush was the one the dying priest had mentioned. Karpo had believed her, and Rostnikov had accepted his belief. The dying priest's Oleg might well be important, but he was not one of the frightened men who had entered the room.

"Would you gentlemen like tea?"

The old men moved forward to accept a cup from the policeman. The sullen man shouted, "What is this about? I just got back to town an hour ago. I've been in Moscow for five days trying to sell my wife's preserves."

"Is that true, Officer Gonsk?" asked Rostnikov.

"It seems so," said Gonsk, keeping a wary eye on the four, particularly the retarded one, who was smiling at him.

"Seems so?" said the businessman. "You can talk to my cousins, the—look at my train tickets."

"Did you know Father Merhum and Sister Nina?"

"Everyone knew them," the man said. "I'm a religious man. My family is religious."

"A month ago he was a party member and an atheist," said one of the two old men drinking tea.

"They lie," said the businessman. "I only pretended."

"Your whole life?" said the other old Oleg.

"A great actor," said the first Oleg.

"A what's-his-name, a Cary Gable."

"Inspector," cried the business Oleg.

Rostnikov put his finger to his lips to quiet the business Oleg and then motioned to the retarded Oleg, who ambled toward him, smiling. Rostnikov sat him down and poured him a cup of tea. "Gonsk," he said. "Go in the kitchen. Find them something to eat. Cookies, something. Then take them home."

"You don't understand, Inspector. These are the only Olegs in Arkush. There are no others."

"Then we must look in Minsk," said Rostnikov.

"Minsk? Why Minsk?" asked Gonsk.

"At the moment it is as likely a place as any," said Rostnikov.

"Minsk?"

"It is a joke," said Rostnikov.

"I don't understand."

"Please, get the cookies."

Gonsk, a befuddled look on his face, headed toward the kitchen.

"When you come back," Rostnikov said, "I want you to find Inspector Karpo."

Gonsk nodded, and Rostnikov picked up the reports Karpo had prepared for him on five men of Arkush, including the missing Peotor Merhum. He had read them once and would now read them again to be reasonably certain of the conclusion he was beginning to draw.

"You may go," Rostnikov said, looking up at the business Oleg, who seemed to be waiting.

"You told Officer Gonsk to get some cookies," he said softly. "I thought . . ."

Rostnikov pointed to an open chair next to the retarded Oleg.

Sasha and Elena entered the apartment of Peter Chesney just after one in the afternoon. They had found that he was, indeed, British and they had located the office from which he worked. The problem was that Chesney was not there, nor was he expected back.

They had then gone to the apartment and knocked at the door. Peter Chesney opened it.

"We would like to ask you a few questions," said Elena. "We are the police."

Chesney was dressed in a perfectly pressed dark suit, a neatly ironed white shirt, and military gloss-black shoes. His tie was striped with a pearl tie pin properly centered. Unfortunately Chesney's silver hair was a mess and his face pale. "What happened to you?" he asked, looking at Sasha and stepping back so they could enter.

"I did not pay sufficient attention to my business," said

Sasha. "I do not intend to make the same mistake again. We have some questions for you."

"Look, someone has been through my apartment," Chesney said, ignoring the policeman and waving his hand at the overturned mess on the floor. "I am a citizen of the United Kingdom. This is intolerable. Can either of you speak a civilized language? I find it difficult to express my anger in Russian. Actually I find it difficult to express anything in Russian."

Elena and Sasha looked around the room. It bore a marked resemblance to the mess they had seen in the apartment of Grisha Zalinsky.

"French," said Sasha.

"German and English," said Elena.

"Good," said Chesney in English. He sat down on the sofa.

"I speak no English," said Sasha. "It is best if we speak Russian. We will be tolerant."

"Since when?" Chesney said in English, and then, reluctantly, in Russian he said, "All right. Someone broke into my apartment. What will you do about it? At least I can say that you came promptly."

"We did not come in answer to your complaint," said Elena. "We are looking for Amira Durahaman."

It was possible for Chesney to get a bit more pale, but just a bit. He achieved the state instantly. "I'm sorry. I don't—"

"You were seen with her at the Nikolai," said Elena.

"Many times," said Sasha, opening his book and looking at a page of notes he could not see clearly with his one good eye. Since he was only pretending to read, it made no difference. "We have six witnesses who have given sworn testimony that you and the girl are lovers," he lied.

"And," Elena added, "two of your neighbors have positively identified her as having been here overnight on three occasions at least."

"Well, perhaps I . . . So what if she did?" Chesney was recovering a bit. He got up from the sofa feigning indignation.

"Look here," he sputtered. "I'm the one whose apartment has been robbed."

"What is missing?" asked Sasha.

"Missing? Missing? I don't know yet, but—"

"The girl is missing," said Elena. "One man is dead. Another man is looking for her, perhaps to kill her."

"You are wrong," said the Englishman, and then repeated his words in both English and French. "We have broken no Russian laws."

"How old are you?" asked Elena.

"That is of no—"

"You are forty-nine," answered Sasha. "You are married and have a wife and three children."

"And two grandchildren," added Elena.

"All of your children are older than Amira Durahaman," continued Sasha. "She is seventeen."

"All of this is no concern of yours," said Chesney. "I think you should leave now."

"I am in a remarkably good mood," said Sasha, taking a step toward the man and feeling a sharp stab across his chest. "But if anything happens to that girl, I will be in a very bad mood."

"You can't frighten me. I'm British."

"God," said Elena with a sigh. "Someone is trying to kill her, Chesney, if she is not already dead. Her father is looking for her. If he finds you before he finds her, you may look worse, far worse, than my partner."

Sasha's smile looked more like a distorted grimace. "This is useless," he said. "I'm afraid you will have to come with us. You can call your embassy from Petrovka Street. You are involved in the murder of a Soviet citizen and the possible kidnapping of the daughter of an important foreign national.

It can be very embarrassing for your country. They may well want to wash their hands of you. It happens frequently."

"You are lying," Chesney said.

"Get your coat," answered Elena.

Chesney looked from Sasha's face to Elena's. While Elena's was far easier to look at, it was no more friendly. Sasha was on his immediate left, touching his elbow. Elena was on his right, her breasts against his shoulder.

"This is ridiculous. I happen to know that Amira is in no danger and that her father is not looking for me. I met with two Syrian gentlemen this morning and did my best to cooperate in locating Amira. I also promised to stay away from her."

"Why?" asked Sasha.

"Why?" repeated Chesney.

"Did they threaten you? Did they tell you what they had done to Zalinsky?" asked Elena.

"No," Chesney insisted.

"Then why should you cooperate?" Sasha asked.

"There were considerations," Chesney admitted.

"Considerations?" said Elena.

"I was compensated for my assistance and given the assurance that no word of my relationship to Amira would reach my family in England or those for whom I work."

"Where is she? What did you tell them?" asked Elena.

"She is working at a café in Zagorsk," he said softly. "I am sure they have found her by now."

"Anything else, comrade?" asked Elena.

"You do not intend to take me in, do you?" pleaded Chesney. "I've really suffered quite enough, as you can see."

"And, apparently, you have been compensated for it. You have enjoyed the company of a very young girl," said Sasha.

"You don't know Amira," said Chesney flatly.

"You had one more thing to tell us," Elena reminded him.

"The Syrian said a man had been following me. They said

they would take care of him. I saw them put him into a black car."

"And what did he look like?" asked Sasha.

"Big. Leather jacket. Rather homely."

Elena and Sasha exchanged a hurried glance. "We will file a report," said Sasha. "We suggest you ask your company to grant you a transfer to another country. Claim possible impending illness."

"You are threatening me?"

"It would seem so," Sasha agreed.

"I will take it under advisement," said Chesney.

FOURTEEN

THE WALK DOWN THE STREET WAS NOT AN EASY ONE FOR Porfiry Petrovich, but he made the time go quickly by asking Emil Karpo a series of questions. "How is your headache?"

"I shall endure," said Karpo, who had been found by Gonsk in the church where the funeral service for Sister Nina was being held. And now, after conferring in the meeting hall, they were heading back toward the four towers of the church. The sound of chanting drifted toward them.

"Does the pain impair your power to reason?"

"I do not think so, but I do not know."

"Let's test it. Where is Peotor Merhum?"

"He has run away or is hiding," said Karpo, "because he was guilty."

"Are there other reasons he might be missing?"

"Many," agreed Karpo. "He could be dead, a suicide. He could be murdered because he himself is not the murderer but has discovered who the killer is. He might even be drunk and asleep somewhere, but we have the evidence of the nun's journal."

"Are you developing a sense of humor, Emil Karpo?"

"I am not trying to be humorous."

"The nun's journal," Rostnikov went on. "It is a strange piece of work, a very curious document. Did you notice that?"

They were walking slowly, ignoring the glances of the clusters of people who watched the odd duo.

"In what way curious?"

"How does the journal refer to the son of Father Merhum?"

"As 'the son,' " said Karpo.

"Yes, never by name. Why never by name? Why not Peotor?"

"I do not know."

"The entry on May second, 1959, refers to the coming of a son," Rostnikov continued. "If the son is Peotor, that would make him thirty-three years old. But Peotor Merhum is thirty. We have his records. I have your notes. He refers to the coming of his son three years before Peotor is born."

"Then there is another son," said Karpo.

"Another son," agreed Rostnikov.

"And he bears a scar on his chest from a trip to the monastery at Pochaev."

They had reached the edge of town. The house where Sister Nina was murdered and Father Merhum had crawled to die was through the woods to their right. The church stood in front of them. A huge crow flew out of the woods and over their heads. Rostnikov paused to watch it. Emil Karpo paid no attention.

"I will bet the Ed McBain novel in my coat that Peotor Merhum has no scar on his chest," said Rostnikov.

"I would have no use for your Ed McBain novel, Comrade Inspector. I do not read English nor do I enjoy fiction."

"Then," said Rostnikov, "let us not bet. Is there a man in the village who bears such a scar on his chest?"

"We can check the birth records for that day and the months before," Karpo suggested. "But . . ."

"Ah, you have an idea?"

"The poem, the poem from the Bible. Perhaps the son was not born on May second, 1959. Perhaps he came to

Arkush around that date. He was not born to Father Merhum on that date, but appeared in Arkush on that date."

"Yes," said Rostnikov. "And now we seek someone with a scar on his chest who came to this town around that date thirty-two years ago."

"Back to the records?" asked Karpo.

"Back to the records, Emil."

Two men and a woman were coming down the steps of the church. One man was carrying a camera of some kind on his shoulder. The other man had a metal box strapped over his shoulder and a microphone in his hand. The woman, eyes eager and determined, bounded toward them with notes in hand.

"The television," said Rostnikov. "Before the reforms we did not suffer the benefits of openness. Go, Emil Karpo. I will weave them a tale and send them seeking shadows."

Emil Karpo hurried away and the trio approached Rostnikov.

"You are Inspector Porfiry Petrovich Rostnikov," said the woman.

Rostnikov had turned and was heading back toward the center of Arkush. "I am aware of that," he said. "But I assume you must ask such questions for your viewers."

The woman, who had on far too much makeup, seemed perplexed but determined. "Do you have any ideas about who killed Father Merhum and Sister Nina?"

"Yes," he said.

"And?" she prodded.

"I can see no good to be served by my sharing such information with you," said Rostnikov. "The curiosity of your viewers would not be well served by my speculations."

"The old days have passed, Inspector," the woman said, sensing that she might have nothing to salvage, so she might as well provoke. "Russian citizens have a right to know what you are thinking."

"I am thinking about the house in which I lived as a child," said Rostnikov. "I've been trying to remember where each item of furniture was and what it looked like. It is like a nagging refrain from a song."

The woman put up her hand and muttered something under her breath. "Turn it off, Kolya," she then said.

Rostnikov limped slowly away.

Through the small window in the tower of the church Peotor Merhum looked down at the policeman who was limping away from the television woman.

Peotor had been hiding for eight hours now, and he had decided to come down from the tower. He did not intend to give himself up, because he wasn't absolutely certain the two policemen were looking for him. However, given what he had been told, there was little doubt that he was the prime suspect in the murder of Sister Nina and his father. So he would simply climb down and go about his business. If they wanted him, they could come find him.

Peotor ate his last unwashed radish. As a boy, he had hidden in this tower hundreds of times among the musty books and furniture parts in storage until they might be rediscovered and thrown away.

Peotor needed a toilet. He needed a shave. He could think of nowhere to run. Panic had overtaken him. But the panic had eased and he had come to the conclusion that he had to bluff it out. Through the thin, dirty window he could hear the voices on the street. It was growing cold, but they were out there, carrion birds waiting to feed on the corpses, to pluck out the eye of a story or the tooth of a rumor.

Peotor was not sure what time it was. He had no watch. But he felt certain it was nearly noon. His legs were cramped but not badly. He tried to think, to make up a story, but his mind just kept going back to the mutilated body of the nun. He had stood over what was left of her in the room that had been his father's. He had stood over her and looked at the blood on his hands and then he had run.

When his legs felt strong enough, he moved to the trapdoor in the floor of the tower and opened it. Below him was a face. He staggered back.

"What are you doing here?" he demanded.

The man climbed up and closed the trapdoor behind him. "Looking for you," he said.

"I'm coming down."

"Why did you run?" The man wiped the window with his sleeve and looked down.

"Why did I run? They think I killed him. When they find out about what he did, they'll be sure," said Peotor.

"How will they find out?" the man asked.

"How? Who knows? Sonia maybe. I don't even know if Alex knows," said Peotor, rubbing his bristly chin. "I hated him, but you know I wouldn't kill him. I should have, but it isn't in me. I rant and complain. You know that. Everyone knows that. But it isn't in me to kill."

"No," agreed the man, turning to him. "It is not."

"Maybe they'll catch whoever killed them. Then I will—"

"No," said the man. "They cannot catch him. If they catch him, they will know our secrets. Do you want them to know?"

"No, but what makes you think the murderer would know that he—no one would believe that a priest, an old priest, would try to seduce his own daughter-in-law."

"Many would believe," said the man. "I believe. People have believed far worse stories about priests for more than seventy years. I have believed such stories."

Peotor shook his head. "Still, the murderer almost certainly could not know about you."

"He knows."

Peotor looked at him, and when their eyes met, he knew what he did not want to know. "You killed them," he said.

"You knew I killed them."

"I didn't."

"You knew. And if the policeman with the bad leg asked you, you would tell him."

"No," said Peotor.

"Yes, you would. You know it. I know it. You would tell him."

The list of those who would have to die was growing longer, but there was no choice. If he stopped killing now, Sister Nina would have died for nothing. At least her death meant the keeping of the secret.

"So"—Peotor sighed, looking around the room—"I must run."

"No," said the man. His voice wavered. "You must die."

Leonid Dovnik sat in the straight-backed chair waiting to die.

He had no doubt about what awaited him. His hands were tied painfully behind him. Of course, given the opportunity, he would try to escape, though these Arabs were clearly skilled in this sort of thing and would allow him very little room to act. Even if he were given no opportunity, he would at least try. To passively let them kill him was beneath his dignity.

The room was small. He had half expected that they would take him to the Syrian embassy, and half hoped that there would be some kind of offer made. They had traveled no more than twenty minutes in silence when Leonid reached the conclusion that he was to be killed.

Before they did this, however, they wanted something from him. He knew this was so simply because he was still alive. He was not foolish enough to think that he could negotiate for the information, whatever it was, but it was keeping him alive for now.

He looked around the room. It had a single floor-to-ceiling

window. If he judged correctly from the view of the house across the street, they were at least one flight up, perhaps two. The room was furnished with four straight-backed wooden chairs, including the one in which he was trussed. A wooden table, once firm and solid, was now shaky on at least one of its three curved legs. A single lamp with a yellow shade stood in the corner. Nothing on the walls. No rug on the concrete floor. He had been sitting alone in this room for at least an hour before the door opened and a dark, well-dressed man stepped in.

"Leonid Dovnik," the man said. This did not surprise Leonid, since they had taken his wallet.

"Yes," he said. "And you?"

"My name is Durahaman. I am the oil emissary from the government of Syria. What does that tell you?"

"That you are the father of Amira Durahaman and that you intend to kill me," said Dovnik.

"I do not deny either statement," said the man. "But there are many ways to kill. There are artists and butchers. You are a butcher. I have men who are artists and will gladly give you a lesson you will never be able to use."

Leonid tried to move his hands, which were tied behind him. The circulation was almost gone in his fingers. They had little feeling besides a gentle electric tingle. "What do you want from me?"

"You killed Zalinsky," the man said.

Dovnik did not answer.

"You may speak," said the man. "It really doesn't matter if this is recorded or not as far as you are concerned."

"I killed him," Leonid admitted.

"For money?"

"For money," Leonid agreed. "I am a professional. I don't kill for fun. I am not some sick terrorist or gang member."

"Admirable," said the man, standing over him. "The

woman who paid you is named Tatyana. She ran the Nikolai Café."

"Ran?" asked Leonid.

"She is missing," said Durahaman. "I think she will not be found. Do you understand?"

"Yes," said Leonid.

"There was an accident," said the man. "She joined the missing before she could tell us. You like trees? The sight of a new automobile? The feel of a woman?"

"What difference does it make?"

"None," said the man. "I'll make a bargain. You get two more days of life, an evening with a woman, if you sign a confession that you and you alone are responsible for the murders of Zalinsky and Tatyana."

"I do not care for women. Or for men."

"Then one last question. Were you also paid to kill my daughter?"

"No," said Leonid. "Though it made no difference to me."

"You do not value your life, Russian."

"Not much," Leonid agreed. "It is dangerous in my business to value anyone's life."

"It is even more dangerous not to," said the man. "One more chance." He stepped closer to Leonid. "Will you sign a confession?"

"Why do you want me to sign a confession? What difference does it make to you?"

"I think you know," said Durahaman.

"I do not know," said Leonid.

"Then what difference does it make to you whether you sign or not? You are a fool."

"All right. I will sign if you give me time to write a letter to my mother, but first I have something I must tell you," said Dovnik.

The oil minister leaned over and Dovnik whispered so

softly that his voice could not be heard. The oil minister leaned even closer and then he discovered why Leonid Dovnik wanted to make him lean very close.

Leonid brought his head up suddenly, smashing it into the Syrian's face. Durahaman staggered back, grabbed his chin, and toppled over a chair. Leonid half stood, still attached to the chair, and shuffled forward as quickly as he could toward the window. Durahaman, utterly dazed, tried to rise.

"Who is the fool?" Leonid shouted. He heard a shuffling of feet outside the door and flung himself, eyes closed, through the window. Shards of glass and splinters of wood dug into him. Cold, cold air slapped his face. As he tumbled forward he opened his eyes to watch the street rush toward him.

The fall couldn't have been more than twenty feet, but it was vivid and complete. He was aware, as he fell, that there were people moving nearby. He tried to turn as he fell, and then he hit. The chair's rear legs struck first, snapping and playing a two-beat as they clattered away to the accompaniment of Leonid Dovnik rolling on his side and striking his shoulder against the pavement. Something inside him cracked loudly and his head hit the ground with a melonlike thud.

He was not dead. Of that he was sure. He did not even feel badly injured, though he tasted blood on his lips and felt the electricity in his shoulder and the numbness of his fingers behind his back.

Someone helped him up, kicked the broken pieces of chair out from under him.

"He's alive," said a woman.

"He looks worse than I do," said a man.

Leonid tried to focus.

"Let's move him," the man continued. Leonid recognized the voice. "I know you," he said.

"The Nikolai Café," said Elena. "Last night."

"Tatyana's dead," said Leonid, gagging on his own blood. "The Arabs killed her."

"You'll be dead, too, if we don't get you to the hospital," said Sasha. "Let's get out of—"

The door to the embassy flew open. Four men came out and hurried toward the two policemen and Leonid Dovnik, who leaned against Elena Timofeyeva.

"He fell," said one of the men, the tallest of the group.

"We saw," said Elena.

"We will help him back in," said the tall man.

"I don't think he wants to go back in," said Sasha.

"No," said Dovnik. His shoulder was broken, and he almost passed out.

"You are on Syrian territory," said the tall Arab.

"I don't think so," said Elena. "The building is Syrian. The ground before it is not. Besides, this man is a Russian citizen."

"He comes back in," said the tall Syrian.

From beneath his jacket Sasha Tkach removed a definitely nonregulation Mauser C-96 and aimed it at the four men who were advancing toward him.

"Stop," came a voice from above, and the four Arabs halted.

Sasha and Elena looked up. Durahaman stood in the broken second-story window, a thin trickle of blood in the right corner of his mouth.

"Let them go," he said.

Sasha looked at the four men, who backed away. He did not return his weapon to the holster under his jacket.

"The man you are helping murdered the Jew, Zalinsky," said Durahaman.

A sound came from the throat of Leonid Dovnik, and Elena thought he might be choking on his tongue. Then she realized, when the sound did not stop, that he was laughing.

"I heard him confess," said Durahaman. "I will be happy to give a full deposition."

And still Leonid Dovnik, who leaned heavily on Elena Timofeyeva and bled upon her coat, continued to laugh. "Come before a Russian judge and tell him who really killed Zalinsky," he croaked. "Tell him where Tatyana is."

"Who killed Zalinsky?" asked Sasha.

"I did, but his daughter paid us to do it." Laughing, Leonid Dovnik tried to point at the man in the window. "She paid Tatyana. She had her Jew lover killed so she could run to England. Let him come before a Russian judge and deny it."

Elena and Sasha looked up at the man in the window, but he made no reply and they could see from his face that the killer in the leather jacket was telling the truth.

FIFTEEN

ROSTNIKOV SAT AT THE TABLE IN FATHER MERHUM'S house where the nun had been hacked to death only a day before. The room had been scrubbed clean, and the icons, those that had not been destroyed, were back on display. Where the ax had been removed from the wall a deep, black scar remained. On the small table in front of the policeman were a pot of tea, two glasses, and a plate on which rested half a loaf of dark bread and an ancient bread knife.

In the chair in which Emil Karpo had sat talking to Sister Nina, Rostnikov drew the same picture for the twentieth time in the last three days. It had not changed greatly, but there were some subtle revisions. His bed did not take up quite so much space. The table had moved closer to the wall and under the window. The rug on the floor was not quite so patterned. All in all the room looked far less exotic than he had at first remembered.

The room was finished. There was an end to it. Now he would have to move on to the next step, remembering the faces of his mother and father. Porfiry Petrovich knew that would be much more difficult. He pushed the small pad aside and looked at Emil Karpo.

"He is waiting," said Karpo.

"Yes," said Rostnikov with a sigh. "You want to be here?"

"No," said Karpo.

"Then send him in."

Karpo got up and moved toward the door.

"Emil," Rostnikov said. "Shall we simply shoot him and say he was trying to escape?"

"You would not do that," said Karpo.

"Would you?"

"No, I would not."

"Because you believe in the law?"

"Because I accept the law."

"Father Merhum and Sister Nina believed in a higher law," said Rostnikov. "They had faith. Does the faith of those you have seen here tempt you, Emil Karpo?"

"One cannot believe what one does not believe," said Karpo. "To pretend to do so fools everyone but oneself."

"Very philosophical, Emil."

"Hegel," said Karpo, and moved to the door.

When he opened it, Vadim Petrov stepped in. He wore no hat. His ears were bright red from the afternoon wind and his hair a brambled bush.

Karpo stepped outside and closed the door. Petrov moved across the room toward Rostnikov. "The other policeman told me you wanted to see me. I came right over," he said.

"Please sit," said Rostnikov. "I prefer not to look up."

Petrov eyed the chair across from Rostnikov and sat wearily.

"Do you know where our Officer Gonsk might be?" Rostnikov asked.

"Looking for Peotor, I suppose," said Vadim Petrov.

"Yes," said Rostnikov. "You look tired."

"I've had little sleep since this began," said Petrov. The darkness under the farmer's eyes looked painted. His hair needed washing and his clothes looked slept in.

"You've had a great responsibility," said Rostnikov.

Petrov looked up at the policeman, who continued, "Party chair, leader of the community, keeper of secrets."

Petrov said nothing.

"May I ask you a question, Comrade Petrov?"

Petrov looked up.

"Do you have a scar on your chest?"

Petrov looked away.

"It won't be difficult to find out," said Rostnikov gently.

"I have nothing to say," said Petrov.

"Then I will speak," Rostnikov continued, looking down at the notes before him. "You came to Arkush in late April of 1959. You were twenty years old. You came in search of your father, the priest. You identified yourself to him and agreed not to reveal your identity. You remained close to him, even accompanied him on a religious mission to protect a monastery. Shortly after you returned, in 1974, you joined the Communist party and became a zealous leader who opposed the church. Then, two days ago, you murdered your own father with an ax."

Petrov turned his gray eyes to the policeman.

"And yesterday," Rostnikov added, "you murdered a nun. At least that is what makes sense to me. If you have any other explanation, let's have some tea and discuss it."

"Then she died for nothing," Petrov muttered.

"I didn't hear. . . ." said Rostnikov.

"Sister Nina," he said. "She died for nothing."

"Would you like tea?" asked Rostnikov.

"Yes," said Petrov.

Rostnikov poured and handed the tepid glass across to the farmer, who took it in his large hand. The policeman waited silently while the man drank.

"My mother lived in the small town near Kiev where my father was born," said Petrov. "Merhum was a boy, but he seduced her, more than once. The son of a priest who would become a priest seduced a married woman, the mother of his closest friend, Oleg Yozhgov."

"Oleg," said Rostnikov.

"Oleg," repeated Petrov. "Merhum, his father, and his family fled the village when Stalin's purge of priests began in the west. He did not know that my mother was pregnant with me. I barely remember my half-brother Oleg. He and his father, Viktor, were forced into the army when the Nazis came. I was a little boy. They died in the war. My mother survived, and when I was eighteen, just before I left for my army service, she told me of my real father. He was not as famous as he later became, but his name was known and she told me of him and where he could be found. She thought if I revealed myself to him, he would take me in with open arms. I had no such illusions, but I wanted to find him, to face him. My mother died when I was in the army. I had nothing to go back to in my village, so I took the name of Petrov and came to Arkush. More tea, please."

Rostnikov poured another glass and Petrov drank it quickly. Then he held out his glass for more.

"He had a family," Petrov went on. "Wife and son. He did not deny me, but he did not want to reveal my identity. I accepted that. I joined his faith, believed in him, and then, little by little, I learned." He stopped and looked down at his empty glass.

"You learned?"

"That he had only begun with my mother, that he had touched many women, girls, taken them, lied to them. Though my wife was ill by then, dying, he even made overtures to her. I turned from him, but I didn't renounce him. And then he had a son, my brother, and later a grandson. I had no children, no family. I befriended Peotor and his family. Helped them. Peotor was weakened, beaten, almost broken by our father's strength. I supported him."

"But you never told him you were his brother?"

"No."

"And then?" asked Rostnikov.

"He set himself upon Sonia, the wife of his son. The mother of his grandson. He took her, tricked her, and then shamed her. He made her . . . I found out about it three weeks ago. I went to him, told him to stop, said I would expose him. He said no one would believe it, that it would bring ridicule upon me, Sonia, Peotor, and Aleksandr. I tried and he said to me . . . he said to me, 'Vadim, there is much that I believe in in this world. I do the work of God and man with my full heart, but the Lord has also given me a lust that age has not ended. It is the burden I carry. I cannot overcome it. In many ways that which I have accomplished has come from the guilt I feel because of what I am.' That is what he said to me and that is why I killed him on the morning when he had planned a meeting in Moscow with Sonia. Sonia looks very much like my own mother's pictures."

"I am sorry," said Rostnikov.

"I killed Sister Nina for the family I never had," Petrov said, his head bowed. "For the secret she had kept for him. I was mad. I killed her to keep that secret and now I've told you and—"

"Where is Peotor?" asked Rostnikov.

"In the tower of the church," said Petrov. "I was going to kill him, to keep him quiet, but I couldn't. My brother is worth more than my honor. I am very tired."

Petrov stood up and looked around the room as if it were some completely unfamiliar landscape. "Comrade Inspector," he said. "Do you have a wife?"

"Yes," said Rostnikov.

"Children?"

"A son."

"Parents?"

"Long since dead."

"Consider what it is worth to destroy the name of a beloved priest and the family of his child,'' said Petrov, leaning forward, both hands on the table.

''You must go to trial. I have no choice, Vadim Petrov.''

''I will give you one,'' said Petrov, picking up the bread knife.

As the knife rose Rostnikov put his hands against the table and shoved. Petrov tumbled backward. Though his leg kept Rostnikov from lunging forward, he did manage to shove the heavy table out of the way as the door opened and Karpo ran in followed by Misha Gonsk.

''Wait,'' cried Petrov, his back against the wall.

The three policemen hesitated and Vadim Petrov plunged the bread knife into his throat.

From the window through which the crow had looked the day before, Klamkin the Frog watched Petrov's suicide. He had heard little of the conversation, but enough for his needs.

He hurried back into town and attempted to reach Colonel Lunacharski by phone, but the colonel had left his office and no one was sure where he had gone.

Instead of waiting for the four o'clock train, Klamkin went to the home of a former KGB informant in Arkush. Colonel Lunacharski had supplied him with the name.

The woman had not been happy to see the ugly man at her door. She wanted to tell him that she was no longer able to perform any duties in Arkush, but recognized that this was not a man one wanted for an enemy.

She let him take her car, a very old Moscova, which he promised to return ''soon.''

Klamkin first drove to the Arkush telephone exchange, a small white stone building on the road back to Moscow. The exchange handled all calls from the region. It took Klamkin no more than five minutes to destroy the new cable into the building. There was no way, he was sure, that it could be repaired till the next day, at the earliest.

Getting to Moscow was not easy. The roads were in need of repair. Buses blocked the lanes and wrecks slowed down traffic, but Klamkin had no choice. He had to be patient. When he finally arrived in Moscow, he called the office of the Gray Wolfhound, identified himself as a representative of the new minister of the interior, and demanded to know where Colonel Snitkonoy was.

Pankov held out for seven whole seconds.

Klamkin caught up with Colonel Lunacharski just as he was about to enter the elevator to the Seventh Heaven Restaurant in the TV Tower.

After listening to Klamkin's report, Lunacharski took the roughly written sheets the Frog handed him and read them quickly. A trio of Japanese businessmen moved past him as he read.

Lunacharski was clad in a conservative gray suit and blue tie. He carried a very slim briefcase that he opened a crack so that he could drop the report into it. "Good," he said. "Very good. Go back to my office. I'll be there when I am finished here."

Satisfied, Klamkin the Frog walked back into the cold Moscow darkness.

Since Colonel Lunacharski had arrived almost an hour before the scheduled meeting with the Wolfhound, he had plenty of time to call the general, give a full report, and still be more than half an hour early. He announced himself to the maître d', giving his full title. The maître d', a dour old man with a white mustache, was unimpressed. He led Lunacharski across the slowly rotating floor to a table near the broad window, where Colonel Snitkonoy was sipping a glass of mineral water.

"Ah, Colonel," said the Wolfhound, rising to his full height and extending his hand to the man who stood nearly a full foot below him, "you are early."

"I was nearby," said Lunacharski, shaking the extended hand and sitting down quickly.

"As was I," said Colonel Snitkonoy. "As was I."

The Wolfhound had chosen to come in full uniform minus the medals. It was clear that other diners recognized him and pointed him out to their companions. Colonel Snitkonoy succeeded in appearing oblivious to the attention. "May I recommend the Strogonoff," he said. "One of their better dishes, though recently a bit deficient in beef."

"I'll have bread and some soup," said Lunacharski.

The opening of this dinner meeting had been a decided defeat for Lunacharski, but the entrée, he was sure, would be his to savor.

"You know General Piortnonov?" asked the Wolfhound. "Special Political Branch?"

"By name only," said Lunacharski.

"Old friend," said Snitkonoy. "Haven't seen him for several years, though I understand he is back in Moscow."

"So I understand," said Lunacharski.

"If you happen to run into him . . ." said the Wolfhound.

"I will give him your regards," said Lunacharski, accepting a glass of sparkling mineral water from an elderly waiter and reaching down for his briefcase. "I really do not have much time, Colonel. I am here to offer you some assistance."

"In these trying times it is reassuring that there are those who wish to offer assistance," said the Wolfhound, smiling sadly.

"I have information on two cases which have been assigned to your department," Lunacharski said. He removed two envelopes from the briefcase and placed them on the table. "I have already passed the information on to my superiors."

Snitkonoy nodded and looked out the window. "There,

look, the Cosmos Pavilion. Impressive. The sun against its dome."

"Very impressive," said Colonel Lunacharski without looking. "The first case involves the death of the priest in Arkush. We have evidence to identify the killer. I have the authority, should you agree, to turn this over to your office. You will have full credit for the discovery, but you will sign a report which is now being prepared in the office of General Karsnikov indicating that I was the source of the information which led you to the arrest and apprehension."

"Vadim Petrov," said the Gray Wolfhound. The restaurant floor slowly rotated away from the Cosmos, and the tip of the Vostok space rocket appeared above the roof of the Mechanization and Electrification Agriculture Pavilion.

Colonel Lunacharski placed his hands in his lap.

"Petrov was an ardent party member who detested the Church and feared its renewed position in a besieged Soviet Union," explained the Wolfhound. "Poor man killed the nun and then, when confronted, confessed to two of my men and committed suicide."

"When did you get this information?"

"Oh, an hour ago, maybe two. The phone lines are down in Arkush. There is speculation that it is the work of angry Marxists," said the Wolfhound. "One of my men, Inspector Karpo, brought me the news by motorcycle. I filed a report immediately with Secretary Panyushkin in President Yeltsin's office."

"Then we will simply forget my offer," said Lunacharski.

"A very generous offer," said the Wolfhound as the elderly waiter approached with two plates of food. "I know you are not hungry. Please forgive me, but I took the liberty of ordering the Strogonoff. It is my treat. I hope you will try it."

"With pleasure," said Lunacharski as the waiter placed the steaming plate before him.

"You said, Colonel, that you have information on two cases?"

"The other is a bit more delicate," said Lunacharski, unsure of how to avoid eating any of the pungent creamed meat before him. "It involves the daughter of a Syrian diplomat."

"The Durahaman girl." On the horizon Snitkonoy just barely caught a glimpse of the sculpture of the *Worker and Collective Farm Woman.* In a moment he would be able to see the Space Obelisk that commemorates the progress of the Soviet people in mastering outer space.

"The case involves the murder of a Russian citizen by a known Russian criminal," said Lunacharski. "However, the criminal was hired by the Syrian oil minister to murder his daughter's Jewish lover. This information has also been passed on to the general."

"The Syrian did not hire Leonid Dovnik to murder Grisha Zalinsky," said the Wolfhound, abandoning his examination of the Moscow panorama and turning to his meal. "Dovnik was hired by the girl, Amira Durahaman. Strogonoff is a bit off I think, don't you?"

Lunacharski looked down at his food, which he had not touched.

"No matter," said the Wolfhound with a sigh. "It is edible. The girl, according to Dovnik, who is now in our custody, wanted to get away from her father and her boyfriend so she could run away with a married British businessman. The boyfriend threatened to tell her father, and the girl paid a woman named Tatyana to have Zalinsky killed. We have reason to believe that the Tatyana woman was murdered by the Syrian in an attempt to cover up his daughter's crime."

"Then we can use the information about the girl to get the father to—"

"I'm afraid not," said Colonel Snitkonoy. "The father has insisted that the girl be tried by a Russian court. He claims that Dovnik's story is a lie. Since the woman Tatyana cannot be found to confirm the tale and Dovnik is a known criminal . . . Well. We have interviewed the girl at the Syrian embassy and she claims that she knows nothing about the murder. Lovely girl, I understand. Quite innocent looking. She suggests that Dovnik and the Tatyana woman did it all in the hope of extorting money from her father. The father claims he has a tape of a phone call made by this Tatyana, offering to find the daughter for a fee. We are now in the process of compiling a detailed account of her whereabouts while she was missing. She went from Zalinsky to Chesney and then moved in with a man named Arbanik who we suspect may be an Israeli agent. It seems the girl is attracted to the enemy, whether to provoke her father or . . . but who can say. Though our information is not complete, Interpol has sent us a preliminary report documenting that when she was fifteen years old a similar situation, including the accidental death of a young man, took place while she was with her father in Paris. Have you anything else that might be of service to us in our work?''

''And this, too, has been brought to the attention of—''

''Secretary Panyushkin, yes,'' said Colonel Snitkonoy. ''A pity you had not come to me a bit sooner, so that your report, which seems to be somewhat in error, could be coordinated with our investigation. Do you have any other assistance you wish to give my department, Colonel?''

''Not at the moment,'' said Lunacharski. He plunged his fork deeply into a square of cream-covered meat that looked absolutely repulsive to him, but he forced himself to raise it to his mouth.

''What do you think?'' asked the Wolfhound.

''Most palatable,'' said Lunacharski.

''You don't find it a little tough? Just a bit too hard to swallow?''

''Not at all,'' said Lunacharski. ''It is delicious.''

Lunacharski had not simply underestimated this great

maned peacock and his staff, he had underestimated him badly. Lunacharski's impulse was to make an excuse, to claim another appointment, to run. He had errors to cover and reports to retrieve, if possible. But he would force himself to stay, to finish the food, even to have coffee with Colonel Snitkonoy.

Lunacharski was a man of patience. There would be changes in his staff and there would be another time, and at this other time Colonel Vladimir Lunacharski would be far better prepared.

At midnight, in the town of Arkush, in the church with four towers, Aleksandr Merhum helped the new priest put on his robes.

The ritual was familiar, for many times the boy had helped his grandfather perform the same ritual.

This priest was young and serious. He neither spoke nor sang under his breath. He neither noticed Aleksandr nor looked away from him, and this was fine with the boy.

When he was ready, the priest nodded to the boy and moved to the door beyond which the soft sound of singing could already be heard.

"You are the grandson of Father Merhum," the priest said.

Aleksandr looked up at the man. His beard was long but showed no gray.

"Yes," he said.

"You know the Gospels," said the priest.

"Some, Father."

"What comes at this moment to the mind of the grandson of Father Merhum?"

Without knowing why, Aleksandr Merhum thought of his father and mother, who were beyond the door waiting for the service to begin. Then he thought of the policeman with the sad eyes and the bad leg. Finally, he thought of Sister Nina and his grandfather, and the boy said, "In the beginning was the Word, and the Word was with God, and the Word was God. He was in the beginning with God. All things were made through him and without him was not anything made that was made."

"*Mir vsyem*," said the priest. "Peace be with you."

"*Spasi gospodi*," answered the boy. "God save you."

The priest opened the door, and the sound of voices came in. As he closed it behind him there was silence again. Alone, the boy continued the passage from Saint John which he had begun:

"In him was life and the life was the light of men. The light shines in the darkness and the darkness has not overcome it."

Then the boy knelt, lifted the loose floorboard, and reached into the darkness. He pulled out the thick notebook he had seen his grandfather put there when the priest thought he was unobserved.

The boy carefully put the board back in place and moved to the table. Beyond the wall the voice of the new priest called out to the congregation.

Aleksandr Merhum opened the book and began to read.

HOLY FATHER, TO ACCEPT THE SINS YOU HAVE IN YOUR WISDOM IMPRESSED ON THIS WEAK VESSEL WHICH IS THE BODY OF VASILI MERHUM, I HEREBY COMMIT THIS CONFESSION IN THE YEAR OF OUR LORD 1962:

In the Spring of the year 1938, in the village in which my father was priest, two weeks and ten days following my 15th birthday I entered for the first of many times the bed of Yelena Yozhgov, the mother of my best friend Oleg Yozhgov.

Since that time, I have committed many sins of the flesh

and mind and sought in vain to control this test you have given me.

I will herein enscribe all of my transgressions in the hope that it will show me the path to righteousness.

In the sanctuary, the voice of the congregation swelled in song. Young Aleksandr Merhum continued to read. He understood little of what he read, but he knew that he had discovered a terrible and powerful secret. The policeman with the bad leg had known, but Aleksandr had not been weak. He had learned well from his grandfather, and the book would teach him more.

But it was well past the time he should have joined the congregation, so Aleksandr closed his grandfather's book. He returned the book to the hiding place below the loose floorboard, straightened his cloak and walked to the side door that led to the narrow street. He would walk around and enter the front of the church.

SIXTEEN

"YOU HAVE TWENTY MINUTES," SARAH SAID. SHE was looking at the table, which was really the regular kitchen table and the metal folding table, covered with the white embossed linen cloth her mother had given her almost twenty years ago. With the help of Lydia Tkach, Sarah had set an appetizing table of *zahkooskee*, appetizers, including dishes of eggplant; caviar; blinis; cabbage mixed with onions, apples, and sugar; egg salad; and sprats. Four bottles of red wine and a bottle of cognac stood in the center of the table.

"It may be years before we eat this well again," Sarah said.

"It looks very good," said Rostnikov. He was still wearing his gray sweatsuit, and he held a large pipe wrench in his greasy hand.

Lydia, who was carrying out glasses and placing them next to each plate, made a disapproving sound. "Sasha may be late," she said. "It is hard for him to walk."

She looked accusingly at Rostnikov, who rubbed the back of his right hand against his already smudged nose. "It is also hard for him to see," she added.

"I'll go wash," Rostnikov said.

"Did you fix the toilet?" asked Sarah.

"Ah," said Rostnikov, looking at his wrench. "It was a

challenge, an exercise in sympathetic imagination. Where was the first curve, the second? Where might the constriction be? I imagined myself as small as a mouse, crawling through this maze. Then it came to me. The problem was on the third floor, where the pipes come together and separate to serve the lower part of the building."

"You fixed it," said Sarah.

"I persuaded the Romanians to let me in," he said with satisfaction.

"Toilets," said Lydia. "He worries about toilets when people around him are being beaten to death."

"Not toilets," explained Rostnikov to Lydia's back, unsure of whether she heard or was even trying to listen. "Plumbing. Plumbing is a hidden universe requiring concentration, expertise, ingenuity. The Chinese are magnificent plumbers. There is a great apartment building in Shanghai—"

"Porfiry Petrovich," said Sarah. "They will be here soon."

Rostnikov nodded. He imagined the grand design of arteries and veins within the walls of the apartment building in Shanghai, bringing in fresh water, taking away waste. The building was almost alive, a pulsing meditation in which he could lose himself.

The small shower stall in their bedroom was nearly perfect. Ideal circulation, even spray. The water was never really hot but it was often warm. He used his rough heavy-duty soap and sang a song in his head, a song from childhood whose words he could not remember, and when he emerged, he felt clean.

He dressed quickly and went back into the living room/kitchen. Iosef and a pretty young woman were talking to Mathilde Verson. Mathilde's eyes wandered to Emil Karpo, who stood at the window looking down into the night.

Iosef was dressed in casual slacks and a heavy gray turtleneck sweater. The pretty young woman had short dark hair and hardly any makeup. She wore a red long-sleeved wool sweater whose sleeves were pulled up to reveal bangly red bracelets. The young woman glanced at Rostnikov shyly, smiled, and touched Iosef's arm. Rostnikov's son stopped his conversation and moved forward a step to introduce the girl. She could not have been more than twenty.

"Karen Vaino," Iosef said.

Karen Vaino held out a pale hand to Rostnikov, who took it and found it surprisingly firm.

"*Zdrahstvooytyee*, how do you do?" said Rostnikov.

"*Ochyeen'khahrhsho*, very well," she replied.

"Karen is an actress," said Iosef. "My next play will be about women."

"Women who work in shops and have little hope for a meaningful life," Karen said.

"I can do it." Iosef looked at the girl and smiled. "With Karen's help."

"I believe you will find a way to accomplish this creative challenge," said Rostnikov with a smile. He looked at Mathilde, who was still watching Emil Karpo's back.

Mathilde brushed hair from her face and looked at Rostnikov. He suggested to Karen and Iosef that they might help Sarah and Lydia.

"He is different," said Mathilde quietly as Rostnikov approached her.

In the kitchen corner the others were talking, drinking, and laughing, even Lydia. Karpo's back remained turned toward the room as he looked out of the window into the night.

"He is different," Rostnikov agreed.

"He is losing his purpose," she said.

"And searching for another, perhaps," said the policeman.

"I almost wish there was no perestroika. Then the statues

of Lenin would still be standing and the triumph of the revolution would still be plastered on the walls. Emil Karpo believed."

She had raised her voice in frustration and Sarah looked in their direction. "I can see him as a monk," Mathilde said with a wry laugh.

"Yes," said Rostnikov quite seriously. "If there were such a thing as a secular monk. But there is not."

"So?" asked Mathilde.

"So, he will work and seek," said Rostnikov. "He will serve and, perhaps, service will become its own end."

"Perhaps," Mathilde said.

There was a knock at the door.

Sarah hurried over to open the door and let in the quite pregnant Maya, the battered Sasha, and a very tired-looking Pulcharia. The little girl held her father's hand and blinked suspiciously at the crowd of adults.

"We are late," said Maya. "I am sorry."

"Don't apologize," said Sarah, ushering them in. She motioned for Rostnikov to take their coats.

As Lydia hurried to help she looked up at her son's eye and made a loud clucking sound to let Rostnikov know that this blight on her son's beautiful face was his fault.

Rostnikov noted that Karpo, now standing alone across the room, had turned from the window and was impassively watching the round of greetings.

Since it was almost Pulcharia's bedtime and her parents were certain that she would not sleep away from her own crib, the guests sat down to eat almost immediately. Everyone toasted Sasha frequently, and he responded with pained smiles.

Karpo stood at the window. He drank only a glass of water brought to him by Mathilde.

During the fourth round of drinks and toasts there was a

knock. Rostnikov motioned for everyone to remain seated, but Iosef leaped to his feet and opened the door.

It was Anna Timofeyeva and Elena.

"We thought you couldn't come," said Sarah.

"A change of plans," explained Anna.

Iosef took their coats and carried them into the bedroom.

Elena, her cheeks red and her hands still cold, was introduced to those she had not yet met: Lydia, Karen, Sarah, Maya, Pulcharia, and Iosef.

"This is the partner?" asked Lydia.

"Yes," said Sasha, loud enough for his mother to hear.

"She is a child," said Lydia.

"She is a very good policeman," said Sasha.

"She had an excellent teacher," said Rostnikov. He nodded at Anna Timofeyeva.

"She is too pretty," said Lydia.

"She is quite pretty," said Maya with a smile. "But it is more important that she is a good policeman."

"Thank you," said Elena.

"This looks like the end of a Chekhov second act," said Iosef. "Now, all we need is a messenger with bad news so we can kill him between acts."

"In Russia today," said Karen, "it is the messengers with good news who are shot between the acts."

The laughter was polite and glasses were held up for a toast.

Karen started off the obligatory round of glasnost jokes. Neither Anna Timofeyeva, who had given her life to the state, nor Karpo laughed, but neither did they show disapproval. Rostnikov watched, drank moderately, and in answer to a question from Lydia, said, "There will be no charges against the Arab girl. She is leaving tomorrow with her father for Syria."

"Ah," said Lydia knowingly. "A man dies, my son is

almost killed, and Arab murderers go home on jet planes, probably Lufthansa. Where is justice?''

"But," said Iosef, "you got the killer of the priest and the nun. Your colonel was on the news." He looked at Karpo and his father and raised his glass in a toast. "And he did it for no reason," Iosef continued, shaking his head. "I've seen men go mad like that in the army. Something inside of them bursts into violence, madness, or suicide."

"Like in your play?" said Sarah.

"Yes," he agreed.

"And now," said Rostnikov, looking at Emil Karpo, "the world will never know why he killed."

"He was the town's party leader," said Karen. "The party is dying. The church is coming back. He couldn't tolerate it, just like they said on the news."

"Perhaps," agreed Rostnikov, rotating his leg just enough to forestall the pain.

"The priest was a saint," said Lydia.

"Perhaps," said Rostnikov. "A toast. To the thirtieth birthday of Sasha Tkach."

"*Zah vahsheh'zdahrov'yeh*," they all said. Sasha looked at Maya, who smiled at him and gently touched his swollen face.

And they all drank.

"To my babies," said Sasha, touching his wife's stomach.

"*Zah vasheh'zdahrov'yeh.*"

And they drank again.

"To Lydia, who has helped when we needed her," said Maya.

"*Zah vasheh'zdahrov'yeh.*"

And once more they drank.

Pulcharia climbed down from her father's lap and looked toward the window. Lydia held up her glass and said, "To Porfiry Rostnikov, who has the responsibility of safeguarding my only child."

"Zah vasheh'zdahrov'yeh."

They drank.

"To my wife," Rostnikov said. "Who today got a job."

"A job?" cried Iosef.

Sarah smiled and looked at her glass. "Nothing much, clerk at a music store on Kalinin near the metro," she said.

"*Zah vahsheh'zdahrov'yeh,*" they shouted.

"To my son," said Sarah, after they had drunk, "who is home safely from the army and has written a wonderful play."

"Zah vahsheh'zdahrov'yeh."

Iosef, rising with some difficulty, held up his glass and said, "To Elena Timofeyeva, a welcome addition to our group."

Karen, a capable actress worthy of a major role in a play about women, smiled, held up her glass, and was the first to say to the embarrassed Elena, "*Zah vahsheh'zdahrov'yeh.*"

And as they were about to drink, Pulcharia let out a squeal, toddled across the room, and threw herself at Emil Karpo, who reached down to pick her up. Everyone stopped drinking and looked at the vampire and the small child. Pulcharia looked at Karpo's drawn face, touched his cheek gently, and put her head against his shoulder.

"It's getting late," said Anna Timofeyeva. "I need my rest and we have two buses to take."

The party broke up quickly then. Everyone asked for coats and Rostnikov motioned for Iosef to help him. Father and son went into the bedroom while the others continued to talk.

"Karen's a very pretty girl," said Rostnikov.

"Very pretty," said Iosef.

"She is also talented," said Rostnikov.

"Very talented," Iosef said. "But you do not understand. The policewoman Elena—I think I love her."

Rostnikov and his son, arms full of coats, paused near the door of the bedroom and looked at each other. "It's possible," said Rostnikov. "But you are just a bit drunk."

"It is true," said Iosef. "I am a bit drunk. But you shall see."

They carried the coats back into the living room.

Anna and Elena left first, followed by Iosef and Karen, whose dancing brown eyes, knowing smile, and unsteady legs made it quite clear that she was drunk.

"I'll take her," said Lydia, reaching out to Karpo for the sleeping Pulcharia as Sasha and Maya moved to the door, supporting each other.

"I will carry her downstairs for you," said Karpo. The child's hair brushed his pallid cheek, and his face was more relaxed than Rostnikov had ever seen it. "Mathilde and I must also leave."

Mathilde looked at Rostnikov and smiled.

"All right," said Lydia. "But be careful."

"I will be very careful," said Karpo, following Lydia Tkach through the door.

"Thank you," said Mathilde, taking Sarah's hand.

"There will be other times," said Sarah.

Rostnikov paused for a moment as Sarah closed the door. Then he moved to the table and began to clear away dirty dishes. "Enough left for two meals," he said.

"Maybe three," she said.

"I can clean up," he said.

"I feel fine, Porfiry. Why don't we do the dishes in the morning. We have both had too much to drink."

It was only a little after midnight when they climbed into bed. It was slightly before one in the morning when Rostnikov heard the knock at the door.

Sarah was sound asleep, snoring gently. He got out of bed as quickly as his leg would permit, put on his ancient blue terry-cloth robe. As he was closing the bedroom door behind him, there was another knock.

This had happened to Rostnikov many times. A murder, a missing child, a terrorist threat. The uniformed driver would be apologetic, would tell what little he knew, and wait patiently while Rostnikov dressed. He unlocked the door and opened it. Instead of a uniformed driver, there were two men. One he did not recognize. The other was Klamkin the Frog, who held a very compact but quite effective 9mm Walther.

"I could shoot you now and walk away," said Klamkin, pushing open the door.

"But you will not," Porfiry Petrovich answered. "Or you would have done so immediately."

The man behind Klamkin was large and young with short sandy hair. He wore a sneer that indicated he knew something you didn't. In this case he apparently did.

Both visitors were wearing heavy coats but no hats. "We can do our business in the hall," Rostnikov said as Klamkin motioned him into the room with the Walther.

"Your wife is sleeping," said Klamkin. "We know. We will be very quiet and we won't be long. She has been ill and we wouldn't want her to have a relapse."

Rostnikov moved slowly back into the room and the young man closed the door. Rostnikov knew that most people in situations like this tried to get as far from the weapon as they could, as if the bullet could not travel just as swiftly across a room. But Rostnikov wanted to be as close to Klamkin as possible, close enough so that if he decided to shoot, Rostnikov would have at least a chance at disarming him.

"We can come back and shoot you tomorrow or the next night or some morning when the sun is shining and the ruble is beginning to mean something again," said Klamkin.

Rostnikov didn't speak.

"The officer for whom I work wishes to make you an offer," said Klamkin.

"I'm listening."

The big man glanced around the room. He was, Rostnikov concluded, new at this kind of work.

"You will provide me with information about your own investigations and others in your department."

"And why should I do this?" asked Rostnikov.

Klamkin did something to his face that made his large lips curl upward. "My superior thinks you might be afraid to die," he said. "He feels you might be afraid we would hurt your wife or your son."

"If my wife or son were harmed," said Rostnikov, "I would kill you and Colonel Lunacharski."

The big man laughed at the absurdity of the threat by the old cripple.

"The help we get now," Klamkin said apologetically to Rostnikov. "We are losing people with training and replacing them with oafs like this who do not know what you could do to him if I allowed him to get too close to you."

"The world is changing," Rostnikov admitted.

"We are of the past, Porfiry Petrovich, you and I," said Klamkin. "Please move back."

Rostnikov moved back a step.

"I had not the slightest expectation that the threat would work," said Klamkin. "But the reward may have a better chance. One year of helping us, and we will get you, your wife, and your son out of Russia—to Italy, America, France, wherever, with money. Conditions in Moscow will grow worse before they grow better. Your wife wants to go and she is still not completely recovered. Who knows how many months or years . . ."

"I'll consider it," said Rostnikov.

"None of your colleagues will be harmed," Klamkin continued. "No criminals will go free. If you wish, your protégés will keep their positions when Colonel Lunacharski takes over. Even the Wolfhound will not suffer. He'll simply be retired. Only you will know."

"The price is too high," said Rostnikov.

Klamkin shook his head and turned to the big man at his side. "Wait outside," he ordered.

The big man did not respond immediately. Klamkin turned his large head toward the man without taking his eyes from Rostnikov and repeated, "Wait outside."

This time the big man left. Klamkin closed the door behind him. "I'm supposed to shoot you if I think you will not accept the colonel's offer," said Klamkin. "We have a scapegoat, a man with a criminal record for breaking into homes. You just met him."

Rostnikov nodded.

"Our department will track him down tomorrow and he will die in an effort to escape. We will be given full credit for the swift action in finding the murderer of a highly respected Moscow police officer."

"You are not going to shoot."

"I am not going to shoot you, Porfiry Petrovich, but neither am I putting my gun away. I'll go back and tell the colonel that you are considering his offer, that you need time. Meanwhile, Porfiry Petrovich, either reconsider or protect yourself."

"Thank you," said Rostnikov.

"Just between us, Porfiry Petrovich," whispered Klamkin, "I like you and I do not like Lunacharski, but . . ."

"Survival," said Rostnikov.

"Survival," agreed Klamkin. As he reached to open the door his Walther was still trained on Rostnikov.

When Klamkin was gone, Rostnikov locked the door. It wasn't a bad door. He had reinforced it himself, but he knew that no door, not even one of steel, could withstand the technology that the KGB had developed.

In the morning he would decide what to do. The world had changed, but in many ways it had not changed at all. For the world to change truly, people had to change, and that was too much to expect.

When he climbed carefully back into bed, Sarah stirred and stopped snoring. "Were you talking to someone, Porfiry?" she asked sleepily.

"It was the television," he said. "I couldn't sleep."

"Sleep now," she said, reaching out for him. "You need your sleep."

He thought of Galina Panishkoya, seated on that stool, the barrel of a pistol pointed at the head of a frightened shopgirl. He thought about the woman's grandchildren. "Sarah," he whispered.

"Yes."

"There are two little girls who may need someplace to stay."

"Yes."

"Maybe we can take them in for a little while."

"Maybe. We'll talk about it in the morning," she said.

He took Sarah gently in his arms as he had at some point each night for almost forty years. He lay on his back, and she rested her head on his right arm and curled up against him. She liked his warmth and purred gently. He liked the coolness of her feet and fingertips.

Then it came to him. Clear and complete. He remembered the apartment he had lived in when he was a child, remembered the sofa with the wooden legs and the spring that hit his back if he moved to the left, remembered the chairs, the windows, the table, the radio with the chip of plastic missing in the front near the dials, remembered even the pattern on the worn-out rug his grandfather had given them and his shoe box filled with lead soldiers. And he remembered quite vividly the faces of his father and mother.

He remembered, and a moment later Rostnikov was asleep.

STUART KAMINSKY

BLACK KNIGHT IN RED SQUARE

A Pulitzer-winning American journalist is poisoned to death at the Moscow Film Festival, along with two Soviet businessmen and a Japanese visitor all on the same night, in the same hotel. An international organization of terrorists has launched its most murderous offensive against both East and West. Foreigners continue dying at an alarming rate, in a huge embarrassment the Kremlin can ill afford. Chief Inspector Rostnikov leads the hunt for a dark-eyed woman of mystery and one very powerful bomb. The trail will take him, along with Karpo and Tkach, to the Soviet Union's most hallowed monument and the terrorist's ultimate target.

STUART KAMINSKY

A COLD RED SUNRISE

At an icebound naval weather station in far Siberia, two grisly murders are committed. Inspector Porfiry Rostnikov is dispatched to solve **one** of the murders, but he is not to solve the other killing even if the two are linked. In a single, fateful day, Rostnikov will hear two confessions, watch someone die, conspire against the government, and nearly meet his own death. All under the watchful eye of the KGB and someone closer and infinitely more terrifying.

Winner of the Edgar Award for Best Mystery Novel

STUART KAMINSKY

DEATH OF A DISSIDENT

For Inspector Rostnikov, the investigation of the dissident Granovsky's murder should be easy. He will simply discover who plunged the rusty sickle into the dissident's chest. Rostnikov almost wishes the investigation won't turn out to be so simple. Before the case is over, Rostnikov will remember that wish and regret it.

STUART KAMINSKY

DEATH OF A RUSSIAN PRIEST

When Rostnikov arrives in the town of Arkush, he finds a community stunned by the murder of the outspoken Father Merhum. The priest's cryptic last words make Rostnikov wonder if this was a political assassination or a home-grown murder. Meanwhile, back in Moscow, Rostnikov's other associates are searching for an Arab girl everyone wants but no one can find. They find themselves in the seedy world of the Moscow night life, following the cold trail of the missing girl and the bloody tracks of a cunning killer.

STUART KAMINSKY

A FINE RED RAIN

Someone is killing the stars of the New Moscow Circus, and the bloody show must be stopped. A deadly stalker threatens the prostitutes of the city. Moscow's top cops take the case as multiple murders sweep the city. Rostnikov was once a great hero in the war against fascism, but too many clashes with the KGB have led to his demotion. And it's up to Rostnikov and his associates to stop the fine red rain of terror that has descended upon Moscow.

STUART KAMINSKY

RED CHAMELEON

A long Russian summer brings crime in Moscow to a deadly boil. The violent and inexplicable murder of an old man in his bathtub and the theft of a worthless candlestick send Inspector Porfiry Rostnikov on a hunt into the past. But as his search narrows down to one feared and elusive man, the trail winds back to the most unexpected and dangerous place for Inspector Rostnikov.

STUART KAMINSKY

ROSTNIKOV'S VACATION

Under orders from his superior, Rostnikov leaves the city for some time off to stroll by the seashore, tend to his recuperating wife, and read American crime novels. When a vacationing fellow officer meets with a mysterious demise, Rostnikov suddenly finds himself unofficially back on the job and on the trail of a murderer. And if his hunch is correct, the powerful winds of change in Russia have begun to carry the ugly smell of conspiracy straight to the steps of the Kremlin.

Also by
STUART KAMINSKY:

LIEBERMAN'S FOLLY

Sixty-year-old Chicago police detective Abe Lieberman has his share of troubles. His partner drinks too much, and his boss is an ogre. Enter Estralda Valdez, a stunning Mexican prostitute who comes to Lieberman with a problem of her own. This "problem" leads to a murder that will plunge Lieberman into the darkest depths of Chicago crime and corruption, and might just get him killed.